Brewbies

KERRIGAN BYRNE
& CYNTHIA ST. AUBIN

OLIVERHEBERBOOKS

Acknowledgments

Our sincere gratitude to the amazingly beautiful and talented Honey Sabina, who was kind enough to share the details of her brave breast cancer battle during the all-important research phase of Brewbies' inception. Additional thanks to Michelle Valory, fellow Hannibal Stan, spooky siren, and aerialist extraordinaire for being one of the most colorful characters we know.

If, like us, you love supporting wickedly wonderful and wise women, shimmy on over to IG and take a peek. @miss.malicious @lolliebombsburlesque @misshoneysabina @mazmorraproductions @barebooksdallas

Very special thanks to Ellay Branton, Mandy Red Fox, Tanya Crosby, and Justin Carlisle.

Dedication

To those of us unwilling to mute ourselves to make the normals comfortable.

A Note

THIS IS NOT A CANCER BOOK

However, there are characters whose lives was torn apart by this insidious disease, and it's impossible to find anyone who hasn't lost someone or battled it, themselves. 1up has gifted people in our personal circles the ability to afford their expensive cancer fight and meet their bills as they fight for their lives.

A percentage of our monthly proceeds from this book will be donated, but if you'd like to help further, please do!

www.1uponcancer.org

Prologue

"No blondes."

To Ethan Townsend, it was a new rule. In the past, he'd preferred blondes. Complex but sweet. Rare. Known for clarity and effervescence and surprising lack of bitterness.

But lately, blondes had been a real letdown.

Especially when they threw you over for a dangerous, vaguely creepy, morally gray ex-soldier who catfished her for weeks—

"What else you like?" queried the pretty woman in her early twenties who'd been a bit too liberal with the lip filler.

"A full-bodied brown, maybe?" he suggested, perusing the inventory. "Or an Irish red or something dark with good head? What's your favorite?"

The bartender had a suggestion at the ready, "New nitro-stout on tap claims to be better than a Guinness."

Ethan rocked back on his stool and snorted. "Big words. Big claim. Now I have check it out."

This would make his third or fifth beer in about an hour, and he was finally feeling lubed up, for lack of a better term, for the night's endeavor.

Taking his stein, he noticed the bartender had written her

number on a cocktail napkin. He very studiously didn't look at her while considering.

She couldn't be older than twenty-two, which, while legal, wasn't the kind of company he was looking for.

Or who was looking for what he was after tonight.

Sipping on the drink teeming with tiny bubbles, he took a moment to appreciate the dark caramel, molasses, and hoppy beverage that, unsurprisingly, *wasn't* better than Guinness on tap.

Still, it took the high-percentage Canadian stout to summon courage of the liquid variety.

Now he just needed to aim it at someone.

The courage, not the beer.

For tonight, he'd stolen across an international border to avoid recognition. Not because he was any kind of celebrity, per se...but because an elected county sheriff shouldn't be prowling around his own citizens, hunting for a quick fuck.

Downside of being a town's favored son? Exactly zero room to be a man.

A person.

With all the foibles and flaws, desires and downfalls that come with the lamentable human condition.

Not that he'd ever had a chance at a different outcome. Or a say into which family he'd been born.

Scandal was inevitable these days... Heartbreak and loneliness her sad suitors, each jockeying for position to tap-dance on his ego.

Drowning the new ache in his chest with a wave of smooth nitro bubbles, he lasered away any blondes from the pool of pretty women weekend-partying on the sticky dance floor.

Big Smitty's was less of a dive bar and more of a hole in the wall the size of a grown man's shadow. The offerings? Local beer and live blues to a small contingency of locals whose morals were too young or too weary to be offended by the establishment. With its all-over grunge vibe and strategically placed slivers of cherry-red light, the bar was a temple to the *now and the next*. A small, echoey strip of nowhere for the songs of today to blare from five speakers in a three-speaker space.

Ethan hadn't marched that far into his thirties yet, and still the music sounded too new for him, not unlike the synthesized, auditory equivalent of a kick in the teeth.

He needed to pick someone up and get out of here before he ground his molars to dust.

Swiveling in the stool he'd dragged up to the bar, he scanned the floor.

What *was* he in the mood for?

A check-in with his recently-not-so-latent libido became a cause for concern.

He was too warm—no, hot. Keyed up. Tense and edgy. Sick of the shit. Ready to be reckless for once in his forsaken life.

And just at a time when he needed to be more vigilant than ever against such toxic traits.

Tonight, he might select someone who could really take it. Who shared his hunger, and his need for anonymity. Who shared his distaste for the apps and the texting games and just wanted to get naked and sweaty with him for a few hours.

Ethan returned a promising smile from a woman in a red tank top with skintight black jeans and motorcycle boots. His hand itched to grip her ponytail and use it as leverage...

Then there was the girl next door out with her friends. Tight white tee and flattering slacks her only concession to party attire. She belonged in this place about as much as he did, and she returned his penetrating gaze with a few shy glances as she played with her hair.

Maybe her? She'd want the gentleman, which would remind him to be one.

A husky, melodic laugh burst over the entire room like shards of a shattering chandelier, audible even above the constant thump of the bass.

Ethan gave the pink-haired woman with pin-up curves a salty glance. She'd been holding court at the other end of the bar for a while now. Surrounded by a pack of panting wolves who talked and tumbled over themselves for the dubious reward of her attention.

Puppies, he scoffed to himself.

They wouldn't know what to do with a woman like her. She'd grab them by the ankles and force them to make a final wish before tearing them apart.

Had to admit, from behind a sip of his beer, that she had a captivating presence—a sensual one that seemed to ripple across the room. She knew how to move her sinuous limbs in a way that drew the eye. How to use her body against men.

She had an arsenal of weaponized sexuality. Eyes of indeterminate color emphasized by charcoal-black liner. Curves for days. Tits that belonged in the hall of fame. If there was such a thing.

Desire surged through his blood, but he turned the firehose on it. He was looking for someone uncomplicated and easy.

Besides, she was flirting with some biker-looking motherfucker who looked like he'd have to hit her up for bail money later.

As if sensing his regard, she glanced over, flipping a tousled, bright pink lock of hair over her shoulder with a saucy move.

Ethan held her gaze, telling himself he *was not* willing her to come over. Or daring her to.

She broke eye contact first, pasting on her sultry smile before she threw her head back and rewarded her captive audience with another wild laugh. The motion shook the abundant cleavage hauled up to her chin by a dress held together by silk straps and a prayer to Satan's sticky brimstone.

Cady wouldn't be caught dead here.

The thought punched through him like a bullet, and he indulged in another swig.

Sweet, sensitive Cady, with her golden hair and genuine heart might as well not exist beneath this wall of neon. She belonged to her dusty bookshelves, her collection of misfit taxidermy animals, and Roman Fawkes, her dangerous disaster of a boyfriend.

No shade on Cady. If she wanted to throw in with someone who would serve life with a side of weird, who was Ethan to judge?

He was the county fucking sheriff, that was who. The heir to the family who'd founded Townsend Harbor, Washington a full six months before ground was even broken across the Sound in Seattle.

The first son of Washington's second incorporated city.

Who couldn't keep the town sweetheart from falling for a walking, talking red flag.

Lifting his pint, Ethan all but opened his gullet to down the brew, hoping to drown all boner-killing thoughts of his ex.

Could she be considered an ex if they'd never made it to bed?

Who cared. He'd find someone in his bed tonight.

It'd taken an hour drive, an hour ferry ride, and another hour drive to reach this bleak neighborhood in Canada, and he wasn't about to waste the trip by getting plastered and passing out in his hotel room.

The third time was never the charm.

Okay... Enough brooding. To business.

Last time, he'd picked a different bar in another forgotten city to hammer out his—er—problems, so to speak. A petite brunette with a generous spirit and effusive gratitude. Taisley? Ainsley? Some uber-modern-ly name. She'd written it in lipstick on the mirror with her phone number, but he'd just wiped it off so the cleaning lady didn't have to and went home.

That'd held him for two months.

Which was, in a word, bullshit.

He'd never been like this before. A man with...appetites. At least a man with appetites he couldn't suppress. Sure, he loved throwing hips as much as the next guy, but he'd been raised a gentleman. Or as close to one as this country could produce.

He'd practiced every virtue he'd been taught. Self-containment. Comportment. Loyalty to family, his badge, his word, and his lady. Duty to his community, his office, and his name as a Townsend.

And for what?

For what?

"Looking for your sister?"

"Huh?" Ethan nearly broke his neck whipping it toward the husky breath against his ear. The pink-haired lady had taken up residence on the stool next to him like a sexy ninja.

"You give b*ig brother looking to kick some ass* energy," she said. One full lip quirked in the suggestion of a smile before she sipped something the color of radioactive piss out of a martini glass.

Probably paid for by another man.

She was out of his league on so many levels. He tended to go for women who favored more natural hair colors and embodied words like *sophisticated* and *wholesome.*

The woman applied her makeup with a precision and skill that left no room for errors—her lips were a boldly hued something that would be called A Dark and Naughty Night or Blood Moon's Kiss.

If Ethan didn't know any better, which he didn't, her body seemed contoured, chiseled and crafted by the deft hands of an expert sculptor and finished by an expensive personal trainer. Fuchsia hair was done up in a series of intricate coils that seemed completely out of place when compared to her—well, he was going to call it a dress. A single silver stud glinted in her dainty nose, while multiple earrings sparkled in her ears. He couldn't even begin to imagine what she had pierced elsewhere...

Oh. Wait. Yep, he could.

Ethan's gaze drifted down her body of its own accord.

She might as well not have been wearing anything, the way the fabric clung to her like a second skin, revealing tantalizing glimpses through strategic cutouts. Cleavage, side-boob, under-boob, even her nipples pressed insistently against the shiny fabric. He hadn't noticed that delicious detail when she'd been surrounded by the herd of rutting stray hounds all waiting their turn to hump her leg.

She smelled like whisky and chocolate, a fact that precluded a stinging in his jaw and a rush of moisture.

"I'm an only child," he said brusquely, not appreciating that his body wouldn't get on board with the brunette with the boots. She was safe. A known entity. They'd know what to expect from each other.

"Soooo, a cowboy, then? If you say yes, Phil owes me a fiver." Pink Hair hitched a thumb at the crowd of fuckbois she'd just abandoned.

Ethan didn't glance up from his beer. He didn't give an old, dusty shit about what Phil looked like.

"Not a cowboy." He avoided the sight of her by going back to scanning the crowd. "Don't even own a hat."

Her laugh was like a waterfall of lust poured over his bare skin. "My mistake. It must have been the flannel." She fingered the collar of his second-favorite casual shirt, and then smoothed it back down. "Looks like you might listen to country and drive a lifted truck."

"Nope. Give Phil my congratulations." Well. Okay. He had a truck, sure, but his dick was large enough to leave the lift kit to the assbags still delusional enough to think they were impressing anyone but each other. Also, he owned an electric Beamer and several other useful vehicles, not to mention the SUV he was required to drive for his job.

After a pregnant pause where his eyes drifted to what was happening below her collarbones only twice, she said, "What do you say we get out of here and I blow your mind?"

Ethan's motor stalled, almost resulting in a spit take. For several embarrassing seconds, he gawked at her, trying to figure out how to ask her to repeat herself. Because he'd probably imagined that she'd just—

"Don't tell me you're one of those guys who is going to pretend he's not here for the sole purpose of finding decent, no-strings-attached ass." She made a face and took a cleansing sip of her drink.

Could she just slow down a hot second? He wasn't left any room to recover before she did something else to overload his circuits.

This woman. She was white-hot and electric. She was something you didn't try at home, but called in an expert.

Everything that made Ethan a male instantly demanded he rise to the challenge.

But an instinct older than the Cascade Mountain Range warned him that she was no quick fuck. She was *Trouble* with a capital T.

"I wouldn't have put it exactly like that, but I won't deny it." He took another swig of his beer, wishing he could hold the chilled glass to his heated cheeks.

"Well, come on then," she said, sliding off the barstool in such a way that lifted her skirt almost up to her hip. Tugging at it, she did a little catwalk turn before reaching for his hand.

He took one look at her ass and forgot what his name was.

Was he doing this? Was this going to happen?

Something whispered to him that this was, indeed, going to happen whether he was ready or not.

It might have been the fact that he'd already allowed her to pull him from his stool and halfway to the door before he realized what was going on.

A chilly night welcomed them as spring threatened to give way to summer. The staccato of her heels made a sensual symphony against the concrete. Each step, each breath, each heartbeat, inhale and exhale, caused the chaos in his core to culminate in his cock.

"Where are we doing this? Your car?" she suggested.

He stumbled. No way. He had weapons in there. Classified paperwork. She'd leave it smelling of whatever herbal musk clung to her atmosphere, no doubt peddled by a French model or an A-lister.

"I have a room." He nodded to the four-star hotel down the block he'd booked for the evening.

Sweet, but with a critical edge, she smiled, her lips curving up into a bow, her pearly whites glinting in the streetlight. "Can't figure you out. Are you a man with a plan? Or an overconfident asshat?"

"I thought you weren't going to ask."

He could tell his answer amused and irritated her at the same time.

Must not have been that big a deal, because she *worked* that satin-covered ass as she set off toward the hotel with renewed purpose.

They didn't speak when the elevator doors closed them in with a Sikh having an intense conversation on his cell. Nor when they were dumped onto the fifteenth floor.

In fact, the next thing she said to him was when he'd thrown the tumbler lock and slid the chain home, securing them in his room.

"Just so you know," she said, "I have a taser."

Cute. He had to pretend he wasn't trained to take it from her. Because the last thing he wanted was to make any woman afraid of him.

"I was perched beneath the bar's camera with you, was seen in the elevator's camera with you, and used my professional discount to upgrade the room. If I'd been up to no good, I'd have made different decisions."

"Fair point." She discarded a clutch on the desk and glanced around, taking in the plush carpeting, glossy headboard, desk, nightstands, and lamps.

A large king bed dominated the room, its heavy four-post canopy reaching to the ceiling like a treehouse, the lush sheets and pillows a welcome invitation.

"Do you care if I open the curtains?" she asked, gliding toward the drapes. "I love a view."

"Sure."

As her arms lifted to catch the cord, the hem of her dress summited her thigh and began to hike up the curve of her ass.

Should be criminal to go out in public looking that fuckable.

"Wait. You're not going to...to charge me for this, are you?"

If he were a coward, he'd turn away so he wouldn't have to face the fallout of that question. If she demanded money, he'd be upset. If he assumed she wanted compensation and she didn't, she'd be upset.

Ugh. He done fucked up.

She again startled him by breaking into a grin followed by a bubble of her infectious laughter. "Believe me, if I decided to charge for this kind of thing, you couldn't afford me. Now take off your pants."

She kicked off her pumps and went to work on removing—peeling off?—her dress.

In a world where nudity was commonplace, Ethan figured he'd grown past being stunned by a woman's body.

Yet here he stood.

Thunderstruck.

Her curves were a testament to sex and desire. Full, enticing hips. Long, toned waist. And those breasts. Fuck him if they didn't defy description. Hell...they defied the laws of physics. Like gravity.

But it was her eyes that captivated him. They glimmered with a deep, soulful intelligence that stole his breath. She was at once a goddess and a concubine. Proud, bold, and wary as she approached and, without another word, grabbed his shirt, pulling him in for a devastating kiss.

Ethan was overwhelmed with desire as their lips locked together. He clenched his hands tightly around her waist, pulling her against his body until he felt the heat of her skin resonate through him. The kiss ignited something frightening as his tongue greedily explored every inch of her mouth. He'd thought to taste her, but ended up savoring and devouring instead.

Her passionate moans vibrated through him, both savage and submissive.

Closing his eyes in pure delight, he cupped her breasts in his hands. Goddamn, the softness and warmth of her skin undid him. Focusing on her pleasure was the best way to distract him from the overwhelming demand for his own. But as he brushed his thumbs over her nipples, her gasp landed right in his groin.

Their kiss turned almost violent as she ripped off his shirt; the seam of their mouths only broke for her to lift his white tee over his head.

When their mouths clashed again, he plunged his hands into her vibrant, astonishingly silky hair, ruining the intricate style and sending bobby pins plopping to the floor.

She didn't seem to care. Pulling him closer, she trailed her fingers down his body to his belt buckle and eagerly unfastened it. When his clothes had been ripped from his body and abandoned to the floor, her hands explored his muscles with a hungry groan of appreciation.

"Body like this usually belongs to some lunk or meathead," she marveled.

"How do you know I'm not?"

A secretive, mischievous expression stole over the delicate features of her face. "I can tell." She winked at him. "Also, you haven't called me *dude, bruh, or babe* yet, so I'm impressed."

That coaxed a laugh, rusty from misuse. "You're easily impressed."

"No," she said, her eyes glinting with an astonishing inner tempest before she pressed the flats of both her hands against the swells of his pecs. "No, I'm not."

With a surprising burst of strength, she pushed him backward, riding him down until his back hit the bed.

Alarm bells jangled somewhere in the dense gray matter of his brain.

This wasn't how these things went. *He* was the driver. The initiator. The one in charge of the safety and satisfaction of all involved. There was consent to worry about. And decency. Birth control. STD protec—

Pulling a foil from her bra, she opened it with her teeth and applied it like it was part of a motherfucking striptease.

A surge of masculine satisfaction rose within him at her appreciative moan when she palmed his cock.

She straddled him, her eyes blazing, the scrap of a pink lace thong granting him a barely-there peep show that expelled the last of his sanity.

He fought a tremor in his hands as they roamed her body, tracing the curves of her hips and exploring her warm skin. His longing was palpable in his kisses as his tongue searched for hers. The pleasure built up inside of him as he tested the weight of her breasts before sampling a puckered nipple with his tongue.

Her flavor was unreal. Some amalgamation of pheromones, salt, sweat, and sex that set his every sense on fire.

Her fingers plunged into his hair, long, lacquered nails scoring his scalp, intensifying their connection. She moaned as his fingers explored her, slipping between her legs. He felt her body quiver and watched her eyes close as her breathing quickened.

Slipping through the drenched ruffles of her sex, he tormented the engorged flesh around the little nub of nerves at her core. Hovering. Flicking. Circling. Never landing where she demanded he go. He loved the way she moved with him, pressing herself against him in a desperate search for pleasure. With each stroke of his finger, her heat became more intense as she built toward an orgasmic crescendo.

When he applied the right pressure, she came immediately, her ecstatic sounds driving him to unparalleled levels of lust. Her back arched and she sobbed for more, her lacquered nails digging and releasing the meat of his shoulders like a delighted cat.

In the midst of her climax, Ethan shifted his weight, positioning himself between her thighs and guiding her down on the marble-hard column of his cock.

He'd expected frenzy. Furious, fast fucking.

But their movements slowed with the intensity of their joining. Her strong thighs flexed as he bracketed her hips with his hands to help with the heavy lifting. The force of their bodies coming together echoed through the air, colliding in a crescendo of passion. With each thrust they connected in a way he couldn't even define, swirling around each other until they seemed truly intertwined. A unified being radiating pure ecstasy.

"*That* was impressive," she panted when they could breathe again.

"Was?" he growled.

Her look of confusion was made adorable by the smear of her lipstick.

Spanning her ribs with his hands, he lifted her full body and chucked her onto her back. "I'm not done yet," he warned as he lifted her knees up before pressing them wide and lowering his mouth.

Hours later, when the last of the shudders had been wrung out of their exhausted bodies, they collapsed to the mattress, her stretching over him like a blanket. His shaft still clenched in the aftershocks of her velvety sex.

A stranger. She was a stranger.

And he'd just had the best sex of his life.

Last thing he needed was another head fuck.

Last thing *she* needed was him in the throes of a head fuck.

But for the first time, he lamented the end of the one-night stand. Didn't want to leave her body, let alone her presence.

God, he was pathetic.

Deciding to rip off the Band-Aid, he ran a hand over the hair now falling a little past her shoulders, taken in by the silken texture.

"You relax," he mumbled with an incredible yawn. "I'll take care of this."

This being the avoidance of a wet spot, the cleanup, condom disposal, pee, and bringing her a warm, wet washcloth to—

"Hello?" he asked his empty room as he folded the washcloth for her.

The answer he found was a pink sticky note and her lace thong on the empty chair back where he'd draped his flannel shirt.

Thanks for the ride. And the flannel. DD.

ONE

Pump Machine

AN ESPRESSO MACHINE THAT USES A PUMP TO
FORCE BREWING WATER AT HIGH PRESSURE
THROUGH A COMPACTED BED OF GROUND
COFFEE.

DARBY DUNWELL STOOD BEFORE THE WINDOW OF HER
vintage camper turned coffee truck, staring at her one-night stand,
and bargaining with a God she hadn't believed in since the tenth
grade.

Her official breakup with a higher power occurred when
Sister Mary Mildred broke a paddle over Darby's ass after she'd
stolen from her reform school's bake sale proceeds to buy cigarettes off an older co-ed. As it had been Darby's mocha-nut
cupcakes that brought in the lion's share of confectionary
proceeds to St. Vincent's Academy, she'd reasoned that she was
due at least a slim margin of the profits.

Sister Eminem (as Darby had not-so-affectionately called her)
hadn't shared Darby's financial assessment.

Still fizzy with her first nicotine high, Darby had flipped up
her uniform's plaid skirt, planted her hands on headmistress's
moat of a desk, and invited the Hand of God—Sister Mary
Mildred's paddle—to do its worst.

The resounding crack echoed through twelve years of her
memory as she looked at *him*.

15

Last in the line of customers, waiting for her to part the Barbie-pink curtains and begin dispensing the life-enhancing elixir, he glowered like he wanted to dick-punch the sun just for rising.

Hungover, she guessed, if he'd necked as much beer the evening previous as he had when she saw him last.

But there wasn't supposed to be a last.

Because she was never supposed see him again.

This could not—should not—be happening.

For once in her life, Darby had done everything right. She had driven three hours away from the tiny coastal hamlet of Townsend Harbor. She had targeted a bar of the kind most Townsendites wouldn't be caught dead in. She had selected her quarry carefully after hours of observation.

Of all her one-nighters, why did it have to be him? The man who'd had her recalibrating her walk for days afterward. The man who'd left her stretched, abraded, satiated, and in such a manically good mood that her colorist asked what kind of meds her psychiatrist had her on.

The man whose name she didn't know despite the fact that he'd been inside her.

Deep, deep inside.

"He sees everything you do, even when I don't," Sister Mary Mildred whisper-hissed in her head.

Whack.

"His justice will be swift and sure."

Crack.

Was that what this was?

Justice?

Some kind of karmic one-upmanship in her lifelong game of chicken with the universe?

One thing Darby knew for sure. She really had to stop inviting wood to come at her as hard as possible.

"To whomever it may concern," she began, fastening her eyes shut. "I solemnly swear I will never have another one-night stand so long as I live if you could kindly make the lumbersnack-looking guy with the icy glare decide to leave in the next thirty seconds." Her throat worked over a gritty swallow. "It doesn't have to be anything super bad. Maybe a mild case of diarrhea? There's a gas station just up the road, and they keep the bathrooms pretty clean, I hear. Thanks. Oh. Amen and stuff."

Feeling completely foolish for hoping he might have magically evaporated, Darby gently widened the narrow slit between the fabric panels.

If anything, he looked more solid from this angle, his broad shoulders juxtaposed against the backdrop of pine trees across the interstate, the sunrise gilding the crown of his head like some kind of small-town avenging angel.

In flannel.

A shirt very much like the one he'd worn that night.

A shirt very much like the one she'd traded for her panties.

Because, unlike the others, she had *wanted* to remember him.

Fondly, and preferably from a great distance.

Darby cast a guilty glance back to the living area of her vintage trailer, where, at that very second, in a cupboard above her bed, the souvenir in question whispered from the confines of a gallon-sized freezer bag. Not to preserve the scent of fabric softener, soap, and a cologne that reminded her of a meadow after a summer storm, but to protect it against the moths that held nightly mixers around the light on the outside her camper.

Or so she'd told herself every time she cracked the zipper to inhale a heady hit of eau d' deep dicking.

Darby bit the pointed tip of her nail as the man who'd renovated her pelvic floor glared at a passing police cruiser.

Maybe he wouldn't recognize her.

Right. Because it wasn't like she had branded her entire business to her two most recognizable features or anything.

Brewbies.

Townsend Harbor's first and only sex-positive, body-positive, bikini coffee camper.

For a cause.

She glanced in the full-length mirror mounted on the door leading to her tiny living area at the camper's rear and let out an anguished groan.

Showgirl tits and hot-pink hair present and very accounted for. Hell, an only slightly exaggerated caricature of her glowed from the top of the camper this very second, blinking neon Las Vegas showgirl, leg kick and all.

Christ, did she have to strangle every single theme to literal death?

The sound of boots crunching on gravel yanked her out of self-speculation and cattle-prodded her into motion.

Her regulars were growing restless.

At the front of the line, the hulking, dark-haired dude who looked like he just stepped off the set of a movie with *Destroyer* in the title. Tucked protectively against his broad chest, the buxom, blonde bookstore proprietress who reminded Darby of Botticelli paintings she'd loved at the Met.

Him: D Cup Slow Grind, extra sweaty—pour-over coffee, black, 180 degrees.

Her: C Cup Vanilla Pump and Dump—regular Italian roast with house-made Madagascar vanilla syrup and extra half 'n' half.

Darby rummaged through the various shelves and cupboards to pull out the necessary accoutrements and scooped a healthy shovel of spicy, cocoa-scented grounds into the compostable paper cone before dispensing the appropriate amount of scalding water. While it brewed, she shimmied through the small door to her dining room/lounge/wardrobe/craft room/library.

Yanking open her "closet," she double-fisted the contents and flung them over her shoulders like a cartoon strumpet, furiously searching for anything to cover her hair.

How could she condense an entire Etsy vintage pin-up boutique into a repurposed broom cupboard but still not own a single hat?

Desperate, she snatched up the baggy Bettie Page t-shirt she'd slept in and hauled it over her bikini top before grabbing another and twisting it around the chignon and victory rolls she'd so painstakingly assembled earlier that morning.

She'd sooner scrape her entire face off with a cake spatula than re-contour, but wiped off her signature siren-red lipstick as tribute.

As she glanced down at the smeared crimson rings on the makeup wipe, her staggeringly unhelpful brain idly wondered if Deep Dicking had seen something similar when he took a washrag to his business the morning after their anonymous feral fuckfest.

Spontaneous under-boob sweat broke out beneath her bikini top at the thought. Darby grabbed a silk fan and beat it against the close air of the camper to cool her furiously flushed cheeks as she lunged the four steps back to the coffee cubby.

Go time.

Allowing herself one last breath, she shoved the curtains aside and slid the pocket window open.

The cool, pine-scented air of an early Pacific Northwest summer felt delicious on her heated skin as she leaned out the window to prop up the cotton-candy-pink mini-awning over the small, brushed steel service counter mounted on the camper's flank.

"Morning," she greeted the customers with considerably less volume than she normally employed. "Sorry about the wait. The grinder was being an absolute dickhole."

Cady Bloomquist met her with a beaming smile. "No worries whatsoever."

If Darby had a six-and-a-half-foot search-and-rescue team/personal space heater following her around town, she suspected she might not have any worries either.

Turning back to her barista nook, Darby quickly finished their drinks and fitted the cups with lids, insulation sleeves, and sip hole stopper topped with a tiny—but remarkably perky—pair of tits.

After punching the order into the iPad, she swiveled it on the lazy Susan base to face them.

Cady's Viking escort stepped forward and held his iPhone up to the screen to complete the transaction with a tip far more generous than she deserved.

"Have the breast day," she said, handing their drinks over.

"I will when you actually come to the Bare-Naked Book Club like you promised," Cady teased with an arched eyebrow.

"Next Thursday, for sure," Darby said, hating herself a little for what she already knew was a lie.

Cady's smooth cheeks lifted in a serene grin. "I'll save you a seat."

They walked off together toward a black SUV big enough to be army issue if not for the uber-tinted windows, Darby's heart squeezing as Conan hooked a finger through the belt loop of Cady's wide-legged denim trousers.

The next three customers were drive-through interstate traffic that represented the bulk of her business. The fourth, a sight that made her face grow longer on her tired skull.

"That timer says twenty minutes," he said in a congested voice dripping with sinus infection. "Your website promises that you never serve coffee that's been sitting for more than fifteen."

On a normal day, when she wasn't having mild, regret-based panic attacks about a man who'd had his mouth on her lady bits lurking at the back of her line, she'd have remembered to reset the timer the second she saw Roy Dobson roll up.

Silver-haired, sour, and perpetually rumpled, Roy was a walking ad for how to die alone.

Tempted as she was to give him decaf, Darby decided that inviting any further karmic consequences might not be in her best interest at this precise moment.

"My sincere apologies, Roy," she said, pressing her hand to breasts he made a show of *not* looking at. "If you don't mind waiting for another ten, I'd be happy to brew a fresh pot just for you." She smiled so hard, her canines poked into her lower lip. "Or maybe I could interest you in a hot pour-over?"

Your face.

Judging by his sigh alone, you'd have guessed that she'd just asked him whether he preferred to move Fort Warden Beach grain by grain, or empty the Puget Sound a thimbleful at a time.

"I guess I'll just take what you've already got." His gaze narrowed behind thick glasses. "But don't microwave it, or I'll know."

He shoved the thermal cup he always brought from home through the window. Darby had the distinct feeling the tempestuous secondhand store owner did this not out of any conscience-driven need to lessen his carbon footprint, but for the fifty-cent discount she offered to anyone who brought their own cup.

"Wouldn't dream of it." If her forced smile got any wider, the tendons holding her jaw on were liable to pop like rubber bands.

Three customers away.

Darby stepped just out of eye line and covertly glanced at him beyond the brassy beast of the espresso machine that had devoured an entire third of her initial business loan.

He hadn't looked at her once.

Something in the distance had his attention. And not in a good way.

Arms folded against the solid wall of his chest, he flexed his angular jaw beneath the tawny carpet of stubble she could still feel on her lips. Just as she could feel the press of his angular hips against her inner thighs. That rough palm clutching the sensitive skin of her throat as his thick fingers slid her panties to the side beneath her skirt, scalding her...thumb?

"Fuck," Darby said, sloshing more hot liquid on herself as she jerked her hand away from the steam wand. "Motherfucking shit-biscuits! Sonova bitch, that hurts."

Darby turned the tiny sink tap onto cold and shoved her hand in the stream to calm her offended nerves. The relief was instant, but wouldn't last, as she knew. Steam burns were the literal worst.

Spotting the lavender essential oil one of her passing patrons had gifted to her, Darby liberally anointed the stinging digit and carefully rubbed in the unguent salve.

"Excuse me." Roy pecked on the aluminum siding of the service window. "Excuse me, but you were planning on refilling my cup, correct? Because I couldn't help but notice that you spilled a significant amount of coffee— *Onyeeep!*"

Darby's head whipped around hard enough for several vertebrae to crunch, her eyes going wide as duck eggs as she saw the reason Roy had broken off so abruptly.

Him.

He stood before the service window with a handful of Roy's button-up shirt gripped in one white-knuckled fist, the other cocked back like a wrecking ball.

"Can't you see she burned her hand you pointless, demanding fuck?" His bicep mounded beneath his sleeve as he hauled Roy's face closer to his.

Roy's mouth opened. Closed. Opened again. "I— But— Tits," he stammered nonsensically.

"That's what I thought." *He* raked Roy with a withering look. "Now you're going to back off and let her take care of it before I forget that I'll lose my job if I rearrange your face."

Roy nodded and was released with enough force to send him stumbling backward. He sat down hard on one of the picnic table benches she'd painted a soothing seafoam teal in optimistic days unsullied by the scene before her.

Still tight with rage, her one-night stand's face swung in Darby's direction. Their eyes met, and recognition surged into his features like the tide. The eyelids lowering. The jaw unclenching. The mouth softening.

He knew.

He remembered her.

Darby stood at the window, her pulse pounding in her ears and her lips parting on a breath that refused to fill her lungs.

In what was perhaps the most shocking turn of events so far, Deep Dicking released his fists and calmly stepped back into line.

Or what was left of it.

Two of the other patrons had mysteriously vanished, apparently uninterested in being pummeled by the coffee bouncer should they ask for an extra shot.

The third seemed completely unfazed.

"Knew Sheriff Townsend had that in him somewhere," she said, wiping lipstick only a shade darker than Darby's fuchsia hair from her top teeth.

Darby's heart skipped a beat.

Sheriff Townsend?

No.

No way.

No way in hell that the man who'd had her leaving dental impressions in a plywood headboard clocked into a county job.

Darby's face prickled with the awareness of his gaze.

"Morning, Myrtle," she said, refocusing on the task before her. "What'll it be?"

The older woman squinted at the menu through the thick frames of her bifocals, the white wisps of her spiky hair glowing like light bulb filaments in the sun. "Can I get a double D Dirty Screw? Oh! And can I add a cream pie to that?"

"One Oreo Frappuccino with a double shot and extra whip coming right up," Darby said, grateful to have something for her hands to do.

"You can hardly blame poor Ethan after that business between Roy and his mother," Myrtle said conversationally.

"I'm sorry," Darby said, scooping cookie rubble into a compostable plastic cup. "Who?"

"Ethan Townsend. The guy who just made Roy's coin purse crawl into his colon."

Sheriff Ethan Townsend.

This was not the name of a man who gave you rugburn.

"Course, he may not be the sheriff much longer," Myrtle said in a conspiratorial tone. "Rumor has it, he's not the favorite to win."

Though she'd only rolled into town a couple months ago, Darby had quickly learned that gossip was a cornerstone of Townsend Harbor's civic structure. "Well, if he doesn't get elected, I can always hire him to do security."

Darby glanced up from her hand blender in time to see—Ethan? Sheriff Townsend? Whatever you called a man whose cock you could sculpt by memory, but to whom you hadn't been properly introduced—making Roy jump just by scratching his jaw stubble.

"If you're looking for help, I'd fill out an application. I know how to work a crowd." Myrtle rose onto the toes of her sassy red mules to peer through the window. "I used to be a dancer, you know."

"Is that so?" Darby asked distractedly.

"Oh, yes," Myrtle warbled fondly. "In Paris. It was a long time ago, but I still have some of my costumes. They might need a sequin or two replaced, but they still fit. I haven't gained an ounce since my wedding day," she pronounced proudly.

On the contrary—she looked like she'd yielded a good deal of adipose tissue and muscle mass to the thieving ass-wrinkle of time.

"Of course, I only danced at the Moulin Rouge before I met my Frank, even though I almost never had relations with my customers. The French are such passionate men," Myrtle said on a wistful sigh.

Darby was so stunned by this new information that she glanced up and involuntarily caught the sheriff's eye over Myrtle's bony shoulder.

He no longer looked angry—he looked like he wanted to retract his head and legs into his ribcage and roll down the road like a sea anemone.

Darby put both Myrtle and Roy's coffees on the counter and took a step back. "I'm not looking for help at the moment, but I'll certainly let you know if that changes."

"Please do," Myrtle said, wrapping knobby knuckles around her cup. "The fertilizer business is in the shitter. No pun intended."

Roy kept his eyes averted as he shuffled up to collect his drink and scuttled away just as quickly.

"Wishing you all the breast!" she called.

And they were alone.

The individual air molecules seemed to thicken and darken despite the rising sun. She was no longer in her cozy little camper, but on a barstool one down from his. Her forearms on the sticky counter. The air hazy with neon-tinted smoke.

The time between then and now dissolved away. Her body came alive under the memory of his touch, her limbs going liquid.

Darby unwound the t-shirt from her head and tossed it to the side. Under a power not entirely her own, she lifted her nightshirt off as well, standing before him in her standard uniform of a cleavage-bearing bikini top that elevated her hardened nipples nearly to her neck.

No point in keeping up a façade now.

His footsteps sounded as loud as gunshots as he approached in slow strides, his eyes flicking to her breasts before finding her face.

"Welcome to Brewbies," she said. "What can I get started for you?"

His jaw flexed, then loosened as he lifted sky-blue eyes to hers. "I'm not here for coffee."

Heat flooded through her, pooling somewhere below the counter but above her ankles.

Had he been driving by when, mirage-like, her glowing neon likeness summoned him for a second round? "What are you here for?"

The man who'd made her come so hard she blacked out reached into his pocket and came back with a white envelope that he set on the counter before her.

"To shut you down."

TWO

Stout

"COME THE FUCK AGAIN?" THE WAY HER HEAD TILTED to the side was terrifying.

Ethan blinked in surprise, then stepped closer to assess her more thoroughly. The words "come" and "fuck" short-circuited his brain for a humiliating second. His gaze drifted down her half-dressed body, lingering on her curves before snapping to her face. "I'm shutting you down," he repeated, more for himself.

Seeing Fox and Cady together was enough to darken his mood. Serving an eviction notice on the one woman he couldn't seem to stop thinking about when he mixed a batch gave him a mood disorder.

Remembering the notice he'd retrieved from the city building, he slid it through the window to her. "I have papers here from the city. They're revoking your permit, but have granted you seven days to shut this establishment down. I'm sorry." It surprised Ethan how much he genuinely meant those words.

"Or what?" she asked, crossing her arms over her chest in a way that did nothing to help with his focus.

"Or you face fines and, if noncompliant, possible jail time."

Her laughter was the last thing Ethan expected, and the first thing he'd thought about when he woke up this morning.

26

Goddammit.

"Come on now, sheriff, you didn't have to make up some old excuse to put me in handcuffs. I'm into it." She leaned over her counter, her arms pressing her breasts together and deepening her cleavage as she offered him delicately veined wrists.

Tempting as the offer was... "That won't be necessary. I'm just here to serve you the papers." When her smile disappeared again, replaced by a guarded disappointment, he felt compelled to add, "I'm sorry. I truly didn't know *you* were Darby Dunwell."

"Most guys ask my name before we fuck, but you didn't seem to need it."

Muting a guilty wince, he said, "I assumed a mutual understanding, but if I was incorrect, I apologize for making you feel disrespected."

"*I assumed a mutual understanding...*" she mimicked, using a stuffy voice he did *not* fucking appreciate. "Don't be that guy. I'm not mad, I'm just wondering what you're trying to pull here, exactly. This is for real? You're telling me I can't run my business on a piece of property I own?"

Ethan didn't know a ton about women, apparently, but he knew enough to be wary when one claimed she wasn't mad.

It usually meant *big* mad. *Punish you later* mad.

"Look, Ms. Dunwell, like I said... I didn't know it was *you* when I set out to serve this paperwork. I'd honestly expected to find that a man owned the business and was demanding that you dress and..." He snapped his gaze from where it'd drooled down her chin, the column of her neck, and back to the offending—though by no means offensive—parts. "And objectify yourself in this way."

When most women frowned, it flattened their lips and creased their brow, but *of course* hers was a sultry pout. Something he instantly wanted to invert.

A fact that irritated him so acutely, he doubled down. "This isn't coming from me. There was a petition circulating around town last week that amassed enough signatures to push this through."

"Petition? But why?" She snapped up the paperwork and used the tip of a claw-like nail to slice the manila envelope open. As she read, her features remained expressionless. The only concession she made to emotion was the speed with which her lashes danced.

It did *not* remind him of how they fluttered when she orgasmed.

Not even a little.

He very much meant to allow her a moment to read and digest, but words exploded out of him before he could call them back.

"I hope you don't take this personally, Ms. Dunwell, but in the spirit it was meant. Townsend Harbor is one of Washington's premier vacation destinations, and there's a reputation to uphold that is closely guarded by a zealous town council. Other than the paper mill and the ship-building school, our economy relies on tourism."

"Exactly why I'm here, sheriff," she chirped with a meant-to-be-charming wink. "Tourists drink a metric fuck-ton of coffee, which in empirical units is still a shit-ton, if you need help with the conversion."

It'd been a long time since someone had insulted him without even glancing up.

He'd need to poke at this from a different direction, but it was almost impossible to strategize when the triangle of her bikini was inching dangerously to the left.

Which was the fucking problem.

"I'm not sure you've considered the consumer base, here—"

"And what would make you think that?" She punctuated her sharp question with a slam of the espresso scoop to discard pressed, used grounds. "You here to mansplain economics to me, sheriff?"

Shit.

"I'm only here because people asked me to be," he said honestly. "Before the petition, there were phone calls. Letters to the editor in the paper." At her expression of alarm, he rushed to explain. "I wouldn't take it personally if I were you. We are a family-friendly town, and a great deal of tourists bring their kids here for recreation. It's a reputation we've all worked hard to develop and—because of the strategic placement and sexual nature of your business—"

"You're saying I'm not family friendly just because I wear a bikini top?"

"No, I'm saying that your *business* isn't."

"I *am* my business. That's me on the sign."

He followed her red nail to the bright pink sign, half again as tall as the fucking trailer. If she hadn't been holding on to both ankles last time he saw her, he'd be able to argue. But that leg kicking out of the coffee cup looked a ton like the one he'd used as earmuffs two months ago.

"Listen here, cowboy—" she started, a lightning storm glinting in her eyes.

"I'm not a cowboy."

"I don't give a good goddamn what you call yourself, you're giving that *me big man with big thoughts and big gun* and *this town ain't big enough for the both of us* energy. Think you're gonna run me out after dicking me down? You can think the fuck again."

Ethan wasn't a stranger to cursing, but for some reason when Darby did it, the words just came out coated in sin. "I didn't... That isn't what I... I have never in my *life* d-dick-er done that."

"Let me guess. You call it 'making love.'" She rolled her eyes.

His gathering temper was the answering thunder. "I call it having sex. Like an adult."

"Oh? You're saying I'm not adult enough for you?" She uncrossed her arms to gesture expansively. "Because I'm trying to figure out just how adult my jaw had to be in order to unhinge to fit your long, hard—"

"*Okay!*" He put up a hand against the word and checked the vicinity. "That's enough. You don't have to say it."

"Why not? Saying it isn't any crazier than doing it. Which we did." She paused to flutter sarcastic lashes at him. "A lot."

"We just don't have to unpack it in public, yeah?"

Leaning out the service window, she made a big show of surveying the scene. "What public? It's only you and me here."

"You know what I mean."

"I obviously don't. So you claim to be 'like an adult.'"

He was really coming to hate the voice she used when imitating him, and the finger quotes were just not fucking necessary.

"But you can't discuss the dirty, sweaty sex we had because you're infantilized by a patriarchal society to want women but not to discuss, analyze, or control your own needs. Why do you think you're alone at this age, driving a million miles away for one-night encounters rather than having a healthy sexual relationship of your own? I put it to *you*, your dick game is strong, but you're riding the emotional short bus, buddy. And that isn't my problem."

Holy fuck. He'd taken right hooks that were less aggressive. "I'm not trying to be your problem, Ms. Dunwell, I'm trying to do you a favor. This sort of"—he waved his hand at the everything that she was—"business works better on the other side of the water, closer to Seattle or Portland."

And away from the property that was sold out from under me.

No, he reminded himself sternly. It was unethical to do this for personal gain. Which it wouldn't be, because if she put the land back on the market, the price increase would be a bitch.

"Hell," he continued, "People in Northern California would *knit* you a bikini and anoint your land with cannabis, and the SoCal set would ask you to pay twelve hundred bucks for two pieces of string. Either way, a woman like you would land on her feet. But Townsend Harbor?" He motioned toward the verdant tunnel created by a canopy of trees one had to wind through before the view of the charming town sprawled, ironically, over two symmetrical hills and the valley between. "We're a tight-knit community of locals who can be as cliquish and myopic as you can imagine," he said, encouraged by her silent, pensive regard. "People either are born here and end up dying here, move away when they launch and go to college, or retire here with discretionary income. Other than that, it's just celebrity or tech giant second homes, artists in yurts and tiny homes, hobby farms, or the seasonal workers who come in with the tide of tourists and disappear when the good weather does."

As he spoke, he did his level best not to notice her brows climbing higher and higher up her forehead. "Women. Like. Me?"

Curling his hands into fists so he couldn't tug on his collar, he stood his ground. "Women who use sex to sell goods and services." He motioned to the paperwork, quoting the legalese verbatim. "Under Article Four, subsection C. Women are forbidden from the public sale of articles depicting female sex organs within a thousand feet of the highway. To do so is a species of indecency and vulgarity that cannot be ignored or controlled by passersby."

"Jesus Christ." Her eyes rolled back in her head, conjuring the several times he'd made them do that in an entirely different capacity. "Are high schoolers not allowed to dance here, either?" She returned to scanning the page. "This law was enacted in nineteen twenty-six under prohibition. I mean, I know there are some retirees in this town, but I bet even these ass waffles who came up with this BS law have kids who are in the ground."

Ethan's air left his lungs as she shoved the half-read paperwork in his face.

"I do not accept the service of this document. Take it back."

"Um. That isn't how this works." She was making it awkward. Could she not just be cool about this? "Listen, I'm not trying to be confrontational here," he said. "I don't want any more awkwardness between us, but this corner has seen almost every sort of business lease this land and try to make a go of it, from taco trucks to fireworks to firewood. They've all failed."

"You're saying you allowed someone to sell wood on this corner? Kick them out, too?"

It was his turn to give the *oh come on* face. "It's not close enough to the picturesque downtown, which is lousy with kitschy coffee shops, nor is it on a corner where people usually stop on 101 for drinks. Did you think of these things before putting up your sign?"

A tightening of her skin over the sharp bones of her face was the only warning he had before she let him have it with both barrels. "I've been doing this a hot minute, Sheriff Small Town. I know what will work and what won't. I scoped this place out very carefully. Bought it with cash in a great deal. And it's not like I'll be mov—"

Just when he was finding his footing and a place to interject, she cut herself off, slamming her lips closed.

"Be what?" he prompted.

She side-eyed the highway. "Nothing. I'll *be* here as long as I feel is necessary. I don't know who signed that little petition, and I don't care. I've already been welcomed to Townsend Harbor by those who matter—in fact, I'll be attending a local book club at the...um...at a bookstore which name I absolutely know, and is owned by my friend Cady."

Oof. Of course Cady got to her—she was still considered a recent transplant after almost a decade, and was the town's self-appointed welcoming committee. But even she had to be grandfathered in by way of a local aunt who owned a business for over twenty years.

"I'm glad for you," he said with a bland bit of nothing. "But that doesn't affect the issue at hand."

"The issue at hand is that I have been doing this a long time, and have the skills and savvy to make this business work, but your concerns are noted."

She jumped a little when he slapped the papers on her counter for emphasis. "These aren't concerns, Ms. Dunwell—these are orders. You have a notice to shutter your stand in seven days until a hearing can be made in front of the town council regarding this issue."

"The issue being a bunch of prudes signed a petition because they still subscribe to the ludicrous idea that breasts are sex organs and not mammary glands, you ridiculous, back-asswards hillbilly."

Sigh. "There's no need for name calling, ma'am. I'm just doing my job."

"Fuck that!" She shoved a finger in his face. "Your job is to protect and serve, not pump and dump."

"That isn't what happened, and you know it."

"It's what you're doing right now. Doing your very best to royally *fuck* me and walking away as if it isn't your fault."

She had it all wrong. He wasn't doing this *to* her. He was doing this *for* Townsend Harbor and the constituents who signed his paycheck. "Again. Not my intention. I didn't know it was you when—when the paperwork was filed."

"You know it's me now," she challenged.

"Doesn't change the law." He tapped the papers with two fingers.

"No one even enforces these kinds of laws anymore!" Because she didn't have room for a good pace, she threw her arms up and spun in a circle, reminding him of how tight her ass was. "Are you kidding? Do you really have so little to do that you have to harass people for showing up to work in a bathing suit?"

Yeesh. The H-word. An officer's death knell. He should go. "I'm sorry, Ms. Dunwell." He turned on his heel, gritting his teeth at the chalky sound of the gravel.

That was not a bathing suit. His grandmother wore a bathing suit. That was a... Well, it was a distraction, was what it was. One he hoped would do them both a favor and hop in the driver's seat and peel out of town ASA-fucking-P.

Or at least before the town found out what they did to each other.

She seemed like the kind of person who overshared.

"Oh, you haven't *begun* to be sorry." Her quiet threat was encored by the loud tears of high-quality paper. "You and your town can take this notice and shove it up your collective twats. Then keep it up there and see if you can turn it into a pearl, because this is *my* land and *my* trailer and *my* business, and I'm not moving. You got a problem with that, I'll see your ass in court." With that, she flung the confetti she'd just made into the air. "I'm going to figure out how to fight this, sheriff. You can count on *that*."

"The info you need is in the paperwork. Have a nice day." It took all his self-control not to take a running vault into his truck and skid out of there. Instead, he kept his pace unhurried, then paused to indulge in a whim. "Keep your eye on the mail, Ms. Dunwell."

She crossed her arms over her lovely breasts. "For what?"

"For your littering citation."

THREE

Tamper

SMALL, PESTLE-LIKE DEVICE WITH A ROUND, FLAT END USED TO DISTRIBUTE AND COMPRESS GROUND COFFEE INSIDE THE FILTER BASKET

"ON YOUR RIGHT!"

Darby flicked the lever of the rose-gold bell to alert the gorp-core-obsessed couple to her presence, but didn't wait for them to shift to the side of the narrow asphalt ribbon before whizzing by them on her bike.

Their startled quacks of outrage were a balm to her still-smarting soul.

Those two had definitely signed it.

It.

The reason she couldn't drive her camper into town for fear of being chased down by a mob waving torches and pitchforks.

The reason why her body felt like a Tesla coil of sizzling outrage.

The reason why the Wicked Witch of the West's theme song had played on repeat in her head as she rage-pedaled into Townsend Harbor.

The petition.

All those names. Rows and rows of them. Handwritten seals of disapproval as distinct as the people they represented.

35

Obsessively small and neat. Aggressively angular and fussy. Slouching and messy. Looping and feminine. All of them sharing one common purpose.

They wanted Darby gone.

Priiing. "On your left!"

The pewter-haired pensioner whipped around, shaking one of his walking poles at Darby as she passed. "This is for pedestrian use!"

"So's your mom," Darby shouted, adding a hand gesture for good measure.

So much for exercise burning off the black mood that clung to her like the briny coastal fog.

If anything, the accumulation of clammy under-boob sweat and a sense profound regret for her choice of outfits had only augmented her fomenting discontent.

The crotch of her romper had crawled so far up her ass, she could practically taste the tiny red cherries printed on the cotton-poly blend.

Given, the halter-topped one-piece would have been a risky selection even if she hadn't been forced to utilize alternate methods of transportation, but since her verbal gutter brawl with Sheriff Dickbiscuit, Darby hadn't exactly been thinking clearly.

Piiing. "Coming through!"

The rangy pack of oblivious skateboard-toting teenagers shuffled along shoulder to shoulder, spilling out into the street.

Darby laid into her horn, and immediately regretted it.

Because rather than opting for the upgraded supersonic safety buzzer the manager at the cyclist store had recommended, Darby had insisted on his installing the old clown horn she'd been given as a gift at the pediatric oncology wing where she'd volunteered. The sound produced by the bright pink rubber ball and dented brass cone fell on a spectrum between pressurized gluten fart and a startled duck.

Darby defiantly squeezed it anyway, galvanized by the sight of her destination in the distance.

Brrippa-brippa! "Guys! Move it!"

Now, the boys not only stopped, but turned around to face her.

Thank God and gravity, five adolescent jaws dropped open and the phalanx of hormone-packed bodies parted like Red Sea.

Darby gave them an appreciative nod, feeling five sets of eyes glued to her various body parts as she sailed up to the metal bike rack just down the street from Nevermore Bookstore.

The playing card she'd secured to metal spokes with a wooden safety pin slowed its ticking as she applied the brakes and steered into one of the slots.

Reaching into the handmade wicker basket mounted to the chrome handlebars, she withdrew a bike chain roughly as thick as those used to tether battleships in the Kitsap naval harbor.

Between the extra-padded, extra-wide vegan leather banana seat, painstakingly restored Holiday Rose paint job, and thick, white-walled tires, the 1952 Schwinn Starlet had set her back almost a grand.

Guilt pricked her as she unlocked the cargo box mounted over the rear tire and lifted a foil-covered plate. It seemed to grow heavier in her hands with every clip-cloppy step of her wedge sandals. Not because the fudgy, salted-caramel squares were packed with a metric shit-ton of butter and bittersweet chocolate.

Because they were packed with deception.

Under normal circumstances, the idea of greasing a couple palms with seditious sweets wouldn't bother her in the least. Even on her best days, Darby's conscience performed about as well as the mediocre-est of government employees. Generally clocking in for its shift, but demonstrating a real lack of enthusiasm for the work.

Unless that work involved Cady Bloomquist, apparently.

When Darby had informed her loyal, decadent-drink-loving customer that she'd be coming to tonight's book club "really for real this time," Cady had been so shamelessly happy, so puppy-bouncing-out-of-a-beribboned-basket excited, that she'd broken into an impromptu happy dance right there at the Brewbies' pickup window.

Like her decision to attend the biweekly gathering of Nevermore Bookstore's Bare-Naked Book Club, the baked goods she'd brought for its members to consume had been made with an ulterior motive in mind.

Bribery.

Pure and simple.

If she was going to turn the tide of public opinion, she'd need allies.

And if she happened to pick up a few useful tidbits that helped her make Ethan Townsend's life a misery in the process... well, that was just icing on the vengeance cake.

Pausing outside the eggplant-purple facade with its ornate Gothic shingle, Darby fixed a smile on her face before pushing open the door. The friendly squeal of old hinges announced her arrival as she was met by the heady bouquet of old books and freshly brewed coffee. Spicy and fruity with a hint of vanilla.

Colombian, most likely.

It paired beautifully with the melancholy classical music filling the seemingly unoccupied space.

Unoccupied, unless you counted the proliferation of unfortunate-looking taxidermy creatures. A ragtag crew of silent spectators, they held their glassy-eyed assembly from the many shelves and tables crowded into the cluttered but cozy sitting area. To the right of the entrance, a beautiful old credenza bearing an ornate antique rotary phone, an iPad on a swivel stand, a small but very new Apple monitor, and several other assorted register-related items sat completely unattended.

A month into her Townsend Harbor residency, and this kind of thing still shocked Darby.

The benign supervisory neglect. The blind small-town trust.

In Boston, if she'd have left her closet of a coffee shop long enough to blow her nose, she'd have come back to a puddle of piss in the entryway and counter stripped of every last cruller.

She drifted over to the large moat of polished wood, as much out of a need to set down her plate of guilt-laden goodies as a compulsive habit to put herself between it and the unlocked door.

Leaning in to examine the glowing golden dial of the beautiful old rotary phone, Darby leapt a full foot when it rang.

"Coming!" Cady's voice sang from the back of the shop. As if the phone itself or the person on the other line could hear her.

Darby quickly grabbed her plate and took a step back into the entryway, attempting to look like she'd only just stepped through the door that very moment.

The squeaking of the building's old floorboards drew closer, and Cady swung into view. As she spotted Darby, her rosebud of a mouth broke into a broad smile.

"Oh my God, hi!" she said, hurrying toward the credenza as she wiped her hands on the apron knotted behind her rounded hips. "I'll just be a minute."

"Take your time."

"Nevermore Bookstore, this is Cady," she rapped out with expert brightness. Darby watched Cady's face light up, her smile deepening into a slow, seductive grin as she listened to the voice on the other end. "Well hello there," she purred. "How was your week?"

Fawkes.

Had to be. Darby was certain of it, even though her asking about his week didn't make one lick of sense.

She'd seen that kind of smile before.

Darby had caught herself wearing one just like it in the bathroom mirror of the hotel room where Ethan Townsend had made her forget her own name.

Heat crept up the back of Darby's neck. Before it could reach her cheeks, she busied herself studying the three-legged armadillo standing in as a bookend for an impressive collection of Nancy Drew mysteries.

Seeing the ghost of a tire tread on his dented shell, Darby felt a pang of sympathy. Since the lumpectomy that had turned her entire world upside eight years ago, her left breast had shot the double-barrel bird at any kind of mammary symmetry.

Me too, little buddy, she thought, giving the scaly shell a pat. *Me too.*

"Is there anything else you'd like in this week's *shipment*?" Cady asked, her voice dripping with suggestion.

The obvious euphemism made Darby smile in spite of the growing ache in her chest.

She remembered this phase. The heady, neurochemical speedball. When everything was new. When you still believed.

When your soon-to-be-ex-fiancé hadn't yet cheated with a rival dancer at the upscale Manhattan cabaret while you were backstage trying to make your custom pasties cover the radiation tattoo on your newly dented breast.

Darby chased the thought out of her head and razed its trail with a mental flamethrower.

She hadn't put an entire country between her and Aidan just so he could slink back into her skull like the oily shit-stain he was.

"Oh, I'll stack them so hard." Cady giggled as she leaned against the counter, her back turned to Darby and her pinky twirling in the phone cord's coil.

The sweetness of their exchange seemed to saturate the air, making it harder to draw air into Darby's lungs. She was having desperate thoughts of inventing an emergency that would allow her to beat a hasty retreat when the shop door swung open.

Gemma McKendrick swept in, her presence as welcome as the rain-scented gust that cooled Darby's flushed skin.

If Cady was a dreamy, doe-eyed Rapunzel, her best friend was a sassier Snow White. Milky Irish skin, dark, glossy, shoulder-blade-length hair, and bright, intelligent eyes of olive green.

The few times Gemma accompanied Cady on her morning coffee run, Darby had admired the knitting maven's boho granny-chic aesthetic. Tonight's ensemble consisted of a pleated purple and fuchsia plaid knee-length skirt, high-necked lace collar blouse, and a chunky magenta cardigan covered in appliqué flamingos.

Her own design, Darby suspected.

As with the bookstore, Darby had honestly meant to stop into Gemma's knitting and notions boutique but hadn't managed to get around to it quite yet. What with all the sexual debauchery and sinful Sumatra she'd been peddling.

"Can I help?" Darby asked, taking in Gemma's precariously balanced armload of assorted boxes and bags.

"Sure." Gemma gingerly transferred the topmost box into Darby's care. "Especially because my best friend is *completely ignoring her guests so she can phone-hump her fiancé.*" The last half of the sentence rose in volume, clearly meant to be an indictment.

Cady rolled her eyes and mimed jerking off an imaginary dick. A gesture that struck Darby as deeply affectionate.

Gemma led her up a small set of steps to a larger room where a folding table had been covered with a tablecloth bearing cursive script declaring, *I like big books and I cannot lie.* In its center, a heart-shaped platter with an impressive assortment of iced sugar cookies and pale pink cupcakes topped with bright red cherries sat.

"Those look delicious," Darby said.

"They are," Gemma confirmed. "But I'd recommend saving them until the end of the meeting, if you know what I mean." Gemma winked at her as she hauled up her burden and swung it onto the table. "I'm physiologically incapable of making more than one trip," she declared, massaging the ladder of pink dents climbing her thin forearms.

"Same," Darby said, placing the box down next to Gemma's bags.

Which was when she realized it was...buzzing?

"Oops." Gemma pawed through the contents, removing several brightly colored knots of wool to reveal an assortment of pocket-sized hot-pink vibrators. "These are from Vee—er— Vivian Prescott. She owns Vee's Lady Garden?"

Darby was used to the precise brand of look Gemma was currently leveling at her. The unintentionally patronizing performance of a Townsend Harbor local, presenting verbal flashcards for the new kid in town. Yet another reminder of exactly what she was.

An outsider.

Which, unbeknownst to Gemma, was precisely how Darby liked it.

After the smothering confines of her blue-blood East Coast upbringing and the spectacular unraveling of her tight-knit Boston circle, she'd enthusiastically embarked on her lone wolf life. Most at home in the liminal space between solitude and civilization. Embracing the edges. Frolicking in the fringes.

Until this bullshit petition dragged her smack into the center of a small-town social skirmish.

"She was super bummed she couldn't make it tonight but wanted to send some party favors in your honor," Gemma continued.

Darby blinked at her. "In *my* honor?"

Gemma's red lips slashed upward in an uneven grin. "Yes indeedy. These are the same ones she's giving away as gifts with every donation to the Brewbies."

Darby's mouth dropped open as she struggled to process this information. "Wait, what?"

Gemma lifted a condensation-kissed bag of ice from one of the grocery sacks and tore a hole in the top before upending it into a brushed metal tub. "So I one hundred percent did *not* tell Cady that this bullshit petition was making the rounds before it went public, because that would be violation of section 2.06 of the city council code of ethics. Which, as a city council member, I would absolutely never do. But however Cady managed to get a hold of this privileged information from a source that definitely wasn't me, she put out a call to the BNBC."

From another sack, Gemma began extracting bottles of rosé and poking them into the ice. "Once Mayor *Spewart's* city council cronies had officially passed the petition's vote to revoke your permit, Cady created a GoFundMe page and shared it with

Nevermore's entire subscribership. Vee contacted all her suppliers, who donated a shit-ton of product, and Myrtle started a phone tree to sweep up the over-seventy constituency who still don't know how Wi-Fi works."

Staring at the snack assortment, the realization careened into Darby with the force of a freight train.

The rosé. The vibrators. The cookies. The sweater.

Pink.

The color of her hair. Her logo. Her life, as of late.

These women barely knew her, and here they were, mobilizing like some kind of badass Amazonian army in her defense.

Darby froze, hijacked by a strange but vaguely familiar sensation. The odd tickling in her nose. The tightening at the base of her throat.

She blinked rapidly to ward off the sneeze, but found her eyes filling instead.

Oh Jesus.

She wasn't going to sneeze.

She was going to cry.

Darby could count on one hand the times she'd cried in the presence of another human and not even need all five fingers. Two of them involved caskets. One of them involved sitting in a doctor's office mid-panic attack, waiting for him to confirm what she already knew down to her bones.

Gemma stepped back, her eyes scanning Darby's face. "Are you okay?" she asked, concern etched on her features.

Darby nodded quickly, her comfortable mask of mannered calm gratefully clicking into place. "Totally fine. I just feel bad you guys went to all that trouble."

"You haven't lived in many small towns, have you?" Gemma asked.

Darby shook her head. "I've lived near them." Usually long enough to make sure whatever property she'd purchased had been developed and then resold at a healthy profit margin.

"Under no circumstances are you to drink any of this coffee."

Cady crested the stairs, the handles of a large thermal dispenser clutched in her hands. "You'll just end up judging me, and I'm already nervous that you'll think the book club is completely lame."

"Give me that." Gemma quickly stepped forward and pried the dispenser from Cady's grasp. "You know you're not supposed to be lifting things," she scolded. "I'm going to tell your husband."

"He's not my husband." A dreamy smile played about Cady's lips. "Yet."

"Well, I'm going to tell your almost-husband," Gemma reported, glancing at Darby. "She has ankylosing spondylitis. It's chronic inflammatory form of—"

"Arthritis," Darby finished for her. "My ballet teacher had it." And had been regularly miserable enough that Cady's sunny demeanor seemed a small miracle by comparison.

"I refuse to let it run my life." A determined look deepened Cady's eyes to the blue of a summer lake. "Just like I refuse to let this town's population of prudes rob me of the barista that vastly improves the quality of it."

Darby shifted, hoping to ease the unfamiliar and supremely uncomfortable feeling of her heart ballooning to fill her ribcage.

"That's sweet of you to say," she said lamely. "But no way is that happening. I don't give a rat's rectum how many notices Sheriff Townsend serves me."

"Ethan served you himself?" Cady's creamy cheeks took on a rosy flush that rapidly climbed toward the roots of her flaxen hair.

Oh, he'd served her, all right.

"Uh-huh," Darby said, her Judas of a body warming in all the wrong places at the memory.

He'd looked so annoyingly handsome in his uniform, the crisp sky-blue fabric of his dress shirt clinging to his broad shoulders and powerful arms, his creased khakis hinting at powerful thighs and not quite concealing the sizable package he dressed to the left.

The way he'd fought to keep his eyes on her face.

The way anger and lust made his jaw clench in exactly the same way.

"I'm pretty sure he irons his boxers, but he's actually not such a bad guy." Gemma twisted the cap off one of the wine bottles and filled three plastic cups, handing one each to Cady and Darby. "He may be the only man I've ever seen literally help an old lady cross the street."

"And there was that time he ran in front of a tour bus to save Kevin Costner," Cady pointed out.

It took a minute for the mental image to take root in Darby's exercise-exhausted brain. Ethan was absolutely the kind of man she could see heroically racing in front of an oncoming vehicle. To imagine the aging actor haplessly wandering out in front of one was a bit more of a stretch.

"That reminds me." Gemma took a healthy slug of her wine. "Is Kevin still shitting in the garden section?"

Darby nearly aspirated her wine, falling into a coughing fit that had both Cady and Gemma looking at her with twin expressions of concern that melted into recognition.

"Kevin Costner is Cady's cat," Gemma explained. "She sort of inherited him?"

"And he's only been leaving presents in the gardening section during thunderstorms, to answer your question," Cady said, after Darby recovered her composure. "But Dr. Hill said that it's probably because the loud noises remind him of the bus's engine."

"That makes sense," Darby wheezed, tapping her chest.

The lull in the conversation that followed seemed to stretch on forever.

This was her opportunity. The moment she'd been waiting for. Phase one of her carefully constructed plan.

So...why wasn't she doing it?

Why wasn't she telling them how their beloved, feline-rescuing sheriff had torn the strap of her vintage cocktail dress with his teeth and sent her buttons scattering across his four-star stabbin' cabin? How he'd made her come before they'd even hit the first horizontal surface? How he'd—

"Sorry I'm late."

In her vivid fantasizing, Darby had somehow missed Myrtle's approach. Quite a feat, considering the vociferousness of the old building's components.

"It's pissin' down rain out there, and of course Roy parked that big-ass Buick of his right in the best spot."

Gemma took the reusable grocery bags from Myrtle and set them on the table before helping the older woman out of her bright yellow rain slicker.

The outfit beneath was no less flashy.

Hot-pink leopard-print leggings, a cotton-candy-pink over-sized sweater, and pink paisley scarf. A hand bearing bright fuchsia nails parked itself on Myrtle's bony hip as she assessed Darby. "Well, catch me up."

"First things first. Would you like some wine?" Cady offered.

"Wine nothin'." Myrtle shuffled over to the table, her wispy white hair poking up like wet feathers. "I brought us a real drink."

"It's not more of your skunk beer, is it?" Gemma's porcelain skin took on a grayish cast. "Last time we drank that, I lost three hours and woke up in bed with a Cady's stuffed capybara."

"I still say you two make a lovely couple." Reaching into one of the bags, Myrtle pulled out a plastic jug full of magenta liquid. "These are pink ladies. Without the egg whites. The only protein I'm swallowing these days is—"

"Is it grenadine that gives it that color?" Cady cut in, trying to steer the conversation away from wherever Myrtle was attempting to take it.

Darby could have saved her the trouble. Having stage-managed the Boston Fetish Ball on several occasions, there was very little in terms of protein or various other fluids that could make her squeamish.

"So," Myrtle said after pouring herself a very generous drink and settling into one of the oversized leather armchairs. "Catch me up."

Gemma did the honors, quickly summing up everything Darby had shared with her about her run-in with Sheriff Townsend.

"Mmm, mmm, mmm," Myrtle said, already halfway through her beverage by the time Gemma had finished. "So what's our game plan?"

Now.

Now was the time for Darby to tell them that she didn't need their help. That she already had a plan of her own and more than enough resources to execute it.

Thanks, but no thanks. All stocked up on strategy. Offer appreciated but unnecessary.

But once again, her tongue refused to tear itself away from the roof of her mouth. Her careful contrivances buzzed around her brain like bees in a bottle.

What the shit was wrong with her?

"The way I figure it, we have two options." Gemma set aside her knitting needles to pick up her glass of wine. "Get the city council to reverse their ruling or get the county to go over their heads and throw it out."

Cady sagged back in her chair. "There's got to be another way. You do remember what an absolute nightmare it was when they tried to take the building from me?"

"It wasn't they, it was Caryn," Gemma pointed out.

"A Karen tried to take your building?" Darby asked, feeling a prickle of irritation on Cady's behalf.

"Not *a* Karen. *The* Caryn," Myrtle said with the wary gravitas typically reserved for creatures who terrified the peasants of medieval villages.

"Townsend Harbor's former first lady and Ethan's mother," Cady said, shifting in her chair to tuck socked feet beneath her bottom.

"After how humiliated those spineless, brown-nosing Mayor

Stewart city council simps were after what happened with her and her Roy-toy, I'd have bet they'd think twice about targeting Darby," Myrtle continued. "No offense," she added, sending a little salute Gemma's way.

"None taken," Gemma said, lifting her glass to Myrtle and draining the last of her wine.

Despite her own difficulties, Darby's curiosity snuffled ahead like an eager beagle. "What exactly did happen with her and Roy?"

Cady, Gemma, and Myrtle all exchanged a look.

"I'm going to need something a little stronger if we're going to go digging in that," Cady said, looking wilted.

"Now you're talking." Gemma was already halfway out of her chair when Darby popped out of hers to retrieve the pitcher of higher-octane pink liquid Myrtle had brought.

After having observed their group dynamic for less than an hour, Darby had already identified the cardigan-wearing knitting virtuoso as the self-appointed caretaker of her less physically able friends.

When all their glasses were filled, Darby settled back into her chair while the three women stripped the scandal bare piece by piece by titillating piece.

The affair between the late aunt and Ethan's (also late) father, the former mayor. The tenuous ownership of the building that housed Nevermore Bookstore and Cady's home. Cady's aunt's passing and probate. Cady's founding of a romance-genre specific rowdy book club in her aunt's honor. Caryn Townsend and Roy's concerted effort to drive Cady out of business and out of town.

All at once, Cady's lightning-fast decision to rally her friends behind Darby made perfect sense. Not only had both their lives been ravaged by the hideous beast that was cancer, because of her beloved Aunt's death, they'd both made the grave mistake of attempting to incorporate celebrations of female-centric sexuality into their healing process.

Darby felt a fresh wave of righteous anger wash over her.

While she'd been hunting tiny scraps of petition from the corners of her camper this morning, she'd entertained the thought of pulling up stakes and hitting the road more than once.

BC—before cancer—she'd have been more than happy to fight just on principle alone, an excess of *you can't tell me what to do* and a stubborn streak a mile wide more than sufficient to arm her for battle. IRL—in remission life—she'd learned to count the energetic cost of such clashes.

But seeing how women like Cady and Gemma had learned to live with and even accept a certain proportion of this misogynistic bullshit?

Not just no, but hell no.

She cleared her throat, choosing her next words carefully. "I don't know how to thank you for what you're doing, but I want you to know that your fight is my fight. Whatever that fight may be."

"Just say you'll keep making great coffee," Cady said with a grin. "As long as I have my C Cup Vanilla Pump 'n Dump, I can fight the entire patriarchy, and read you my favorite gothic romance when I get there, bad back and all."

"Amen to that," Gemma echoed. "Give me a B Cup Thick Shaft, and I'll fight the entire patriarchy and knit you a goddamn cardigan when I'm finished, ADHD be damned."

Myrtle, who had been uncharacteristically silent during the last part of the discussion, lifted her rheumy eyes to them. "With my Double D Dirty Screw, I can fight the entire patriarchy, turn seventy years of their bullshit into compost, and grow you a goddamn garden of divine feminine rage watered by king baby tears."

Her words vibrated with a quiet power that turned their half-teasing boast into a vow.

Though Darby had at least a few years on Gemma and Cady both, whatever outrages and injustices the three of them had endured, a woman Myrtle's age had survived far worse.

Darby stood and topped off their glasses before lifting hers in a toast. "To dukes, double-pointed needles, and divine feminine rage."

They went around the circle, clicking plastic cups and sipping Myrtle's contribution, which proved to be as powerful as her part of the toast.

Remembering the rain and her long ride home, Darby nursed hers slowly, making it last through the arrival of additional BNBC members and a local population of Townsend Harbor's un-homed regulars, with whom Darby's brownies garnered praise bordering on worship.

The discussion of *Venus in Furs* was lively, the conversation colorful, and the company so pleasant, Darby actually forgot to be worried about her predicament. Until, armed with a box of Gemma's THC cupcakes, she floated down the sidewalk toward her bike.

And ran tits-first into Sheriff Ethan Townsend.

FOUR

Mouth Feel

A SENSATION OF THE CONSISTENCY OF VISCOSITY OF A BEER.

PATROL WASN'T EXACTLY IN ETHAN'S PURVIEW AS sheriff, but he'd loved it since his first starched-shirted day out of the academy. Though a creature of routine, he'd take different routes home from work every day. Sometimes whimsy led him along suburban streets so crowded with trees one would think he was in a national forest if not for the laneways.

Other days, he drove along the jagged coast, mentally challenging battleships, yachts, crab boats, or pleasure crafts to a race.

A part of him longed to join them.

Most of him recoiled at the very idea.

If every twit with a trust fund wasted all his time on a boat, who would run things? Who would keep communities together when Main Street small businesses were shuttering all over the country at an unprecedented rate?

This time, he cruised the touristy thoroughfare of Water Street as the daylight made its gradual departure. The Victorian-style streetlamps powered up in an attempt to take over, though they were no match for the graphic colors of day's end. Damp brick buildings gleamed after a savage five-minute cloudburst. Windows glowed with anticipation for the advertised boat, music, art, and various upcoming festivals and events that flooded the town with summer cash.

Though it could have been a peaceful scene, a certain flamingo-haired problem kept popping into his mind's eye.

Darby Dunwell.

Darby Dunwell, who was supposed to be in town tonight at Cady's now infamous Bare-Naked Book Club.

Darby Dunwell. who could be currently describing his (gulp) bait and tackle to a group of women he'd known since birth, one of whom was sort of his ex.

Tossing his head back against the headrest of his unmarked SUV, he let out a rare groan of mortification.

Darby Dunwell, whom he'd done *pretty fucking well*, if he could say so himself. Though since their very salacious—very slippery—encounter, he hadn't been able to think of anything but her pink hair in his clenched fist.

Her pink sex in his mouth.

Her pink lips around his cock.

Even...when driving her out of his town.

He was off duty. Had no reason to patrol streets all but deserted before the summer deluge. All was peaceful. He should head home.

After another three rotations around the downtown area, the doors to Nevermore Bookstore burst open and a man in a dingy coat plunged into the blustery evening.

Visible through the shop window and glass door, a dozen women spilled down the stairs to the Nevermore foyer like a litter of unruly kittens. They ricocheted off and reached over each other for goodbye hugs and kisses, exchanged food and phone numbers, books and squeezes.

Which was why they didn't notice him parallel-park two doors down in front of The Mean Bean Coffee House behind a VW bus with a mural of a peacock and a yin/yang on the side.

Ethan stepped out onto the pavement, doing his best to shut

his car door gently, though he couldn't fathom why. It wasn't like he was hiding from anyone. Or lurking. Watching.

Hell no. He wasn't the kind of guy who lurked.

Lurkers were creepy, problematic motherfu— Uh oh.

He stepped back into the shadow of the bus when Nevermore's doors opened again. Better to let the tidal wave of libido-laden ladies scatter to the wind in search of wealthy werewolves or bodacious billionaires or whatever the fuck they got off to in those romance novels.

But not because he was hiding or lurking. He needed to make that very, *very* clear to himself.

"It's freezing out here." Cady Bloomquist pulled her cardigan around her generous frame as she pushed her glass door open with her hip and held it. She eyed Darby's antique bike with a dubious expression. "I can drive you home and Fawkes can bring you your bike in the morning when he comes back from cutting trails in the Hoh Rainforest."

"No need." Darby breezed out of the bookshop and dumped an armful of what he could see were leftovers and books before turning to crush Cady, Gemma, Vee, and Myrtle in a hug. "I've ridden old Lola down side streets in Ann Arbor, where the snow drifts were taller than me. Compared to that weather, this is just a little PNW pizzaz."

She *squonka squonked* her little bugle horn to everyone's delight, and stood stubbornly until the others had moved on, and Cady sought refuge from the water-chilled evening breeze.

Ethan watched in silence as Darby turned her gaze back toward the bookstore, a contemplative expression on her face. Her dazzling, painted smile faded, shoulders lifted and fell, lips parted on a beleaguered breath.

Lonely.

The word would have tripped him if he'd been walking.

Her loneliness must be bland for her to dress it up with such vibrant colors and season it with an outlandish lifestyle. She belonged to the violent throbs of light and rhythm that kept big cities alive. Hell, that kept them awake past nine p.m.

His loneliness was, in a word, vivid. Palpable. It screamed through the cavernous halls of the Townsend manse. It shivered in the cold press of his sheets. Pulsed through him now as she bent to unlock her bike.

He needed to go before the memory of them fucking in downward dog made him do something stupid.

Just pull away and let her be about her business. At least until her business moved on and she wasn't his—er—*Townsend Harbor's* distraction—er—*problem* anymore.

Part of him wanted to dive behind the van in case he should be recognized, but he shook off the thought as quickly as it appeared. He was a goddamned adult. A sheriff. How could he do something like hide from a hookup and still keep his man card?

His job was running toward the danger, for the sake of every fuck.

He strolled toward it, instead, despite the insistent voice in his head demanding he run—not walk—the other way.

She ran right into him without looking up.

"Here." He put his hand on the cold chrome of her handlebars to steady them as she regained her composure. "Let me take you home."

Shit. Wait. That hadn't been the plan. Had it?

Darby looked up at him, her gaze flicking over his features before settling on the logo of the sheriff's office on his shirt. He felt her stiffen, and her face clouded with suspicion. Straightening, she tossed the lock in her wicker basket and dislodged the bike from the rack. She folded up the kickstand with the toe of her wedged sandal (who the actual fuck wore sandals in this weather?) before turning away toward her edge of town.

"No thanks," she tossed over her shoulder as she kicked a leg over the ridiculous banana seat.

Something about the way her toned ass hit the seat had him biting down on his lip.

Hard.

Ethan furrowed his brow, confused by her response. "But it's not safe to be riding on the outskirts this late at night."

"Why, because half the town is going to burn me at the stake?" she challenged.

"No, because it's a dark-trying-to-be-stormy night, and you have at least a mile to bike once you hit the edge of town through that dark tunnel of trees." He did his best to soften his features. "Look, I know we're at odds right now, but the least I can do is get you home safe."

After studying him for a moment, she lifted her finger and twisted it into her dimple, adopting an old-timey voice and over-pouty lips. "Oh, you mean li'l old me might be all vulnerable and female and I need a big, strong man like you to protect me from the nighttime?" She cocked a smirk at him and fired, "*Please*. I started this gig in Boston next to an Irish pub with probable mob ties. Believe me, I know a thing or two about danger."

Of that, he had no doubt. "Hate to break it to you, but we're fresh out of Euro-American crime families...but close to the Olympic Mountains as we are, you might run into a pack of coyotes, or a mountain lion looking for fat racoons, or the herds of town deer that eat everyone's yards."

"So that's why everyone's arbor vitae look like mushroom-tipped dicks. Little bastards can't reach high enough to eat the top." Chortling, she positioned her sandal on the pedal.

"That's what you took from my warning?" He scowled.

"I'm not getting in your car," she said, raking him with an acerbic look. "I barely know you."

An expression of irritation burst from his throat as if she'd launched her words at his solar plexus. "You know you have nothing to fear from me. I'm a cop."

She lifted one perfect brow. "I think we both know that isn't the flex it used to be."

"Fair." With the longest sigh he'd ever summoned, he cursed the name of the ass-faced goddamned motherfuckers who wore the badge and sullied it. "Look, the deer weren't the point. The predators are. They're very real and very close. Also, that's the route drunk drivers take when they're finished for the night."

She held up a hand against him saying anything else. "Okay, so you've mansplained inclement weather, wild animals, and drunk drivers to me. Anything else we need to go over before this ABC After-School Special is done?"

"Last year we found a den of coyotes on the forested hill between downtown and uptown." He ignored her sarcasm and pointed toward the four-story staircase that connected the beach-front shops to the rest of the town. "They chased a couple of kids down the stairs, and we had to call Sequoia Forrester to reloca—"

"That's fascinating and all, but bye." Darby was pedaling down the block, waving a hand that was definitely more a *fuck you* than a farewell.

Ethan growled. As in an actual low, rumbling, throat-clearing sound that didn't seem to reach her as she stood to give her pumping feet more strength and speed.

Damn, the sight of that ass bouncing would follow him to his grave.

Her toes had to be freezing.

Not my problem, he reminded himself.

There were limits to protect and serve...in that you often couldn't protect people from their own stupidity until it was too late.

Feeling at a loss for what to do next, Ethan left his eyes glued to the glutes powering Ms. Dunwell up the curved slope beyond Water Street toward the shipyard. A gust leapt from the water and hit her sideways, causing her to overcorrect. Had a car been speeding down the hill, it would have hit her.

Spitting on the pavement, he let his string of curses follow him like a kite as he stalked back to his vehicle and wrenched the door open. She wouldn't get in the car? Fine. Didn't mean he still couldn't escort her home.

It took him no time to catch up to her, then pull to the shoulder to inch along two car lengths back from her banana seat.

A quick glance behind her sent her legs chugging even harder up the hill.

Ethan met her speed exactly, his headlights illuminating the path ahead as she stubbornly refused to acknowledge him.

He followed her past the little hospital on the second hill. Past the famous Dungeness Diner, where people ate butter-drenched crab with mallets and no dignity. Past three different bed-and-breakfasts, all of which had been featured at some time or other in *Travel* magazine. Past the organic pet store and one of four packed antique shops. Past a couple fuel stations, and the handful of competing nurseries perched at the edges of the animal rescue and lavender farms that made for the brilliant violet welcome party to the tourists.

When Darby crested the second hill, she looked over her shoulder again, her expression furious and fatigued. She yelled something at him, but the wind snagged it away before it could reach him.

He just waved.

She flipped him off.

Ethan couldn't help but grin. Kept her safe and pissed her off. That was what they call a *twofer*.

When she reached the hollow of trees that tunneled a mile out to the highway, she braked and put her foot on the road to steady herself.

He pulled up beside her as she fished in her basket. "Had enough of the wind?" he asked.

She didn't look up. "Nope. Fuck off, please."

Counting in for five and out for six, Ethan breathed through his aggravation as she secured a little headband around her forehead and clicked on a headlamp. "Come on, Ms. Dunwell, just get in the car."

"You do understand what *no* means, correct, sheriff?"

And she was off again. Launching her bike down the deep

slope, which bottomed out by the marshy riverbed before lifting out of the tree tunnel to meet the highway.

Being here tore a few of Ethan's synapses from Darby's ass and repaved the well-worn pathways back to the task at hand.

Raven Creek.

The very estuary toward which they currently sped.

Ethan used to own this tree tunnel and everything for one hundred and fifty-five forested, fertile, and spring-fed acres of property along the internationally famous Pacific Coast Highway 101.

Or his family did.

To hear his grandfather, Ethan Townsend II, and father, Ethan Townsend III, speak of it, Townsend Harbor was their birthright, and Raven Creek their investment in the future of the legacy.

Until his scheming, appearance-obsessed mother sold it out from under him without so much as a whisper of care for his future...

To Darby Leighton Dunwell.

Just as Ethan eased his foot off the brake, he slammed it on again as a black-tailed stag bounded out of the trees and, in two leaping sprints, connected with the bicycle. The power of the impact knocked both Darby and her bike off the road and out of reach of his headlights.

Before Ethan put a coherent thought together, his instincts kicked in. Jamming his lights on, he grabbed his gun, radio, and flashlight before diving out of his vehicle.

"Ms. Dunwell?" he bellowed, scanning the tree line with his flashlight and wrestling with his runaway heartrate. "Darby?"

When she didn't immediately answer, he lifted his radio to call for medical backup.

Fuck, fuck, fuck. If she wasn't okay, he would—

A pained moan filtered from the reeds on the right and a little down the hill.

Ethan plunged into the marshy flora to find Darby already

struggling to retrieve her bike from where it'd tangled in the moss and mud.

A relief so confoundingly potent struck him dumb for the several seconds it took for her to realize her handlebars were not only bent, but her back wheel was mangled.

"Son of a bitch."

"Don't move," he commanded. "I need to assess the extent of any injuries."

She rolled her eyes up to where he shined his flashlight down at her and lifted her hand against the glare. "Oh, I'm fine. I'm an aerialist and a dancer. We *know* how to fall. Hell, we know how to fall and make it look good." She kicked a mud-stained hip out and perched her hand on it in a vixen pose.

He could argue with no particular point of that.

As he scanned her for wounds, he couldn't help but notice that the tumble had only turned her into his fifteen-year-old fantasy after he'd discovered bikini mud wrestling for the first time on cable.

Not that she had on a bikini at the *moment*, but merging the fantasies was something his brain did before he thought to suggest it.

"Take my hand," he said, bracing himself on the slope and reaching down toward her.

She handed up the corpse of her bike. "Take Lola first."

He lifted the wreckage with one hand and discarded it behind him before reaching back down for her.

The roadside ravine was a bit too deep for their fingers to reach.

"Grab my flashlight," he said, extending it.

"Thanks." She snatched it from his hand, and bounced the light off every part of ground she could safely reach.

"No, dammit, so I can pull you up."

"In a minute," she snapped, as she shined the light further down to where the creek turned into a river this time of year.

He blinked. "A minute isn't going to help you get back up the hill in those shoes."

"No, but it might help me get my basket. It fell down the side of the goddamn hill, and I need a goddamn stick long enough to get it." She gesticulated an impressive tantrum that had him catching his breath that she didn't go tumbling down the hill.

"We'll get you a new basket. Come on." He reached out again.

"Getting a new one would defeat the entire point. I found that basket at an estate sale." She looked up at the sky and shook her head. "Not to mention, the baked brownies inside it were so good, they nearly restored my faith in a higher power."

Yeah. Well. He wasn't climbing down a ravine in the middle of a soggy night so she could get high.

With a deflated sigh, she turned to him and reached out.

"Hey!" she gasped as he lifted her bodily, and didn't set her down until he'd taken her the five or so strides to the road.

Once her sandals touched the ground, she squirmed out of his grip and lunged for her bicycle. The handlebars came off in her grip.

Ethan caught the frame before it fell over again. "Looks like the bolt holding it on is sheared clean through."

"You don't say," she droned, examining the damage.

"Your back tire is shot. The rim looks bent. You will probably need to replace it."

Her eyes went round and owlish in her dirt-smudged (and still adorable) face. "Oh? Is that so, sheriff? Tell me, is the earth round? Is water wet? Is there any other wisdom you can share with me where my lack of a dick would have hindered my own deduction?"

A defensive retort jumped to his lips, then he bit it back.

Well. Shit. She kind of had a point. He was being Captain Obvious, but he couldn't tell her it was because he needed anything else to focus on but how much he wanted to kiss her.

Running a tired palm over his face, he lifted the bike. "At least let me throw this in the back now and take you the rest of the way home."

He was still too shaken by her near-mishap to enjoy the fact that her coat reminded him of something his dog shat out when he'd eaten the tinfoil with the dinner inside it.

"You don't want me in your car," she said. "I'm filthy."

Yeah, she was.

"It's okay. Motor pool will clean it. The inmates at the jail like to get outside and wash cars. Sometimes we get them fast food and let them play in the sprinklers like kids."

"Well, in that case." She marched to his vehicle and opened the passenger door—before he could get there to hold it for her, goddammit—and slid into the seat.

After retrieving the two pieces of her bike, he put the back seats down flat and tucked it into the SUV's trunk.

He mouthed a little prayer for both of their survival as he made the tiny journey to the driver's seat and folded himself into it.

She clicked the lights off a beat before he could, and the red and blue flashes went dark.

"That's a crime, you know," he grumbled.

"Arrest me." She pulled some moss out of her hair and chucked it out the window.

"Most women thank me when I rescue them from such a predicament," he pointed out, apropos of nothing.

"Most women have been conditioned to respond deferentially to men in positions of power for survival reasons. Not sure I'd brag about that."

"I'm not," he muttered. "Put your seatbelt on."

She didn't move.

Had she heard him?

"Buckle up," he said again.

She snorted. "It's only a half-mile, and the road is empty."

He gaped at her. "Did you learn nothing from what just

happened here? You should have been wearing a helmet, by the way. And probably some sort of rash guard."

"Yeah. Okay, Daddy," she said in a voice usually employed by angsty teens.

You'll call me Daddy.

Ethan coughed as if the thought might have burst out of his mouth instead of his lizard brain.

"Excuse me if I don't fall all over myself worshiping my enemy," she continued. "So typical. You want some sort of reward for helping when it's your fault I biffed it in the first place."

That snapped him out of it. "I'm sorry, you think I summoned that deer out of the forest to knock you over? You could have been killed!"

"I'm amply aware of that fact," she snapped. "Thank you for condescending to me about it. But I wouldn't have been there in the first place had you not been following me like some fucking police escort I didn't need or ask for."

"You don't know that. You'd have ridden home either way."

"But I wouldn't have been rushing to get away from you. I wouldn't have been in that spot at that *exact* moment...ergo, that's your fault." She crossed her arms over her chest.

"It isn't—!" Ethan stopped himself. Counted to ten. And then did it again in French. "Put. Your. Seat. Belt. On."

She sat there looking straight ahead.

"Of all the fucking stubborn..." Because he was brought up well, he didn't say the words that followed as he reached over to strap her the fuck in his own damn self.

Immediate mistake.

All sorts of warning bells sounded the alarm, and red flags painted his vision crimson as his torso came into contact with hers.

Mud transferred. Her breast touched his arm. Her breath tickled his hair.

And fuck an entire flock of ducks if he didn't have a semi by the time he clicked her in.

Motherfuck.

He tapped the pedal harder than he usually did, and the vehicle leapt forward. Half a mile was nothing. He wouldn't have to look at her or speak until he could drop her off and peel away.

"Why not go after Vee?" she asked.

His brain stalled for a second. "What?"

"She has a vagina store, for fuck's sake. If boobs bother you this much, then pussy must send you into outer space."

His mouth pressed into a grim line. "From what I understand, Vee's Lady Garden is a medical sort of deal."

"Okay, C-Creepy-O, explain to me exactly how a thirteen-inch strap-on is medically necessary?"

He slanted her a smile. "Didn't think I'd have to."

"Oh, fuck off. You know what I mean."

He did know what she meant. "But there's...other stuff too. Like how to take care of your...lady business stuff." Not that she had anything to worry about in that department that he could tell. And he'd thoroughly examined the area.

Darby suffered a dramatic seizure. "Lady business stuff? Give me strength."

"I'm trying to behave myself, here."

"What you're trying to do is fuck me again. This time out of my livelihood."

Glancing over, he noted the defiant lift to her chin, the tension in her every muscle, the ire radiating off her in palpable waves.

She was right. Tonight she hadn't needed him at all. He had no doubt in his mind that she would have made it home on the strength of her will alone.

So, why didn't he leave her to it? Why did the idea of her being too cold, too alone, vulnerable to the elements and the whims of the night, make him a little crazy?

Maybe because they had boned.

Maybeeeee...because he wasn't the kind of guy who did the one-night-stand thing very comfortably. He was the kind of guy who got attached. Who cared. Who fixed things, took out garbage, opened doors, and drove his lady around.

His lady?

Darby Dunwell was many things, but *his lady* was not one of them.

He pulled through to the cleared corner of land upon which her trailer hunkered behind a few tables whose chairs had been stacked out of sight. The offending vintage sign was dark, but outdoor patio lights strung around the little picnic area gilded the surrounding trees with gold.

"I'm not your enemy," he said, remembering what she'd called him earlier.

"Okay, well, with friends like you, who needs them?"

He grunted as the hit connected. "I'm saying...this isn't personal..." Wait. That wasn't exactly true, was it? "I mean, this isn't meant as an indictment upon you as a person. It's important."

"It *is* about me," she argued passionately. "It's *happening* to me. And regardless of how you and a couple of prudes feel about what I do, I love it. And I'm proud of it. And I truly believe it doesn't hurt anyone. In summation, you and the rest of the moral police can eat my entire ass."

Ethan was smart enough not to mention he already had.

She'd picked a great parting shot, and would have looked amazing stomping off into the night...

Had she not been hindered by a door latch.

"Child locks," was all he said by way of apology. Frigid claws wrapped around his wrist. "You let me out of this car, Sheriff Townsend, or so help me I'll slap you with a lawsuit faster than you can say—"

"Is that blood?"

She blinked, her expression frozen between bewildered and alarmed until she looked at where he was studying the cuff of his shirt.

Peeling her hand away, she stared at the drying dark red stains on her hand that'd transferred with some of the mud.

"I thought you said you weren't hurt," he accused, undoing her seatbelt.

"I didn't think I..." She paused for a mental scan of her person and then drew her knee up to find a few layers of dermis was missing in a gnarly case of road rash. "Oh, I must have put my hand on it. I didn't even know that happened. You know how it is when you fall...it's like...everything vaguely hurts but also doesn't until the adrenaline wears off."

"Let me get you something for that," he said.

"No, don't bother, I have stuff insi—"

He was already out and shutting the car door on her arguments. He set her bike parts against a tree and grabbed a first-aid kit from the back. He did his best not to enjoy how much racket she made trying and failing to open the door.

He lifted the latch but put out an arm when she made to get out of the car. "Look. I could lose my job if I don't assess your injuries and something awful ends up happening to you tonight."

"Oh please, it's road rash. I'll shower off and be fine."

"You have waterproof flexible knee bandages in your trailer?" he challenged.

She didn't answer him, but the flicker of her lashes did.

"Okay, then." He squatted down as she swung her feet over the doorjamb and placed her knee at eye level.

Every hot, bendy, naked, thrusting, throbbing thing they'd done crowded into his brain and short-circuited his fine motor skills as he tried and failed eleven times to separate the bandage wrapper from the bandage.

Once he'd managed, he wet a gauze with disinfectant and cupped the back of her knee.

Darby's face contorted in pain, and Ethan felt a pang of guilt. He had been responsible for this, after all.

Gently, he began to clean the wound. His touch was soft but firm, and he took his time wiping away the dirt and gauging the depth of the cut. Once it was clear that the damage was very surface level, he blew on the wound lightly.

Her breath hitched and her entire leg erupted in goosebumps.

Ethan had never tried so hard in his life not to remember someone's nipples. Never.

"Apparently the pandemic taught you nothing about how your breath just dis-disinfected my knee," she grumbled.

She was silent as he pressed the stuff to her wound, and he didn't dare look up until he'd applied the waterproof seal like a second skin.

"Boom. Dis-dis-disinfected."

"Ninja Turtles?" she asked with a lifted brow.

He chuffed and shook his head, still pressing the edges of the bandage in place. "Fresh out of Peppa Pig and Wonder Woman."

Finally satisfied with his work, he sat back on his haunches and looked up.

She met his gaze with an expression that seemed to reflect his own thoughts—equal parts attraction, fiercely regretted choices, and a concoction of emotions they hadn't quite put names to yet.

Her eyes turned liquid as her posture grew stiffer by the second, and tension settled into her body like a heavy mist.

Staring into those evocative eyes filled Ethan with an overwhelming urge to protect her. To kiss and soothe, stroke and caress her worries away.

Which really pissed him off, because he was one of those worries.

I don't want to be your enemy.

The last thing in the world he expected to follow that thought was the rush of her breath caressing his lips.

When had they leaned in so close?

For three seconds he sat like a pile of spare parts as she inundated him with the aroma of chocolate brownies and strawberry lip stuff, the scent of her underscored by the loamy moss still clinging to her hair and bits of her clothing. It was like the air after a storm. The beach after the pull of a wave deserted it.

Ephemeral. Intoxicating.

I want to be free to want you.

As if she could read his thoughts, she leaned forward, her eyes locked on the lips he'd accidentally just moistened with his tongue.

No. Nope. Nuh uh. If she kissed him, he'd forget his name, and possibly all the reasons they were wrong for each other.

Right before they might have connected, he turned his head slightly, allowing her kiss-ready lips to land against his clenched jaw.

She jerked back, touching her mouth as if his chin bristles had drawn blood.

If he was in such proximity, he was in danger of forgetting that kissing her would be a betrayal of them both.

And that would be wrong.

Ethan heaved himself to his feet and put the car door between her eye line and his erection before she noticed. One look at her told him he'd failed.

Everything they'd done and left undone swelled between them, but a beloved oak tree bristling in the wind cemented Ethan's tongue to the roof of his mouth.

Wordlessly Darby stood and brushed off her backside, her tongue still making enticing sweeps over her lips.

"Why Townsend Harbor?" he lamented. "You could have picked anywhere else."

"I came because I thought I needed to get away from everything and be in the trees," she said. "I'm staying because this town needs someone like me."

FIVE

Drip Method

BREWING METHOD THAT ALLOWS HOT WATER TO SETTLE THROUGH A BED OF GROUND COFFEE.

DARBY SAT AT HER TINY KITCHEN TABLE, A STEAMING cup of coffee at her elbow, and Ethan Townsend on her mind. The sun hadn't yet peeked over the horizon, and despite an icy shower in her tiny bathroom cubby, her body still hummed like a tuning fork. Every time she blinked, the immaculately maintained interior of the sheriff's SUV assembled itself around her. Slow, fat tears of rain sliding down the windows and beating on the roof. The air between them heavy with the scent of him—an intoxicating brew of briny wind and woodsy soap emanating from skin heated by richly earned irritation.

Laced with lust.

Darby's throat still ached from the fat crow she'd had to eat after the obviously suicidal and/or masochistic buck decided to tear ass directly into her path.

Hit by a goddamn deer.

Of all the lousy luck.

A shiver worked its way through her as flashes of the nightmare that had rolled her out of bed before the ass-crack of dawn flickered through her mind. Wide, startled eyes. Sharp-pronged

68

antlers. Scrabbling hooves and an unearthly scream of animal terror.

Okay, that last bit might have been churned out by her fevered subconscious, along with the "Watch it, lady" that had fallen from its black-lipped maw in a Southie accident remarkably similar to Tony Two Toes, the bookie who had frequented her very first coffee shop in Boston.

In the real-life version, the buck had bounded off, its white flag of a tail held up like a stiff middle finger, completely ignorant of the damage both Darby and her beloved bike had sustained.

Darby made herself focus on the heartbreaking image of twisted metal and the lingering throb of her wounds instead of the memory of Ethan's deft and tender fingers on her knee as he'd dressed them.

Instead of the awkward, shearing kiss she'd planted on his stony jaw when he deliberately turned his head.

Her lips still stung with the ghost of his eight o'clock stubble, the sensitive skin imprinted with the memory of about 1000psi of tension in the muscles bunched beneath it.

The rejection stung as much as the paper spread out on the seashell-pink 1950s metallic-flecked Formica tabletop before her.

The official order allowing her exactly six days before the county intended to shut her down.

Six days until Sheriff Townsend would force her to close her service window and shut down her espresso grinder. Reaching for her mug, she took a sip of double espresso, a brew as black as her mood.

Knowing she had allies in Cady, Gemma, Myrtle, and Vee was a comfort, but not a cure.

Taking a deep breath, Darby smoothed out the creases in the copy of the order Gemma had sourced, since Darby had torn up the last one and tossed it at Townsend Harbor's sheriff like so much confetti.

She'd stared at the text until her eyes were in imminent danger of going crossed, reading and rereading the legalese for even the tiniest of loopholes. As Tony Two Toes, dear friend of the infamous Kelly family whom she'd rented her coffee shop from, had taught her to do.

...sexually inappropriate business... shall refrain from selling...

Her gaze snagged on a word and doubled back.

Selling.

Selling.

Sheriff Townsend might be able to stop her from selling her coffee, but he couldn't stop her from giving it away.

A deluge of ideas rushed into her mind on a tidal wave of caffeine-driven inspiration. Darby reached for a notebook and began furiously scratching them down.

Item one: Name??? Carnival for the Cure. Benefit for the Boobs.

Item two: Action Plan

1. *Next six days: business as usual. Send strippergram to sheriff's office?*
2. *Reach out to performer friends: Ben Dova (her hyperflexible contortionist/tax guy), Mary Anette (her former yoga teacher/body suspension artist), Gabe "the Babe" Kelly (kid next door/ex-con turned carnival worker who could erect a Ferris wheel faster than shit through a goose), Miss Malicious (sideshow stage manager and pet sitter extraordinaire), et al.*
3. *Mobilize Zoomers — Sex-positive TikTok? FetishTok? BookTok? CoffeeTok?*
4. *Raise shit-ton of cash*
5. *Fuck Ethan Townsend*

Realizing this could be taken several ways, Darby scrawled in an addendum: *in the strictly karmic sense.*

Satisfied, she set down her pen and scooted out of the booth to rinse her coffee cup and fill her pale pink watering can at the sink in her kitchen cubby.

The hollow sound of the water climbing up the sides lowered her blood pressure by several points.

Let Ethan think he'd won.

Then, the morning after he'd triumphantly driven off into the sunset in his county-issued SUV, she'd wait for word of the circus to reach him.

Imagining the look on his face when that same SUV crunched back up the crushed-shell-lined circular drive before her camper sent a little flutter rippling through Darby's middle.

Ethan would fix that icy glare on her through a windshield even bugs wouldn't dare sully by dashing their tiny brains out mid-flight. His angular lips set in a scowl, the muscles of his stony jaw flexing as he clenched his teeth against words she knew him perfectly capable of saying, given the right provocation.

And dear God, did she enjoy provoking him.

Just as she had when she'd refused his offer to give her a ride home last night.

The reason was embarrassingly simple.

Ethan Townsend brought out the brat in her. And though she doubted he recognized the patterns or would even know what to do with them if he had, Darby now knew she couldn't trust herself alone in the confinement of a vehicle with a man who quietly and obliviously radiated dom energy by the ass-load.

Because her virulent dislike of the man had done not one thing to dampen—poor choice of words, all things considered—her desire for him.

Finished watering her indoor menagerie of plants, Darby slipped her feet into the feathered mules that matched her pink silk kimono, and stepped outside to address the various flower-pots and planters. Seeing how pretty the camper looked in the pale light of dawn only redoubled her determination.

She had quite literally poured her own blood, sweat, tears—not to mention a healthy supply of cash—into the old Airstream's renovation smack in the middle of her radiation treatment. An act that had proven utterly incomprehensible within the small circle of friends she'd accumulated during her brief Ivy League under-grad education.

To her, it was a symbol of freedom. Of a life lived outside the long shadow of a trust fund her parents had treated as both a bit and bridle. Of a life lived without dependence on another living soul.

And Darby had no intention of allowing Sheriff Townsend or anyone else to tell her where she could park it.

The birds had taken up their warmup exercises for the dawn chorus. Meadowlarks. Robins. Song sparrows. Chickadees.

"Breakfast," she sang, lifting the lid of the metal garbage can where she kept her industrial-sized bag of birdseed.

"You should put a lock on that."

Darby shrieked as a rainbow of birdseed flew from the cup in her hand and rained to the ground at her feet. She whirled around, ready to clock whoever had startled her, when her brain gradually matched the giant, hulking shape and voice with a name.

Roman Fawkes. Cady's Viking.

He sat on one of her picnic tables, his size-eighty-three boots propped on the bench and his hands gripping the table's thick edge.

Had she really walked right by him? Given he was roughly the size of a backhoe, she didn't see how that was a possibility.

"Jesus fuck," she said, pressing her hand to her rioting heart. "What the hell, fella? You trying to kill me?"

"Something tells me it would take a lot more than that." The deep voice rumbled out of the darkness.

"Way to make this even creepier." Darby's body issued a series of detailed complaints as she stretched sideways to flip on the camper's exterior light.

The golden glow bounced off the craggy angles of Fawkes' weathered face, but only cast his deep-set dark eyes further into shadow.

"What the hell are you doing here so early, anyway?" she asked.

Fawkes' voice was a smoky rasp against the sweet early-summer morning air. "Wanted to talk to you before the hordes descend."

Darby reached into the pocket of her robe and pulled out her cell phone. "For the record, this right here works at all hours of the day and is 99.99999 percent less likely to result in a broken nose and/or perforated testicle than sneaking up on me."

"I wasn't sneaking," Fawkes said. "I was waiting."

"Maybe wait a little louder next time?" she suggested, bending to refill her cup with birdseed. "A good throat clearing always works for me. Maybe a courtesy cough. Hell, a fart would have reverberated rather nicely on that table."

The faintest tinge of color haunted Fawkes' sharp cheekbones as he cleared his throat.

"Yeah, see? That would have worked perfectly about three minutes ago."

"Noted," he said. "I won't take up too much of your time."

"I appreciate that, seeing as you've already stripped a good five years off my life," she said, picking her way over to the bird feeder. Already, her regulars were bouncing like feathered ping-pong balls between the branches of the ancient oak overhead, waiting for her to move off so they could move in.

"Cady told me about the petition," he said.

Straight to business, this one.

Darby bent to crank the handle of the water hookup pipe jutting out of the ground behind her strategically placed flower planter. After a groan and a hiss, the collapsible garden hose began to fill, drawing with it the memory of a certain part of Ethan's anatomy as he'd reached across to buckle her seatbelt.

"Did you come to offer your condolences?"

"My assistance."

Darby lifted the hose's brass spray nozzle and glanced at

Fawkes over her shoulder. "Are you volunteering to crumple Ethan into a sheriff wad and stuff him into a sewer grate?"

"I'm officially retired from that kind of assistance," Fawkes said.

"I have plenty of other ideas." Darby twisted the spray tip from "could probably peel flesh" to "rain shower" and aimed it at the next pot. "But some of them require specialty equipment."

"Like cement galoshes?"

Darby arched an eyebrow at him, wondering whether his question was a general nod to her East Coast roots, or a hint at specialty research on his part.

"Like Vaseline and a nine iron," she said. "Or KY and a pitching wedge. I'm not picky."

An enigmatic almost-smirk tugged at one corner of Fawkes' lips. "As much as I'd like to see that scenario play out, sporting equipment isn't your most effective weapon in a place like Townsend Harbor."

"Slander?" A guess based on her own recent experience. "Blackmail?"

"Information."

"Like when the tides are coming in so you can figure out when to dump a body?"

"Like who stands to gain the most from your loss," Fawkes said cryptically.

"The whole goddamn town, apparently," Darby muttered as she hauled the hose to the next planter.

"Or the person who tried to get his grubby hands on this land before you bought it."

Darby's stream snapped off as her thumb slipped from the grip. "Is this information you have?"

From some unknowable environ on his hulking form, Fawkes produced a manila envelope and held it out to her in one massive paw.

Darby slung the hose over the back of an Adirondack chair and picked her way over to him, feeling a little ridiculous about her choice of footwear in his presence. With one pointed finger-nail, she flipped open the envelope's flap and pulled out the paper within. She made it halfway down the page before a prickling chill stole down her spine.

"Roy Dobson?"

Fawkes nodded. "Kind of odd that Roy Dobson frequents your establishment despite being one of the most vocal members of Townsend Harbor's self-appointed morality police, no?"

"I mean, yeah. But then, odd is kind of Roy's thing, right? Cady told me all about his creeping around the bookstore like some kind of discount bin poltergeist."

"That's not all he's been doing."

Darby looked up from the document in her hands, studying Fawkes for a moment before he spoke.

"Always struck me as strange that he was so willing to be Caryn Townsend's fall guy when there's no proof that money ever changed hands."

"Maybe she paid him with nature's credit card," Darby said, tucking the paper back into the envelope and sandwiching it beneath her arm.

Fawkes' heavy brow lowered. "Or maybe Roy wanted the leverage."

"For what purpose?"

"The Townsend family has steered Townsend Harbor like a private yacht for centuries. And yet a guy as universally disliked as Roy seems to have his fingers in just about every pie in town."

Darby shuddered. "I'd rather not think about where Roy puts his fingers, if it's all the same to you."

Fawkes' flannel-clad shoulders bunched toward his ears. "Might be worth looking into, is all I'm saying."

"Any suggestions as to how I might go about that?" Darby asked, picking a brown leaf from a pot of slut-red geraniums.

The table creaked as Fawkes shifted his weight forward. Better the table to bear his considerable mass than the bench, she supposed.

"Seems the people who were chummy with Roy while Caryn was trying to get control of Nevermore haven't spent much time with him lately."

"And you know that because..." Darby trailed off.

Anger transformed Fawkes' already brutal features into something more primal. Lethal, even. "Because they fucked with Cady. Once you fuck with Cady, I will never not have eyes on you."

A smile creased Darby's lips despite the graveness of the sentiment. Every heart as sweet and kind as Cady's should have one as fierce and loyal as Fawkes' protecting it at all costs. Darby of all people knew how rare and precious such a thing was.

"Any suggestions as to how I might best approach our friend Roy? He doesn't seem to like anyone very much."

From the same ether that Fawkes had materialized, he now produced a small plastic-sealed box and held it out to her.

Darby set the hose aside and took it. "Cigars?"

"Cohibas are his favorite. Smokes one every evening in the alley next to his shop."

She resisted the urge to tease him about liking to watch after a particular memory a pink-cheeked Cady had shared during their discussion of voyeurism in Christina Lauren's *Beautiful Stranger* came to mind. A novel Myrtle had pronounced "a first-class snatch soaker," to Darby's delight.

"Anything else you can share?" she asked.

"He's not a local. He moved to town about ten years ago."

This surprised her. His run-down secondhand shop occupied a primo spot on Water Street. Darby had assumed Roy owned the building since before efforts had been made to double down on Townsend Harbor's allure as a tourist trap, and had flatly refused to sell.

"I'll keep that in mind," she said.

Fawkes pushed himself off the table and turned to leave.

"Wait," Darby said. "You at least have to let me send you home with some coffee."

Fawkes only shook his head. "Appreciate the offer, but Cady likes to look at the menu to decide what she wants."

"But she orders the same thing every day," Darby pointed out.

"Yep," he agreed. "But it adds an extra five minutes to our trip."

"That's so fucking adorable I think I might actually vomit," she said, tucking the cigar box next to the envelope. "See you later, then, I guess?"

"See you then." He turned to go again but paused at the edge of her tulip border, his gaze swiveling back toward her camper. "Where's your bike?"

Darby glanced at the hitch where she'd secured her mangled bike the night before. Sure enough, it was missing.

The chain was still there, lying in a loop on the ground like a discarded snakeskin. It had been cut cleanly with something sharp and strong enough to slice through the steel chain like butter. She bent down and ran her fingers over the cuts, knowing in an instant who had taken it and why.

A florid string of curses escaped her then, Ethan Townsend's name strung between the various insults like pearls.

She was panting when she finished, her bathrobe sticking to her with the fine sheen of sweat that had erupted during her tirade.

Fawkes had observed all of this silently, a shadow passing behind his eyes and vanishing just as quickly before he spoke.

"Be careful of Sheriff Townsend. He's got the nice-guy act down. But he's a lot more brutal than anybody knows." Fawkes' hands tightened into ham-sized fists at his sides as he glanced back at her over his shoulder. "Even himself."

Darby gave him a brittle smile and managed to remain upright until he disappeared back into the darkness. Only once he'd faded into whatever mist superheroes were always fucking off into did Darby allow herself to swoon onto the bench that he had occupied so stealthily.

If he only knew.

SIX

Head

"RHODODENDRONS CAN SUCK MY DESERT-DWELLING DICK," Deputy Trent McGarvey muttered as he deadheaded another pink-gone-brown blossom as if it'd insulted his voluptuous mother.

Ethan gritted out a sound of mirth but didn't add any complaints.

Much as Deputy McGarvey, a city-born former MMA fighter, hated donning gardening gloves on his off-hours, Ethan loved it.

The best part of being a sheriff was the community outreach. So many officers put too much stock into the "protect" part of their creed. Why there wasn't a better emphasis on "serve" in this country made no fucking sense. Establishing that a community leader was willing to serve made the protecting part a hell of a lot easier. In his experience, anyhow. Ethan lived for emergency preparedness mock training, for tsunami drills and anti-bullying assemblies at local schools.

And every spring, he looked forward to Deadhead Sunday, a Townsend Harbor holy day where Townsendites, from Water Street, to uptown, to the lighthouse and the state parks, all put on

78

their gardening gloves and clipped the damp and dying rhody blossoms from their intensely green bushes.

After, a beer tent and food trucks appeared like magic, and the town called in some incredible band from across the Puget Sound in Vancouver or Seattle for the Concert on the Docks.

The docks being the three wide piers along the boardwalk where cruise ships on their way to Alaska mingled with the occasional celebrity yachts to unload their shoppers—er—tourists to Water Street's several blocks of shops, galleries, pampering, and eateries.

"I like to do something physical on Sundays," he replied carefully. "And the more people see us willing to help, the more likely they are to come to us when they need it."

Ethan thought he might have seen a little admiration before McGarvey rolled his eyes. "You'll have to understand if my people aren't as enthusiastic about mandatory gardening."

Hesitating, Ethan straightened. Something he didn't even consider when handing out an invitation for obligatory labor to a Black man.

"Know what else can suck my dick?" McGarvey continued, his bad mood picking up steam. "Azaleas, hyacinths, lilacs, and whatever the fuck these puffballs are that keep sticking to my legs. And those goddamn proselytes damaging my calm."

"Met Pam and Janet, did ya?" Ethan chuckled before bending over to discard a rock he'd dug up. He'd been wondering where the town's sandwich-board-toting, end-of-days-fearing, Bible-verse-spouting contingent of old and wooly women had been.

Festivals were like their Super Bowl.

"They refused to pull the weeds by the weed bakery," McGarvey marveled, as if Ethan might be hearing this for the first time. "Said they were afraid of the 'devil's lettuce' and that the metaphysical shop owner kills small animals and, after her satanic rituals, fertilizes the marijuana with their corpses. I poked around, and all I found were a few composted eggshells and some fluff that looked suspiciously like one of Kevin Costner's hairballs."

"Welcome to Townsend Harbor." Ethan sighed as he remembered just how fucking relentlessly "Pammit and Jamela," as the dispatcher, Judy, called them, clucked at him.

Not half so much as they did the town police, but seventy times more than they should. Not only that, but they also made it their self-appointed mission to rouse the rabble whenever they felt a witch needed to be burned.

McGarvey hadn't finished his tirade. "It took all my training not to tell them how much they can fuck the hell off."

Ethan grunted from where he curb-stomped his shovel into the ground. "So can whoever put this sign here."

It was several months until election day, and already someone had broken a hundred-and-fifty-year unspoken truce by putting up a political sign on Water Street turf. Politics tended to slam tourist wallets shut, and that was a fact any side could agree on.

KIKI FORRESTER FOR SHERIFF

Any other name and he'd have fed the sign to a trash compactor.

"Who's tryna have a sheriff named Kiki, anyhow?" McGarvey asked. "That's like naming your kid Billy Bob and expecting them to be president someday. Though...way things are going..."

Ethan made a motion for his newest deputy of eight days, a transplant from Tacoma by way of Albuquerque, to keep his voice down. "Her name is Kikisoblu Nootka Rose Forrester, after Chief Seattle's daughter."

"That's different, then." Trent's granite eyes gleamed with only half a sense of humor and the other half a wince. "Wait. Please tell me she's not some new-age white lady."

A snort escaped Ethan when he thought about how many of those white ladies McGarvey was going to have to deal with. How many of them would chase him with Sadie Hawkins intensity.

"Her brother is right over there."

McGarvey glanced over as Ethan hooked a thumb to where Cypress "Cy the Tree Guy" Forrester had fastened himself to a redwood almost twenty feet off the ground by a sling and the strength of his legs. He didn't wear his blue-black hair in a long braid, like his father, but his ochre skin gleamed with a burgundy undertone as he topped the tree for the sake of a view.

Cy, the town's premier arborist, was a gentle giant, until you said something about one of his sisters. Come to think of it, no one knew exactly how many sisters Cy's had. Anyone who thought they knew all the Forresters seemed to find themselves introduced to one they hadn't met before.

"Kiki Forrester is the chief of police over the S'Klallam tribe, which is technically part of the county." He tossed his head in the westerly direction, where a thirty-minute drive along the jagged coast would land you in Bryn, a picturesque inlet where the Strong People, or S'Klallam tribe, had turned a reservation into a resort that would rival almost any place on Victoria Island or even Alaska.

"Hmm." Trent nodded, the chilly spring sun gleaming off skin like polished obsidian as he flashed his brilliantly white smile. "Sorry, boss. Might have to vote for her."

Trying to push even half of his heart into a laugh proved too much effort. So Ethan barked out something he hoped passed for genuine, and returned to churning up the earth around the lawn sign so summer blooms could be planted beneath the towering, newly bare bushes.

Ethan searched for something to change the subject. He always evaded any talk of elections to his deputies. He never wanted them to feel pressure not to vote their conscience. He never made signs. He didn't raise money. And any funding he dumped into his pitiful campaign was from his own trust.

He used to be proud of the fact that his name, alone, made him a de facto winner in this town. That his family's subsidies to the fairgrounds, community sports, music programs, and tourist boards would do his talking for him.

Now, while looking at Deputy McGarvey and his kind-if-wary eyes, or thinking about how much he respected his colleague Kiki Forrester and her entire family, a wedge of shame propped open the door he wanted to slam on the glaring reality of his immense privilege.

"You ever been to the reservation?" Ethan asked, landing on a subject. "It's stunning. A great place to take visiting family or a date if they get sick of small-town entertainment." On top of their five-star accommodations—or the next-door three-star hotel for the budget conscious—they offered what so many in the U.S. could not. Legal and recreational marijuana, magic mushrooms, a gleaming, tasteful casino, skiing on the Olympic Mountains, hunting, fishing, hiking, and dining that would impress the most finicky of epicureans.

"Yeah," Trent said, karate-chopping a flower into little pink confetti. "They really lucked out in the reservation department."

Ethan cringed. "Not speaking from lived experience, obviously, but I don't think any Native considers their rez good luck."

"You've never been to the Southwest," Trent said, giving effortless side-eye.

Humiliatingly aware that he looked like a television Viking come to rape villages and pillage women—not to mention he came from a long line of wealthy colonizers and captains of industry—Ethan opened his mouth to apologize for every un-melanated human alive when a sharp sound cut him off.

"Oh my Gawd!" squealed a girl with aqua hair and a bow tie who waved a disposable coffee cup with a bright pink lid. "Which one did you get? Mine's the Tiramisu Toffee Tits with a shot of dark desire!"

An Asian kid traveling in a pack of youths toasted her with an identical paper cup, and raised her squeal with a glass-shattering squawk. "Honey almond Hard Hump. But my favorite is Salted Caramel Quickie."

"So cute, right?" asked the first.

"So fucking cute!" agreed her new friend.

"Mama, what's a quickie?"

A mother holding hands with a preschooler cast the kids a look of distress and disapproval.

A stab of irritation picked Ethan right in the chest, and he used his shovel to attack the ground with renewed vigor.

Darby's coffee.

So.

Bury.

Fucking.

Stomp.

Cute.

Dig.

"I bought a Mount Me Macchiato on ice coming into town this morning." McGarvey picked up the clear plastic cup in which floated half-melted ice and the spiced remnants of betrayal.

"Not you too."

He shrugged. "Not only is the coffee good, the barista is a smoke show." He wrapped his lips around the straw and slurped loudly. "We flirted this morning, I think."

Good for him. Good for *fucking* McGarvey and his laid-back voice that was as smooth as his Bic'd head and southwestern patois.

"She flirts with everyone," Ethan muttered.

"Yeah?" McGarvey's eyebrows went up. "Well, hate to tell you that she had one of these Kiki Forrester signs front and center in her parking lot this morning, and had a few...spicy things to say about you when she saw me in uniform."

"You're not wearing a uniform," Ethan pointed out blandly.

McGarvey puffed out his cheeks and averted his eyes. "Yeah, but I was every other morning I stopped by this week."

Ethan had opened his mouth to launch into a full on anti-Brewbies tirade, when a weasel pushing a wheelbarrow arrested his attention.

"Hold down the fort," he said, placing the handle of his shovel into McGarvey's palm before stalking toward his prey.

"What fort?" McGarvey called after him. "It's a botanical garden!"

Ethan handed out five and a half disingenuous greetings to

various shop owners and residents before catching up with Mayor Stewart and his wheelbarrow empty of garden implements.

And full of KIKI FORRESTER FOR SHERIFF signs.

"What the actual fuck, Stewart," Ethan growled under his breath as he crowded the man out of the walkway and into a break between the trees and gas lamps that lined the boardwalk. "Does Caryn know you're putting these signs downtown?"

"Your mother doesn't tell me what to do, sheriff." Mayor Stewart carried his egg-shaped skull tucked low between thoroughly average shoulders made wider by the lies his suit jacket was tailored to tell. His title was the only thing that distinguished him from the legions of invisibles that climbed over each other in the homogenizing presses of small-town politics. He was as fine as anybody, in no way memorable, and perfectly devoid of loyalty.

Or a soul.

Beady eyes beneath comically curled eyebrows flicked from side to side, as if he were wary of a secret being drawn out.

"My mother tells everyone what to do, Stew," Ethan drawled. "What it looks like you're doing is renting out your henchman skills out of town because no one here buys your bullshit anymore."

The mayor lifted himself as tall as his tight-ankled khakis would allow, which still only brought him eye to Adam's apple with Ethan. "You can't be surprised that the town would be searching for a new favorite son." Mayor Stewart adopted an expression of faux sympathy. "After all, your father was an adulterer and your mother a criminal, though she hasn't been arrested..."

Letting that insinuation hang in the air like a rotten cabbage fart, Stewart bent his knees to take up the wheelbarrow again. "I'll be on my—"

"No one pressed charges against Caryn, Stewart, and you know it. Don't be hinting that I didn't arrest my mother after what she did because of nepotism."

"I would *never*." Stewart placed his hand over his heart as if it'd been pierced. "But not everyone is as attuned to nuance as I am. Caryn was a woman scorned, after all. And you know what they say about fury and hell…"

"That it's where you're going to burn when you die of the terminal condition of being a little bitch?" Ethan snarled.

Mayor Stewart blanched a little at Ethan's uncharacteristic intimidation. "An exact example of why Ms. Forrester is a superior candidate to you in every way. She's well educated. Well spoken. A classy woman with a first-rate vocabulary and endless wells of professionalism."

"You want to hear more of my vocabulary, Stewart?" Before he could think better of it, Ethan stepped closer.

The man dropped the wheelbarrow handles and jumped back. "Touch me and your career is over!" he squealed in the range of the young Asian girl from before.

"Oh, I'm not going to lay a hand on you," Ethan said, his voice dropping dangerously low. "But I am going to make sure everyone knows what a worm-tongued liar you are."

"That's rich," the mayor scoffed. "You think anyone will listen to your slander after who your father was and what he's done? Your family used to mean something in this town, but now you're just a joke."

Ethan's temper flared from some place deeper than his restraint could reach. "You keep my family's name out of your mouth, you son of a bitch."

"Or what?" the mayor asked, his bravado only buttressed by the handful of passersby watching their exchange with interest. "Tell me one thing you could do that wouldn't see you canceled faster than reruns of *The Cosby Show*."

It would almost be worth it just to wipe the smarmy expression from the mayor's face with his fist.

"How the fuck did you get to working for Forrester, anyhow? You voted against the tribe in the Snake River Dam case. You're the reason they are having problems with their water supply."

The mayor shrugged as if he weren't shaking in his boots. Which he was. Visibly. "The enemy of my enemy and all that."

"Kiki and I are not enem—"

A flash of pink had Ethan swiveling his head like an owl in time to watch the luscious Darby Dunwell saunter right up to the one door on Water Street always caked with dust and grime.

Roy Dobson's You Want It, Take It.

What—and he could not stress this enough—the fuck?

SEVEN
Hard Bean

COFFEE GROWN AT ALTITUDES OF 4,000 TO 4,500 FEET THAT PRODUCES A SLOWER-MATURING FRUIT AND A HARDER, LESS POROUS BEAN.

DARBY STOOD IN THE ENTRYWAY OF YOU WANT IT, Take It, her mouth open in full gape.

Anemic light shone through the dusty front window onto haphazard piles, the glass foggy and hazy with dirt and years of grime. Cobwebs clung to every corner of the ceiling, spreading to some of the furniture and boxes belching their contents from age-swollen bottoms.

The cramped shelves and counters bore an assortment of items that defied explanation. Valuable pieces crammed in among filthy, old stuffed animals and toys. Water-damaged posters green with sun damage leaning up against oil paintings that would have been perfectly at home at her parents' Hamptons estate.

A single word echoed in Darby's head as a clock ticked quietly somewhere in the strange hush created by Roy Dobson's hoard.

Depression.

She could feel it coating everything as thick as the blanket of dust settled atop various items in the shop. She could smell it as strongly as the dank mildew creeping up at the walls.

Below it, the sweetness and spice of tobacco.

Darby had waited until the exact moment when Roy stepped out into the alley to smoke his cigar to slip in through the front door, shocked when she found it unlocked.

But then, maybe Roy assumed he didn't have anything worth stealing.

How wrong he was.

Even just a cursory glance around the store had revealed several pieces her father's stodgy auctioneer would have wet their starched shorts to get their greedy hands on.

Outside, the laughter of a group of pedestrians provided a surreal soundtrack to this profoundly disorienting moment.

As if in a trance, Darby found herself pulled deeper into the mess, her fingers drifting over random objects as she made her way toward the ticking sound. Tucked behind a large armoire out of sight from the main part of the shop, she found a glass case bearing a strange assortment of items, all in pristine condition and carefully arranged in a thoughtful display. A woman's vanity set with ornate silver hand mirror and matching hairbrush with dark strands still woven between its bristles. An ivory comb with delicate floral embellishments and perfume atomizer with the residue of golden liquid at its thick glass base. A collection of chic hats and cloches perched atop the black velvet display podium.

Through a door beyond it, she spotted what must be Roy's work desk—a cluttered mess of paper and knickknacks, illuminated by an old desktop computer monitor and grimy keyboard. Darby stepped into the room and noticed a set of blueprints pinned to the wall with several pieces of string tied around pushpins. She walked closer and saw that they were detailed plans for an addition to You Want It, Take It. A space for a kitchen and dining area with living quarters at the back.

The sight of the thermal coffee mug he brought to her camper every morning sitting among the mess next to the dried-out husk of a sandwich hit her like a sledgehammer to the gut. Peeling her eyes away from the painful sight, she ran her fingers over a dusty paper bearing the words *My Family Tree* below an elaborate crest.

"Get away from that."

Startled, Darby dropped the cigar box. It hit the floor with an accusatory thump as she spun around to find Roy standing in the doorway behind her, his face a mask of fury.

"What are you d-doing in here?" His gaze shifted to the desk's abysmally cluttered surface.

Darby could feel her heart pounding in her chest and tried to recall the excuse she had practiced on the way over, but found her mind utterly empty until her eyes darted toward the window.

"My bike," she blurted. "I just picked it up from Pedal Pushers, and those assholes replaced my vintage chrome handlebars with cheap-ass mass-produced aluminum alloy. I know it's a long shot, but I thought you might have something more period appropriate?"

Darby's teeth caught her lower lip as she waited through a stony silence.

At last, Roy's perma-scowl softened into something like a skeptical frown. "I might. What kind of bike you got?"

Bingo.

"A 1952 Schwinn Starlet."

Roy's eyes narrowed. "Twenty-four or twenty-eight-inch frame?"

"Twenty-six-inch frame," Darby said, returning his shrewd look with one of her own. "Schwinn didn't make a twenty-eight-inch Starlet. You'd need a Spitfire for that height."

Silvery brows shot up toward Roy's surprisingly abundant pewter gray hair.

Suck it, secondhand snob.

"I got a set in the back," he said begrudgingly.

"Splendid." Moving robotically, Darby stooped to pick up the cigar box and shoved it toward Roy's pearl-snap-clad chest. "Here," she said. "These are for you."

Roy's gaze fixed on the box like it might contain a bomb instead of a dozen hand-rolled Cuban cigars that had probably set Fawkes back a pretty penny.

"What for?"

Over the course of her illustrious career as St. Vincent Academy's resident bad girl and the blue-blooded Dunwell family's black sheep, Darby couldn't even begin to figure how many lies she might have told. Ranging from your harmless little fibs to your absolute save-me-a-seat-in-the-back-row-of-hell whoppers.

Why, then, the completely unvarnished truth should come spilling out of her lips in such a completely inopportune moment was an utter mystery.

"They're a bribe."

Roy's watery blue eyes blinked at her from behind the smudged lenses of his gold wire-framed glasses.

"A bribe?"

"Yes, sir. Cady Bloomquist's fiancé said they were your favorite and that I should bring them to you so I can try to find out why the entire town dances around you, even though you don't seem to get along with anyone, because it might help me get the petition against Brewbies overturned."

Shit, shit, *shit.*

One bushy silver brow lifted. "That all?"

"Also, he thought it was strange that you agreed to help Caryn try to get control of Nevermore Bookstore when you didn't have a single thing to gain from it."

"I see." A current of smoky-sweet tobacco leaves drifted over to her as an ancient window AC unit cranked to life.

"Personally, I think it's kind of bullshit that she and Mayor Stewart have avoided you like the plague since you basically took all the blame during the city council meeting," Darby added when Roy didn't say anything else. "According to what I've heard."

The silence that stretched out between them lasted approximately a millennium.

"You're wasting your time." Roy herded her back into the shop with an outstretched arm.

"Because you won't change your mind about the petition?" Darby asked, praying she didn't end up going ass-first into one of the piles.

"Because I didn't sign it."

EIGHT
Pitter

ETHAN CROSSED WATER STREET TO DOBSON'S SIDE, so intent on where Darby had disappeared into the secondhand shop that he nearly knocked over his own mother. Immediately, he broke his vow not to allow his first words (post-scandal) to Caryn Townsend be an apology.

Steadying her, he couldn't help but notice how thin her shoulders had become beneath her silk blouse and tailored blazer.

"Ethan." She regarded him as if she'd sent him off to war and never expected to see him again.

"Are you okay, Mom? Did I hurt you?"

Her lips curved beneath her celebrity-in-search-of-invisibility sunglasses, but the smile was as brittle as the rest of her. "Of course I am," she said. "I'm just a bit tired."

Ethan frowned. He'd never seen his mother look so fragile before. Her delicate frame seemed almost insubstantial, and her skin was pale, stretched tight over her Greta Garbo bone structure. Even her usually voluminous hair had thinned and lost its luster, though she'd styled it with her usual eye for perfection.

"Have you been eating enough?" he asked, concerned for her health, despite everything. She'd aged a handful of years in a handful of months.

Accountability could do that to you.

Caryn waved away his worry with a long-suffering sigh. "I've been eating alone. Doesn't leave me with much of an appetite."

And here he'd forgotten to pack his luggage for the guilt trip she was about to take him on.

Should have known better than to ask.

"Well, you'd have plenty of dining companions in jail, if that alternative appeals to you," he muttered, doing exactly nothing to keep the bitterness from his voice.

Caryn Townsend had been a "Karen" before Dane Cook had canonized the name as the invocation of every middle-aged white lady with an entitled chip on her shoulder and a burning need to talk to a manager.

Her meager—if perfectly lined—smile disappeared as she pressed her mouth into a thin line, indenting every groove of age beneath her nose. She stepped out of the way of a pack of dogs intent on sled-team-pulling a teenaged walker down the main thoroughfare, nudging them closer to the streetlamp from which swung a basket of begonias and rosemary.

Though her glasses were dark enough to hide the darting of her eyes, Ethan could feel that they didn't stay focused on him, but frequently slid over to Roy Dobson's dingy shop windows.

"I'm going to talk to Anton Gilmore at the city building about taking the Kiki Forrester signs down from Water Street," she offered. "Really, Ethan, Mayor Stewart knows better."

The door through which Darby Dunwell had only just disappeared yawned like a hellmouth in Ethan's periphery, but he could only handle one infuriating woman at a time.

"Don't bother," he muttered. "I doubt your inquiries or suggestions will hold much weight at City Hall these days."

She winced as if he'd slapped her, and he had to stuff down a wellspring of compassion.

"I know you're still upset with me about the Townsend Building," she ventured, pulling a burgundy cashmere wrap from her tote and draping it over her shoulder when the sun disappeared behind a traveling cloud. "But I thought after some time had passed, we could discuss—"

"This has exactly nothing to do with the Townsend Building, and you know it." He said the harsh words in the gentlest tone he could muster, though his enunciation was entirely too sharp to use when speaking to a matriarch. Karen or no Karen. "I'm not upset, Mom. I'm fu—I'm freaking pissed." Welp, emotional honesty wasn't a Townsend family practice, apparently, but he'd fucking grown in the past few months.

Kinda.

"I'm pissed that you set me up with Cady Bloomquist in the mercenary hopes of gaining access to and ownership of the Townsend Building."

Blanching, she fluffed her chic bob to cover her distress. "I thought the two of you would be a good—"

"Then, when she wouldn't cooperate," he interrupted, in no mood for excuses, "you used me to gift her that camera *through which you illegally surveilled her.*"

Not that Cady seemed to have a problem with illegal surveillance, seeing as how she didn't press charges against Caryn... And she was shacking up with Roman "binocular boy" Fawkes, the huge, shaggy hermit who broke into a cold sweat at the sight of a closed door.

Caryn's throat bobbed beneath her silk scarf in a difficult swallow. "I didn't think—"

"*And then* you had your henchman, Roy Dobson, sneak in and search for papers that would substantiate your claim, scaring her half to death. And do you know what happens when women are afraid of intruders?"

"We've already been through all—"

"That's right! They call the cops. So, I run around town investigating like a clueless douchebag while my *mother* is her terrorist the whole time."

At this point Caryn was squirming, her head on a swivel in search of eavesdroppers. "I think terrorist is a bit of a strong—"

"And if that wasn't enough, you go and do the same thing to me that Dad did to you, selling the Raven Creek property to a woman who makes coffee damn near topless for every pervert from here to Forks not a stone's throw from Grandpa's ashes."

"I didn't know what sort of business she planned to put there. I'm not informed of the buyer's occupation. I had no idea that plot meant so much to you."

That ratcheted his temper up to eleven. "You would have," he snapped. "If you'd actually listened to the plans I had for it."

Caryn stepped back a little, which made him acutely aware that he'd been gesturing more than normal. A man with his wing-span had to be careful.

"Oh, Ethan," she said, her expression changing to either regret or squinting at the newly unveiled sun, he couldn't tell. "You made so many different noises when you were young about what you wanted to do, and I knew you had the skills and smarts to do any of it. But, darling, you didn't. You became the sheriff. You rented that workshop and an apartment on Taylor Street. I assumed you'd pivoted on your plans since your twenties."

Because his father had a stroke, and Ethan came back from college to help, because the pressure to become an "influential Townsend" had begun in the womb, and because he could never in good conscience live off his trust in a post-Occupy Wall Street world, he'd dutifully joined the force. It was the only thing that'd appealed to him out of the civic positions he was all but gun-to-head coerced to pick from.

He'd never intended to abandon his dreams, but once old Sheriff Holt had died, his senior deputy, Dick Chambers, had immediately began campaigning.

And that guy was a gun-happy racist on a good day.

Then the years passed, like they do. And here Ethan was in his thirties, further from his ambitions than ever.

Unsure of how to respond, he shook his head, glancing back toward the secondhand shop with a world-weary sigh. "It doesn't matter, Mom. I should probably get back to the botanical gardens before McGarvey gives up and goes back to the desert."

Caryn's arched brows dipped below the rims of her sunglasses as she scowled at him. "I know you don't appreciate what I did, but the Townsend Building was your legacy. It bears your name," she spat, gesturing across the street to Nevermore Bookstore's lovely edifice. "I couldn't let that stand."

"No." Ethan sliced the air with his hand. "You couldn't stand that Dad gave it to Cady's Aunt Fern while having an affair with her. And I don't blame you for feeling that way, but taking it out on Cady was unacceptable."

"I know it was," Caryn said. "I know it was! I already apologized to Cady, and she was very gracious. More so than you, it must be said." She lowered her sunglasses to spear him with a glare from the blue eyes she'd genetically gifted him.

"Yeah, well...that's Cady." They'd been perfect for each other. The town hero and the town sweetheart. It was like a fucking Hallmark movie. Hell, they already had the idyllic small-town setting.

Opening his mouth to reply, he spotted the Ravencroft Art Gallery across the way taping a Kiki Forrester sign in their window. "If I lose my job, it's because of all the Nevermore bullshit, you know that, right? As much as you and Dad cared about legacy, you sure aren't leaving me much to work with..."

The Caryn Townsend he knew would have sliced him in half with a scathing remark. This one only swallowed twice and said, "I know."

That rocked him back on his heels a little.

"Then...why did you do it?"

"Because, as much as your grandfather was a dear, he'd never had to make money, and so he'd never learned to manage it. He passed that trait, along with a horrible sense of entitlement and devil-may-care attitude, to your father, who turned it into a gambling problem and apparently spent the rest of his fortune on mistresses."

If Ethan felt bitter, his mother was a truck full of roasted hops.

"Wait." He held a hand up as her words sank in properly. "Are you saying you sold Raven Creek because you needed money?"

She shifted nervously. "I'm saying it was either sell the Raven Creek property, or lose it due to the taxes your father hadn't paid. The liens were already in place, and the lawyers said that selling was the safest thing to do for all involved."

Taking in a deep breath, Ethan pinched the bridge of his nose. *Of course* his philandering father had fucked this all the way up one side and down the other. The Townsend Family lies were stacked as high and deep as bodies beneath Paris. That land had been the central component of his entire life plan, and his father had known it. "What's done is done, Mom. All I can do is try to get the property back."

"I can help—"

"Immediately, no." He shook his head vehemently. It was her "help" that got them here in the first place. "You would do well to stay as far away from town politics and interested parties as possible for the time being."

Caryn's chin dipped toward Roy's shop before she caught herself and checked the sidewalk for imperfections.

Ethan's spider-sense was more of a zap than a tingle. "What were you doing, skulking around Roy's shop?" He narrowed his eyes in suspicion. "You two cooking up something new? Do I need to be worried?"

"I have never skulked in my *life*," she huffed. "You know I love the rhodys and came down to see them before the blooms disappeared for the last time."

"Likely story," he muttered.

It actually was. Because she did it every year.

Still. He wasn't letting her off the hook. Crossing his arms over his chest, he demanded, "Tell me just exactly what's going on here... The truth this time."

NINE
Fair Trade

COFFEE PURCHASED FROM FARMERS AT A "FAIR" PRICE AS DEFINED BY INTERNATIONAL AGENCIES

"THOSE WERE YOUR WIFE'S HATS, WEREN'T THEY?" Darby sat on an old steamer trunk next to the grandfather clock, her knees still wobbly with shock at Roy's asking her to sit in the aftermath of her compulsive confession.

He nodded and handed her one of the two delicate porcelain teacups he'd rinsed under the hot tap of a water cooler that had seen better days. Decades of them, from the look of it. "Gwen loved antiques."

Darby smiled as she took the cue, enjoying the warmth that radiated from its delicate surface. She gave Roy a sidelong glance as he poured them each a generous helping of whisky from a tarnished silver flask in his shirt pocket.

"Is that how you got into the secondhand business?" Darby asked before taking her first sip. The smoky-sweet liquid slid down her throat like honey.

"Sort of." Roy's silvery mustache brushed the brim of his teacup as he lifted it to his lips.

"How'd you end up in Townsend Harbor?"

"Came here on our honeymoon. Gwen always talked about

moving here once we retired. Said we'd open a little antiques shop. Buy some land and build guest cabins."

Darby suspected it wasn't the whisky that deepened his voice.

"Some land like Raven Creek?" she ventured.

Roy's bushy silver brows lifted above the foggy lenses of his glasses. "Yes." He took another sip of his whisky. "We'd already bought this place when she got sick."

Sick.

Such a deceptively simple word for the battery of conditions it comprised.

"May I ask with what?"

A crease appeared in Roy's ponderous forehead. "Breast cancer," he said. "Same as you. Not like I'd have driven all the way out of town every morning to pay for overpriced coffee from a half-naked woman otherwise."

Darby's cup paused halfway to her mouth.

That Brewbies donated a portion of its proceeds to breast cancer research was included in the general information available to anyone who happened to go looking, but she hadn't wanted to make it her entire marketing strategy any more than she wanted to make being a "survivor" her entire identity.

Learning Roy had somehow come across this information and elected to drag his curmudgeonly ass out of town to buy his coffee from her shop each morning to honor the wife he'd lost to the same disease was blowing her entire mind.

She figured his backhanded insult just now and her suspicion that he might have a secret hat fetish earlier just about canceled out.

"She went fast."

Darby watched as Roy's blue eyes misted over, his gaze fixed on the hatboxes stacked in the corner of the room. She wondered how many memories were stored in those boxes, how many stories they held. The silence stretched between them once again, broken only by the ticking of the grandfather clock and the distant sound of cars passing by on Water Street.

"I'm sorry," Darby murmured, not sure what else to say. She had never been great at comforting people, and especially not people who had openly expressed dislike for her general person. But something about Roy's quiet grief tugged at her battle-scarred heartstrings.

He waved a hand as if brushing away her sympathy. "Helen didn't want any pity, and neither do I."

"I understand," Darby said. And she did. To a painful degree.

They both took healthy swallows of their whisky.

"Anyway, since I made it through that, I decided I would just do whatever the hell I want." Darby shrugged. "And that's what landed me in my current mess."

Roy looked her intently in the eye, his expression softening. "You're a brave kid," he said. "I'll give you that."

"Please," she scoffed. "I can't even—"

"Son of a bitch." The venom in Roy's tone brought her up short. His knobby knuckles had gone white as he clutched the teacup. His jaw creaked and popped as his teeth ground together.

Darby pried the cup from his hand, afraid he might be having a stroke, until she followed his gaze. Through the murky window, she saw Ethan and a stunning middle-aged woman with a chic blonde bob standing on the sidewalk across the street from Roy's shop. The woman had her arms crossed and was shaking her head emphatically while Ethan gestured wildly with his hands.

It was the most animated she'd seen him since...since it was definitely better not to think about.

"Tell you what." The palm of Roy's hand rasped as he ran it over a stubble-flecked chin. "You convince Caryn Townsend to meet with me, and I'll give you a piece of information juicy enough that the city council will not only reverse their decision about the petition, they'll beg your apologies *in print* in the *Townsend Leader*."

"You could do that?"

A sly smile lifted the corners of Roy's lips below the walrus-y moustache. "That," he promised, "and a hell of a lot more."

"How do I know you've really got something good?" Darby leaned forward on her box, putting her face between Roy and the object of his fascination. "You could just be putting me on."

Roy rose and disappeared into the back of his shop. When he returned, it was with the sleek mauve felt cloche from the display case in his hands. "How's this for collateral?"

Darby reverently took it, gently placing it atop her head. Glancing at herself in the age-crazed mirror behind the register, she almost hoped Roy would fail to come through.

She looked fucking *fabulous*.

"You've got a deal," she said, holding out her hand. Roy clasped it in a surprisingly warm and gentle handshake. Darby shot the rest of her whisky and stood. "Pleasure doing business with you."

Get Caryn Townsend to talk to Roy Dobson.

How hard could that be?

* * *

ETHAN

"Roy—Mr. Dobson—and I are not in contact anymore." A flush rose above her scarf only to disappear beneath her airbrush makeup.

They were probably too ashamed of themselves. Or, at least, Ethan's mom was ashamed that she, the wealthy woman who bore the town's name, had teamed up with Roy Dobson, the *Duck Dynasty* reject with the scruples of a coyote.

"I wonder, though," Caryn said, peeking around Ethan's shoulder, "what kind of business the new coffee shop owner and Mr. Dobson have with each other."

Curiosity was too kind a word for what radiated from both mother and son, though he couldn't bring himself to admit it was what drew him over here in the first place. He looked at the door through which Darby had disappeared, and then glanced down at his watch.

She'd been in there a long time. Alone.

"She's one of those nomadic, free-spirited types who is really into vintage stuff," he explained, mostly for his own benefit. "She's probably just shopping for...for...whatever whatnots sexy coffee shop owners like."

Next time he looked over at his mom, she was studying him with a look he'd never seen before. Something landing in the middle of fondness and concern.

"Sexy coffee shop owner?" she echoed quietly.

"Owner of a sexy—er—sex-themed coffee shop," he corrected himself, hoping she couldn't see the heat rising to his cheeks.

"Ah," was all she said before she joined him in a much-too-long examination of the opaque glass down the way, behind which just about anything could be discussed by two unlikely allies.

As if summoned by intense Townsend regard to the second power, the hydraulic arm squeaked as Roy held the door open for Darby to step through before following her out into the intermittent sun.

Everything about her gleamed, from the healthy sheen of her pink victory rolls, to the polka-dot sundress, to the genuine affection in the smile she gifted Roy.

Bastard didn't deserve that smile.

That was *Ethan's* smile. She smiled at *him* like that.

Or she did, before he tried to run her out of town.

What a fucking mess.

"Thanks for everything, Roy. I'll see you in the morning." Darby lifted up on her tiptoes to plant an airy kiss on Roy's silver-stubbled cheek before she gathered her things and damn near skipped off in the other direction.

"Gotta get that premium roast while I still can," he said after her, waving a hand she didn't look back to see.

Possibly because both Townsends froze like they'd been

dipped in liquid nitrogen, and Roy melted back into the gloom of his shop without noticing them.

"Now what the hell do you think that was all about?" Ethan wondered aloud.

"Do you think he told her?" His mother sounded legitimately afraid.

"Anyone's guess." Ethan's lips thinned. How had he not noticed the overabundance of secrets in his family?

"I have to go," Caryn breathed.

He glanced over. "You okay?"

She nodded jerkily, yanking the sagging strap of her designer tote over her shoulder. "I'm just peachy. So much to do. You know how it is." Fumbling with her sunglasses, she turned away from him before hesitating. Then turning back. "I hope we can speak again soon?" she ventured, her tone as soft as he'd ever heard it...which was to say, not very. "When you're ready?"

He nodded.

She nodded.

And then they turned their backs to each other like duelists about to walk ten paces.

The last thing he needed to notice was how Darby's ass swayed in that hip-hugging skirt before it flared and flowed down her smooth thighs.

He'd cupped the back of her knee just last night, tested the thin, delicate skin there and bathed in her subtle but delicious response.

He'd almost given in to the intense desire to kiss her.

Aaaaaaand...that was why he should run—not walk—the other way.

Except his mom was that way.

Right. He needed to get back to the botanical garden and help McGarvey.

An exclamation of surprise drew his attention back to the curb, where Darby had doubled over. Two buskers on the bench close by couldn't be bothered to put down their accordion and whatever those tiny asshole guitars were to help her.

Hissing, she examined the bottom of her foot and rolled her delicate ankle as if to test to see if it was still working.

Her beige and white shoe lay on the ground a step behind her in two distinct pieces.

She hissed again as she picked an errant pebble from the pad of her foot, giving Ethan time to act.

Before she knew what he was doing.

Hell, before he'd even figured out his own plan of action, he'd swooped over and retrieved the broken shoe from the ground before she could limp back to it.

"Hey," she called after him. "What the fuck, you just can't take that!"

Watch me, he thought, striding away without so much as a glance.

TEN

Slurp and Spit

THE TERM FOR SLURPING THE COFFEE FROM THE SPOON, TASTING IT AND SPITTING IT OUT

"**WHAT THE HELL DO YOU THINK YOU'RE DOING?**" Darby limped after Ethan, feeling something cold and slimy that she dearly hoped wasn't tobacco spit squelch between the toes of her bare foot.

Stupid vintage shoes with their promise of superior craftsmanship.

She'd chosen her footwear the same way she'd chosen her outfit. With Roy, not Ethan, in mind.

That she opted for her oldest pair of vintage pumps to appeal to the sexagenarian's sensibilities felt a bitter irony now.

Ethan and his broad back ignored her, marching down the alley next to Roy's shop with a purposeful stride. Glancing at the overflowing garbage can, Darby was sorely tempted to grab the slimy fast-food bag on top and hurl it at the back of Ethan's fastidiously barbered head.

Only her total lack of accurate aim and a memory of how delicious the smooth skin of his neck had been just beneath his starched collar prevented her from exacting her well-deserved revenge.

She clomped faster when he turned the corner, shuddering as she splashed through a gritty puddle.

A blast of briny air off the water hit her full in the face as she rounded the corner after him just in time to see a door swing closed.

The load of ammunition cocked in both barrels of her sharp tongue abruptly jammed when she yanked open the door and saw what hid beyond it.

A woodshop.

Bright, airy, and so completely *him*.

Polished mahogany shelves. An impressive array of hand tools hanging from pegboards in surgically precise rows. Chisels, awls, handsaws, hammers, brushes, stains, and sanders.

Darby's eyes moved over the impressive array of hand-carved items ranging from standard plaques to classic rocking chairs to elaborate porch swings. Every single object felt like an extension of Ethan Townsend's actual person. Built with a sturdy economy. No extraneous ornamentation, no unnecessary frills. Only undeniable art in the expertness of its craftmanship. Of its precision.

And yet, seeing the pieces all together, something tugged at her.

"The welcome sign on the edge of town. You made it."

Ethan's reply was little more than a grunt. "Yep."

Darby stepped out of her other shoe and bent to hook the strap with her finger. "I'm going to guess 'Get Knotty' wasn't your choice of tag line?"

Ethan's body tensed as if bracing for a blow. He didn't answer at first, instead turning to the window overlooking the harbor. His gaze seemed distant, almost sad, as he watched a sailboat bobbing in the gentle waves against the backdrop of an orange sky at sunset.

Finally, almost reluctantly, he spoke into the silence between them. "Nope."

Her need for cobblery outstripping her desire to needle him about it further, she decided to wander around the shop instead. The concrete floor was smooth and cool beneath her bare feet, and absent of so much as a single wood shaving.

"This a side hustle?" she asked, leaning in to examine a scale model of what looked to be a roomy banquet hall with a tall, tapered brick chimney.

"Nope," he repeated.

"Then why do you make all this?"

A metallic clang echoed through the space as he elbowed a drawer in his large standing tool cupboard closed. "For fun."

Darby leaned against the counter and narrowed her eyes on Ethan's stony face. "Are you absolutely sure?"

"Yep."

"I ask, because I've got to be honest, you look like you wouldn't know fun if it leapt up and bit you in the taint."

"Being bitten in the taint doesn't sound much like fun."

"Was that a joke?" Darby asked, blinking rapidly at him. "That was a joke, wasn't it?"

"Maybe." Ethan's eyes lifted from the shoe he held as gently as a baby bird.

Darby felt a sympathetic twinge as she watched him turn it over in his big, capable hand to expose the denuded sole.

Those same fingers had buried themselves in her hair as he'd leaned in to devour her mouth. They'd compressed the column of her neck as he'd driven into her against the wall of his hotel room. They'd relieved her of the weight of her breasts as he buried himself to the hilt from behind, that deceptively tight mouth whispering the most delicious filth against her sweat-damp neck.

"You supervising?" Ethan's truculent question was just the bucket of ice water her libido needed.

Darby blushed and cleared her throat, quickly averting her gaze. "Do you know how much longer it's going to be?" she asked, coating her words with all the impatience she could muster.

"Hot date?" Ethan drawled.

With your mother, Darby thought but didn't say. "That's none of your business, sheriff."

The knuckles wrapped around her shoe began to whiten. "Might go faster if you weren't hovering."

"Am I disrupting your concentration?" she asked, folding her arms beneath her breasts.

Ethan's Adam's apple bobbed above his starched collar. "No, ma'am. I just work faster when I'm not talking."

Liar.

"Excuse me all to Poughkeepsie for being sociable," Darby said, sauntering toward a wooden porch swing next to his work area. "Can I sit in this?"

"Kind of the point, isn't it?" Ethan muttered without turning to her.

She decided to let that one slide. Between Roy's whisky and the adrenaline rush of nearly eating a piece of Townsend Harbor's historic sidewalk when her heel had broken, a sudden drowsiness had stolen over her.

Darby boosted herself up to the platform and settled into the swing, lifting one leg onto the bench to stretch it out long and using the other to give herself a push. The well-oiled chains barely squeaked as the bench glided back and forth. Darby rested both feet on the arm closest to Ethan.

She allowed her fingers to play over the silky wood, running them along the raised bumps and gnarls in the grain.

The sense of strangeness she'd felt looking at his pieces earlier came crashing back to her with a sudden realization.

Every single item she'd looked at until this one had been completely free of organic knots, scars, or other imperfections. Each and every one of them painfully, obsessively, free of flaws.

Talk about a metaphor.

"This is a beautiful swing," Darby said, gazing up to admire the thick crossbeam that had to be an entire tree trunk.

"Didn't make it." Ethan set aside some kind of resin and reached for his hammer.

"You just babysitting it so it doesn't get lonely?"

"It was my grandfather's."

"Would that be Ethan Townsend the second? Or is this on your mother's side?"

His back stiffened beneath the crisp fabric of his dress shirt. Touchy subject, apparently.

"My father's father."

"He's the one who taught you how to work with wood?"

"Yep."

"That must have been nice," she said, still determined to draw him into conversation. It was almost a game now. "Both sets of my grandparents passed before I finished elementary school."

"Sorry to hear that."

"Don't be," Darby said. "I'm not."

"Weren't close, I take it?"

She shrugged, returning her foot to the ground to give herself another push. "My dad's mom was already dead when I was born. And his father I barely remember. We only saw him on Easter and Christmas for mass. My mom's mom was also dead before I was walking, and her father was an asshole. So no big loss there."

"Don't much get along with anybody, do you?"

A rebuttal rose instantly in Darby's throat but was blocked by a word that had been stuck there for the last seven years.

Estranged.

From her mother. From her older brother, Daniel, who had once watched over her as carefully as a manic hen. To know he was out there in the world waking up every morning putting on his suit and tie, going to work in the Dunwell law firm, fully aware of her presence but deciding his life would be better without it, opened an ache in Darby's chest that threatened to swallow her whole.

The distance that her refusal to let her parents stage-manage her illness had created had been firmly cemented by her lifestyle choices in the wake of her recovery.

Ethan cleared his throat, snapping her out of the unpleasant memory.

"Did you say something?"

"I asked you if you wanted me to put a new top piece on this," he said, holding up her shoe. "Looks like the other one's worn down to the nails."

Though she had no idea what a top piece was, she deduced by context that it was the bit on the bottom of the heel. She'd known one had gone missing from this pair, as she sounded somewhat pirate-like when she'd been walking across the marble floor of Townsend First National Bank earlier this afternoon.

"Sure." Darby shrugged. "Knock yourself out."

"I'll need your other shoe. Don't want them to be uneven or it could potentially impact your gait."

Darby leaned down and scooped her other vintage peep-toe pump from beneath the swing's bench. "Catch," she said, lobbing it toward Ethan's head. He got his hands up just in time, she was only somewhat sorry to note.

Ethan planted the heel of the shoe on his workbench with slightly more force than may have been strictly necessary and set to work.

Darby watched as he pried the top piece off and applied the resin to the stump, his long fingers quick and sure. She could feel her eyelids getting heavier with each stroke of his brush. Without meaning to, she began to drift off, lulled by the steady creak of the swing as it glided back and forth.

Daylight was failing when Darby woke, the shadows cast by Ethan's pieces stretching long purple fingers across the floor. Sunset light poured a honeyed glow through the windows, making the wood shop look like a storybook illustration. Her freshly polished shoes perched on his worktable's gleaming surface like something left by a helpful elf in a fairytale.

Only when she shifted on the bench did she register that a flannel shirt had been draped over her like a blanket.

Stealing a guilty glance around the empty shop, Darby fisted a handful of the supple fabric and pressed it against her nose. Her eyes fell closed as she inhaled deeply, drawing the scent of Ethan out of its fibers. Damned if the sheriff wasn't some kind of manbrosia, forever emitting a pheromone speedball that hit her hormones like a cattle prod.

"It's Downy."

Darby nearly leapt out of her skin at the sound of Ethan's voice. Jerking the flannel away from her face, she quickly swung her legs off the bench to turn herself.

He stood in the doorway with his hands in his pockets, a half-smile playing at the corner of his lips as he regarded her with a mixture of amusement and curiosity.

He'd changed from his dirt-streaked work clothes to well-worn jeans and—oh sweet Jesus—a plain white undershirt.

Her very own sartorial kryptonite.

Alarm bells clanged in her head.

If she didn't get out of here, and fast, she was in imminent danger of chipping one of her caps on his abdominals when she tore that t-shirt with her teeth.

"How long was I out?" she asked, smoothing her hands over her dress as she scooted to the edge of the bench.

"Half an hour," he said, walking back to his worktable. "Found the time to do a little more on your shoes." Lifting one of the pumps, he aimed the bottom toward her. "The outsoles were pretty shot, so I replaced them with a weather-treated leather and hit it with a little PVC sealant. Should provide better traction come winter."

Darby cocked her head at him. "You seem to know an awful lot about women's footwear. If I didn't know better, I'd say someone has a fetish."

Something in his expression shifted, the playfulness abruptly evaporating from his features. "Do you?"

"Do I what?" Darby asked.

"Know better."

"I know that I paid off a mountain of medical debt by selling my used socks on eBay."

His lips twitched. "That so?"

"Yes, sir." She stood and gave into the delicious full-body

stretch that pulled her limbs like taffy. "An extra ten dollars for every additional hour. Twice that if any of the hours happened to be in the gym."

The sheriff stared at her as if she'd sprouted a second head. "You're not serious."

Darby grinned at him, savoring the way his eyes widened in disbelief. "Not if I can help it. But yeah. It's not as much as I made selling pies I'd stepped in, but the packing and shipping overhead on those was outrageous."

Amazing how similar jealousy and disapproval looked on a man's face.

Ethan slowly shook his head and walked over to the industrial sink in the corner. Water gushed from the faucet, and steam curled up from the basin. Darby couldn't help but feel that he wanted to wash his hands of this conversation.

Or of her.

And could she really blame him?

Glancing down at her feet, she saw herself through Ethan's eyes. The sidewalk silt and God knew what else she'd picked up and dragged into his spotless shop. Like the smudges of mud and moss she'd left in his vehicle after her less-than-graceful ride the night before.

The realization made her insides twist with a feeling she couldn't name but cared for not at all.

"I should probably get out of your hair," Darby said, quickly making her way over to where Ethan stood by the sink.

His hand closed over her wrist as she reached for her shoes. "Wait."

She waited.

Ethan released her hand and turned back to the sink. Water spattered in the basin as he wrung out a rag obviously made from an old towel that had outlived its original purpose. He draped it over the basin and turned to her.

Before Darby registered what he was doing, Ethan gripped her hips and lifted her effortlessly to his worktable.

Her mouth dropped open more out of surprise than objection as his fingers circled her ankle and lifted her foot.

Ethan swaddled it in the warm towel and began to gently massage her instep. Its heat seeped into her skin, relaxing every muscle in her body, and Darby couldn't help but melt into his touch.

The sensation sent tingles of pleasure rippling up her leg, making Darby suck in a breath as his gentle grip lingered on her tired arch.

"How much you think I could get for this?" Ethan asked, his voice low and a little gravelly as he held up the rag with a grayish footprint.

"Hundred fifty, at least." Her voice sounded distant to her own ears as he repeated his ministrations on the other foot.

"I'll keep that in mind." Setting the cloth aside, he reached for one of her shoes. His fingertips brushed her ankle as he slipped it on her foot and fastened the impossibly tiny buckle.

"Tell the truth, Sheriff Townsend. You've done this before."

Ethan looked at her below the pale tips of his long sable lashes in a way that made Darby's heart beat faster. "Yep."

Warmth spilled through her middle, pooling low and heavy in her belly. Under normal circumstances, this would have lit up her mile-wide jealous streak.

But here, in the rare golden light of this workshop that felt like a scrap of his soul made manifest, she couldn't help but feel strangely honored by the personal revelation.

And more than a little turned on.

Seduced by the mental voyeurism of imagining him handling another woman this reverently.

Ethan finished with the second buckle, but instead of releasing his grip, he trailed his hand upward. Fingertips lifted to avoid the nasty bruise on her shin, he pushed back the hem of her dress, revealing her bandaged knee.

Darby's mouth went dry as the moisture seemed to relocate itself to other places.

"How's it feel today?"

If she could concentrate on any sensation other than the subtle pulse that had woken within the damp silk of her panties, Darby might have given him an honest answer.

It had throbbed like a bitch all morning.

That pain had mysteriously evaporated sometime between their confrontation on the sidewalk and the present moment.

"Fine," she managed, shocked at smoky rasp that had crept into her voice.

Ethan must have heard it too. His eyes had darkened, deepened as they found hers.

Darby didn't move, couldn't breathe, wanting him more than she wanted air, but determined to avoid a repeat performance of last night's stinging rejection.

Kiss me.

Kiss me like you did when you didn't know my name.

The small cry of surprise died in her throat as Ethan's mouth crashed against hers in a raw, hungry rush. His hands seemed to be everywhere at once. Behind her knees to drag her to the edge of the table. Beneath the backs of her thighs to anchor her legs around his waist. Buried in her hair as he plundered her mouth with deep, silky strokes of his tongue.

In that moment, she tasted the chaos below the placid surface of his self-enforced calm. Met the frenzied, starving animal inside the man who denied its very existence.

Darby moaned against his lips, dizzy with pleasure. Desperate for more, she curled her fingers into his shirt as the heat from their bodies mingled like merging storm clouds. Alive with electricity that was almost too much to bear.

Ethan groaned, a deep, guttural sound that vibrated through her as he pressed the hard ridge of his arousal into her core, making Darby gasp with pleasure and surprise.

Shifting his weight, he crowded her back to the worktable, freeing her breasts from the halter top of her dress with an efficiency that suggested experience. Darby sucked in a sharp breath as he closed his mouth over one tight peak, teasing it with his tongue, incinerating the last of her logic.

She clawed at his back, rocking her hips against his as Darby pressed her mouth to the hard curve of his jaw—on purpose this time. Kissing and licking. Scraping lightly with her teeth. Needing the taste of him. The feel of him. The heat of him.

Darby jerked at the hem of his shirt, her greedy hands delving below the waistband of his jeans to find the silky head of his erection and the pearly bead of moisture already gathering there.

With a growl feral enough to raise the fine hairs on Darby's arms, Ethan pinned her hands above her head. Even through her haze of pleasure, she felt her knuckle brush something cool and smooth, felt the object shoot over the edge of the table and heard an ugly, splintery crash when whatever it was hit the floor.

Ethan stiffened and broke away from her, a look of confusion on his face, as if he'd just woken up. His eyes fixed on the floor, and the lingering heat in his gaze was snuffed as quickly as a candle.

Darby sat up, quickly rearranging her top and smoothing her dress back down her thighs.

"I can't do this..." His voice sounded thick and hoarse, his words aimed at no one in particular.

As if she were already gone.

Darby blinked at him, following his gaze to the floor where his model ship lay broken, its wooden hull split in two.

"I'm so sorry," she said dumbly. "I—" But the words froze in her throat, victims of the arctic chill spreading from Ethan's eyes.

"You have to go," he said. "Please."

She wanted to grab him. Demand that he talk to her. That he tell her what he was thinking.

What he was feeling.

But the old, stubborn pride had risen inside her, welding her jaw shut.

Palms planted on the table, Darby pushed herself off the

counter without a word and marched out of the shop on her newly repaired shoes.

* * *

Darby woke with a start, her sheets glued to her body and her heart racing in her chest. She'd been having the nightmare again.

It was always the same. She was running down a seemingly endless maze of hospital corridors, chased by a shadowy figure she could never quite make out. The walls were white and featureless, the lights flickering and casting eerie shadows that seemed to move with her as she ran.

The fear in her dream was overwhelming, like an icy hand clutching at her throat and squeezing until she could hardly breathe. Her legs trembled beneath her and sweat stung her eyes as if it were real.

It always ended the same way. Just when Darby thought she had lost the figure chasing her, it would suddenly reappear in front of her, opening a hole in the waxed linoleum floor beneath the soles of her hospital-issue surgical pressure socks.

But this time, something had been different. It hadn't been the dark figure that woke her, but a sound. A strange and unfamiliar creaking noise that her mind had attempted to weave into the strange landscape of her dreams.

Darby peeled back her tangled covers, rubbing her eyes groggily as she squinted into the darkness. When nothing leapt into her field of vision, she scooted to the end of the bed and slipped into her kimono.

On her way through the kitchen, she paused at the counter and fished inside her cookie jar for the .45 Patrick Kelly had given her as a going-away present.

That she was about a thousand times *less* likely to need it once she'd left Boston hadn't seem especially important to point out at the time.

The weapon felt reassuringly heavy in her hand as she tiptoed into her slippers. She was indescribably glad she'd taken a can of WD-40 to the hinges of the camper's front door the day before.

Darby crept out into a starless night filled with the faint sigh of the wind off the water, her heart speeding when the strange creaking sound came again.

From directly over her head.

Mountain lion, her nightmare-addled brain suggested helpfully. *Cougar. Black bear.*

Swallowing hard, Darby clicked the safety off her gun and tipped her chin upward to look.

What she saw instead was considerably more alarming.

Sheriff Ethan Townsend was in her tree.

ELEVEN

Specific Gravity

A MEASURE OF DENSITY IN A LIQUID OR SOLID

No, I am not *being creepy.*

Ethan's argument with himself escalated into devil's advocate territory as he used the strength of his legs to propel himself up the ginormous branch of the thousand-year-old oak.

Talking to yourself was normal, or so he heard. But if someone were to eavesdrop on the conversation in his head, he'd be branded certifiably nuts.

In fact, the longer Darby Dunwell lingered in Townsend Harbor, the more likely he was to catch a few diagnoses.

And possibly a straitjacket.

Because she was driving him out of his damn mind.

Returning something wasn't the same as surveillance. *It's not like I brought binoculars or anything,* he justified to himself.

No, you just drove past here an hour after nightfall to see if her light had gone off.

That was because—

Then, two hours later, you waited in your personal truck for the length of a particularly good PB&sugarfreeJ sandwich and a scotch ale from your own stock to give her enough time to establish a healthy REM cycle. Tell me again you're not creepy.

"Fuck off," he told his conscience out loud.

118

Looking fifteen feet down at his disarray of tools, he had to admit that it *might* look like the Night Stalker Serial Killer's beginner kit... Complete with rope, tape, flashlight, and an impressive cacophony of blades, hammers, wrenches, and other things horror movie villains used to drain buckets of blood.

Shaking himself, Ethan focused his flashlight on the task before him.

He'd threaded a rope the diameter of a baseball bat through a hole Grandpa Townsend had drilled what must have been a million years ago. After securing it with a washer and bolt the size of his own fist, he moved one scoot to the left to secure the second one.

He'd found out the property had slipped out of his grasp when his mom had the old swing delivered to his shop with a note:

I know this was important to you, so I took it down before closing on the sale. XX, Mom.

What he'd read?

I sold your dream out from under you. Here's a swing no one but you wanted. XX, Mom.

She'd never taken his plans seriously. Neither had his father, his coaches in high school and/or college, his handful of semi-serious relationships, his coworkers, or his friends.

Somehow, he'd allowed those dreams to linger in an empty lot with an empty swing playing a lonely pendulum for the passing of time.

After glancing over to the Airstream both shadowed and gleaming in the nearly full moon, Ethan took a moment to listen to the night.

The birds had all gone to roost, but the wind still carried the scent of new blooms and a hint of wood smoke.

It was like this particular night was a gift from somewhere else —maybe from a universe that understood he was trying to reclaim something vanished.

Or maybe find something he'd been missing all along.

Understanding and empathy weren't incredibly forthcoming in his experience, which was why he'd often found himself in this particular tree when he felt lost.

Besides, brooding was well done on a beautiful spring night in the Pacific Northwest with a star-strewn sky above him and an old oak beneath him, lending its sturdy branches to hold up his bulky frame made weightier with heavy questions.

So many people found solace in nature when faced with problems.

But to him, the acres of land on the corner of Highway 101 and the Townsend Harbor Tree Tunnel had been his refuge.

A crossroads, his grandpa had said. *People used to know that is where you go when you need direction.*

Crickets chirped in perfect harmony with the hooting of owls and the murmuring of Raven Creek. Frogs croaked and stars shimmered in an endless night sky, free from smog or light pollution.

Steeping in the fresh fragrance of petrichor that hung in the air like a sweet fog, Ethan closed his eyes and tilted his head back to the sky, feeling like he could breathe for the first time in—

"What the fuck are you *doing* up there?"

Startled by Darby's sudden question, Ethan dropped his wrench so he could use two hands to keep him from falling out of the tree.

It landed in the soft moss below with a muted *whump.*

Gravel crunched beneath fancy slippers as Darby strode from the shadow of her doorway out into the night, her kimono flaring out behind her like a cape. Moonlight painted blood-red shadows in her hair and gilded her eyes like diamond-cut glass.

Bracing himself for an unwanted confrontation, Ethan squeezed his eyes shut, awaiting the barbed tongue lashing that would accompany the pin-up fantasy exterior.

The chalky sound of gravel gave way to soft squishes of the mossy ground set back from the road. The stretch of meadow where people on road trips would pull over and let their kids and dogs out of the car to frolic by the creek and climb this old oak.

Quiet stretched out long enough that he cracked one eye open.

Darby stood directly beneath him, fingers tracing a spackled groove in the swing with uncharacteristic reverence. "Did you make this?" she breathed.

"No," he answered automatically, before pulling the cord on his stalled brain motor a few times. "I mean. Kinda."

She tilted her head back to look up at him, and he felt his breath hitch as he took in the sight of her. The way the moonlight played on the curves of her body was intoxicating.

And he shouldn't be noticing.

"It was the first thing my grandpa let me help him make in the woodshop," he said, mostly surprised that he'd revealed something personal to her. "It hung here since my eighth birthday until..." He cleared his throat, not wanting to beat a dead horse on such a nice night.

Her brow dipped as if his answer troubled her, then she looked down, concealing her expression. "And you're hanging it here to...to what? Make a point?"

That was what he told himself.

So why did it feel more like a gift? But to whom? Her? The tree? His dead grandfather?

A beam of light appeared in the distance as a car approached from a half-mile away. Ethan followed its progress through the snaking, mostly deserted highway. "When people used to ask my grandpa how to get to Townsend Harbor, he never gave them street names or maps. He would just say, *Start at the top of 101 and turn when you find the oak grove where the oldest tree has a big swing over Irish moss.*" Even after the years without him, Ethan's throat could still thicken at the mention of the old man. "It's keeping me up nights, thinking people have been looking for this swing for over twenty years as a landmark to turn, and they won't find it anymore."

He fell quiet, awaiting her response.

She was going to tell him he was trespassing and kick him off her property. That he was a fucking psycho for climbing a tree that no longer belonged to his family in the middle of the night to hang a swing. She was going to douse the swing in fuel and set it, and the tree, on fire.

With him still sitting in it.

Probably what he deserved.

"And here I thought you'd crafted an amazing apology for leaving me hanging earlier," she said, nudging the swing as if to test its mobility. "Get it? Leaving me hanging?"

He blinked down at her, waiting for the other shoe to drop.

"Okay. Bad joke," she admitted. "Still shaking off sleep brain."

Not knowing how to answer, he said, "I'll be out of your hair in a sec. Sorry if the noise woke you."

"You didn't make any noise." She shrugged and encircled the thick rope with her hand, testing the rasp of the frayed fibers with a porny stroke.

Yup. Time to go.

Ethan lowered himself from the branch with the strength of his arms, until his feet were close enough to the ground to let go. Dropping into a crouch, he immediately retrieved his wrench, level, and a couple of other tools to return to the toolbox in the back of his truck.

"Your grandpa, Ethan Townsend?" she teased. "Son of Ethan Townsend and father of Ethan Townsend?"

"The very same," he droned mirthlessly, plodding to where he'd parked his truck a few yards away and unlatching his toolbox. If he looked at her, he'd have to think about why she sounded so breathless.

A shiver of awareness lifting the hairs on the back of his neck told him she'd shadowed him to his vehicle.

Nope. Didn't want that. She needed to stay over *there*.

Where he couldn't savor her perfume or appreciate the

texture of her cheek in the silvery moonlight without its usual dusting of makeup.

He very carefully *didn't* look while he returned his tools to their designated spots with careful precision.

"Oh my God, do you alphabetize them, too?" she asked, peeking over his shoulder. "All I have is a wicker basket that I chuck hammers and stuff into."

His fingers paused as he examined the pristine case that looked as if he hadn't used it almost every day for a decade. "This is an expensive toolbox."

"*You're* an expensive toolbox."

Sighing, he shoved the truck bed shut and circled around to the driver's side.

"Wait!" She ran around him with the tiny, quick steps her ridiculous—if sexy—slippers would allow. "Wait. I was trying to lighten things up between us a little. Sheesh, whatever crawled up your ass and died must be decaying your sense of humor."

Her levity seemed out of place when the scent of hydrangeas and honeysuckle threaded through the stony loam of fresh spring water and the musk of her sleep-warmed skin.

"Noted." He reached for the latch and tugged at his truck door, but she threw her entire weight against it, forcing it closed.

Raised not to use his strength against a woman, he stood motionless, waiting for her to move before attempting to leave again.

Instead, she stood watching him, her eyes narrowing as if she were refining the view on her microscope. "This tree means a lot to you, doesn't it?"

Almost as much as the land it lived on.

"My grandpa's ashes were scattered there." Christ, was there some sort of truth serum in her perfume?

A speculative sound melted from her throat as she turned away and drifted back toward the tree, the little heels of her slippers wobbling on the uneven ground.

Drawn by the train of her kimono, or maybe by the fireflies in the tall grass, or the whispering stream, Ethan followed as if in a daze. A gentle mist kicked up from the ocean, turning the atmosphere dreamy and ethereal.

Darby bypassed the wide swing to splay her palm on the tree. Against the leviathan with long, gnarled branches thick enough to support Ethan's two-hundred-plus pounds, her pale hand was a wisp of nothing. It glowed against the rough bark as if transferring messages through the ancient veins.

For a breathless moment, Ethan felt like the interloper.

A car passed on the other edge of the grove over by where her camper was visible from the road. During the day, the swing could be seen when coming from the direction of Seattle, but at night it remained in the shadows, as the roads never directed headlights this way regardless of what direction it turned. Once the late-night traveler had passed, only moonlight illuminated them both.

When she glanced over her shoulder, Darby's face was distressingly cherubic as she studied him. "Why did he pick *this* tree? Most people don't want to be buried this close to an interstate highway."

That was easy. "It was my Grandma Tove's favorite," he answered. "She used to call it Yggdrasil."

"The tree of life," she murmured. "I can see why. It looks old enough. Sacred enough."

He nodded, reaching out to place his large hand opposite hers, feeling the scrape of the ancient bark against his calluses.

"I like the name Tove," she told the tree.

"She was Scandinavian. Died when I was maybe six."

"I'm so sorry. What happened?"

Because she sounded like she meant it, he answered. "Lymphoma. Took her so young."

Darby snatched her hand away as if the tree had bit her.

When Ethan would have asked her about it, she dropped it to her side and turned to him with a sultry look. Approaching, she spread her arms to catch both ropes and tested their strength. "Come sit," she invited him. "I'll push you."

Ethan's brows slammed together. "Uh. I'm good."

"Oh, come on." Her smile gleamed a bit too brightly, and her voice was a smidge too effusive. "Don't go dishonoring your Townsend grandparents. They'd love to see your tight ass in this swing again."

"Gross," he harrumphed as he went to her, turned himself efficiently on his heel, and plopped down on the shellacked seat. "I'd appreciate your not mentioning my sainted grandparents and my butt in the same sentence."

"Noted." She used his word against him, but waited until he gripped both ropes before nudging his shoulders with her palms.

Not surprisingly, the swing didn't get too far, but that didn't seem to bother her—she just tried again, this time leaning her body in closer.

"Tell me about your grandpa. Was he also a Big Man About Town?"

"Actually, not really." Ethan didn't know if it was the night, the beer (probably not; he'd only had one), or the proximity to the tree that had him floating in his own nostalgia. But here in the presence of the woman he didn't trust himself around, he felt safer than he had in years. "Grandpa was...himself. A good man. A pilot in Vietnam. A loving and devoted husband and father..."

"But?" she prodded when he'd allowed his thoughts to drift for too long.

There wasn't a but. Not in the way she meant. "Looking back now, I realize...he never gave two ripe shits about being a Townsend. He was a simple guy. Not great with paperwork or money. Liked to work with his hands, instead. He listened to good music. He spoke too quietly and laughed too loud. Loved fishing and camping."

The swinging had picked up a tiny bit of speed—meaning his boots had begun to drag in the moss a couple of inches.

"I remember one of the last times we hiked through here, he took me to where Raven Creek springs from the ground. Water's pristine enough to drink." He should know. He'd had it tested back when he was talking to architects about building a spring-fed brewery or distillery.

Just like Tove's father, Leif, had owned in Norway and passed down to his gigantic ginger sons.

In the north pasture, he'd wanted to plant his own hops. In the east he'd had plans for an orchard in which he could grow cider apples and fruits for infusions. Raven Creek Brewery. It would have been something he could pass on to his own kids. A legacy they could work with their own hands. They'd make something, contribute rather than rest on the laurels of the Townsend name.

It was a dream he was finding he couldn't give up just yet.

Planting his boots on the ground, he stopped swinging. Her next push brought her body in front-to-back contact with his.

The imprint branded on him, immediately.

The smart thing—the right thing—to do would be to hop off the swing like she'd cattle-prodded him in the taint, sprint to his truck, and peel out of there.

But the two perfect breasts pressing into his shoulder blades, combined with the honeyed breeze of her exhalations tickling the wisps of hair at his nape, froze his tush to the swing.

"Thank you for this," she murmured against his ear. "The swing is really lovely."

He swallowed, hard, doing his best to douse a warm glow trying to ignite behind his breastbone. "I didn't hang it for you."

"Doesn't matter. I still love swings. Always have. Check this out."

His shoulders missed the warmth of her body the moment she left, but she returned right away, pressing her shoulder blades to his.

"What the—?"

"Hold still and keep your boots planted," she ordered him before seizing the ropes above her head and doing little hops as she counted, "One. Two. Three. Hup!"

Through some kind of bendy magic and a miracle of biblical

proportions, she flipped her entire body upside down. Using only the strength of her toned arms, she stretched her legs up the ropes of the swing and then hooked her ankles to secure herself above him.

Ethan looked up, astounded to find her face smiling down at him, her hair creating a lush pink curtain around them both. He couldn't bring himself to break eye contact long enough to wonder about the kimono's location.

"What the..." he repeated poetically.

Strong as he was, he probably couldn't even do that.

He checked the way she'd splayed her legs against the ropes, soles of her now bare feet to the sky.

Correction, he could most definitely *not* do that.

No one did that.

No one in his life hung upside down at one a.m. on a swing with her fragrant fuchsia hair pleasantly feathering over his upturned face. Setting nerve endings on fire. Blocking out the illusions of the past and the opaque, unsteady path to the future.

Five days.

In five days she'd be compelled to wander away. To find the next place that called to her restless soul. To set up this caravan of coffee and carefree sensuality to a community in need of her.

And he would be the one who'd driven her away.

Something like regret reared in his gut, tinged with a frenetic note that might have been panic.

Five days, and he might never see her again.

That was the fucking plan all along. It was what he dearly wanted.

Wasn't it?

"You're thinking too loud," she accused him with a grin, her voice raspy by the effort it took to remain inverted.

"Oh yeah?" he murmured, his voice thinned by the arch of his throat. "What did you hear?"

"You were thinking about how you can't wait to be rid of me," she guessed blithely, adjusting her hands on the ropes to slide a little closer. Her eyes were dark, but he knew what he would read in them if he could see into the depths.

"You a mind reader, too, huh?" he rumbled, the spell cast by the night and her scent, by the brook and the waft of her sweet breath, threatening to carry away the last of his rationality.

With a smooth, if abrupt, move, she hinged at the hips and tucked her body around with the grace and strength of a gymnast, unfurling as she flipped herself upright. Splitting her legs, she locked them around his torso and slid down to face him on the swing, releasing her feet to dangle behind them.

Straddling him on the swing, she finally released the ropes, shaking out her hands before resting them on his shoulders for balance.

Shit. He should have done the safe thing and stayed home. A good man knew his own weaknesses and was extra vigilant against them.

Darby Dunwell exploited every single one.

And uncovered a few more he'd not known he had.

"You're thinking you never should have come here tonight," she purred against his ear, grinding her ass against the erection he'd been ignoring for longer than he'd like to admit.

Ethan was instantly suffused with tension. His muscles locked as she enfolded herself around him. His jaw locked against a moan.

Her thin cotton pants and matching strappy camisole were the shittiest barriers to her curves, providing easy access points to the skin he could *see* was bare beneath.

He should say something.

Do something.

Stand up.

Set her down.

Walk away.

Any one or a combination of those things.

Any minute now.

But it was her eyes that did him in. Liquid pools of desire

underscored with something he was convinced must be a trick of the moonlight. A latent vulnerability. Unspoken need.

"You're thinking about how much you want to kiss me," she informed him in a breathy timbre. "Despite everything."

A wild, whispered breeze carried away the last of his doubts and fears, replaced by an armed calm that made everything else seem insignificant.

They both should be somewhere else.

And yet here they were. Together, connected, alive.

Releasing the ropes, Ethan moved to cup her face, barely daring to touch her lest he break something precious beyond repair.

His breath shook.

Her fine muscles twitched.

The moon shone.

The air moved.

He didn't take her lips, but sampled them first. Small, brushing strokes. Delicious little tastes interrupted by the passing caresses of his thumbs over the sensitized rim of her mouth.

A deeper kiss. And another. Pressing his lips to hers with a sensation so soft and glorious it felt like coming home.

Darby's reaction matched his. Tentative. Searching. Questioning.

This was a discovery they'd not slowed down to make before. Different flavors and textures. Curious reactions.

She slid her hands up his shoulders and threaded her fingers through the crisp-cut layers of hair at the base of his neck. A firework of sparks and heat ignited from the inside out, consuming him with its intensity until not even ash remained of his past self or future plans.

All that mattered was this moment between them. Just them. Not fighting, but embracing the unexpected gift of stolen time under starlit skies near a babbling brook surrounded by nature's symphony.

Darby undid his shirt and pushed it off his shoulders. She

visibly appreciated the sight of his sculpted muscles, her gaze drawn to every ripple of corded flesh. His body heated beneath her admiration, and a flush spread across his chest and neck. He held still, savoring the sensation of being seen.

Wondering what it would be like if he bared everything to her. Not just physically.

She trailed her fingers over his chest like a whisper, leaving behind a trail of goosebumps in their wake as she leaned forward to place a tender kiss on the center point between his collarbones. Her lips were soft, yet firm—gentle and teasing all at once—sparking another surge of heat that left him craving more.

He felt alive like he hadn't in years, suddenly overwhelmed with emotion that threatened to break the surface if he wasn't careful. His heart thudded against its cage as Darby continued to explore him with reverent touches, tracing sweet circles against his skin until they were both trembling with desire and anticipation.

Finally, she looked up into his eyes with a daring half-smile. He could read the silent invitation in her gaze and knew there was no turning back.

Hungry for a touch of her milky skin, he slid his hands beneath the hem of her shirt and followed the curve of her waist up to her ribs. He caressed the undersides of her breasts, smoothing a thumb over the taut nipple.

She gasped, clenching her thighs.

Despite the layers, Ethan felt the heat between her legs intensifying.

Claiming her mouth, he cupped each of her petal-soft breasts, intent on finding every curve and divot left yet unexplored. He found an inexplicably large divot where her breast met her ribcage, and curious fingers dipped against the ridge. What was this?

With a strangled sound, she seized his hands and wrapped them around her, anchoring her to his lap.

The kiss deepened as their tongues entwined, and they

devoured one another with an intensity that felt like it had been brewing since the last time he'd been inside her incredible body.

The kiss spiraled out of control as their passion followed.

Ethan leaned back, allowing Darby to slide her hands over his body as she moved to undo his belt. He groaned in pleasure when she exposed his hard length.

Her cotton sleep shorts disintegrated in his hands, and with a reverent groan, he slid a finger along the soft, downy seam of her sex before delving inside the wet heat. Finding her clit immediately, he circled the tiny aperture with the pad of his thumb, bathing in the sweetness of her response. Keeping his thumb busy with her pleasure, he stroked a finger inside the inviting flesh, then two, setting an exquisite tempo that soon had her arching her neck to beg the stars for release.

He fell on her throat like a vampire. Nipping, sucking, and savoring the salt and sweat of her skin.

Her pleasure was a puzzle to be solved, and he watched every twitch of her muscles, every hitch of her breath and shudder of her limbs for direction. He let the intensity of her responses swing them gently, establishing a rhythm organic to their own bodies.

When it seemed like she was about to come, he drew his hand away.

Darby moaned in frustration and curled her hips in search of him.

Their eyes locked together with a force he hadn't known existed before Ethan lifted her hips and lowered her onto his cock. Sparks of pleasure blinded him as she enveloped him in the warmth of her body. Sensations overwhelmed him as her tight walls clenched and released in a rhythm that felt as ancient as the first song.

Ethan opened his eyes to find Darby regarding him with an awestruck expression, one that seemed to hold all the secrets of the universe and a thousand more questions besides.

Filled with a foreign and infinite tenderness, he cupped the back of her head, pressing his face into the silk of her hair as his knees and hips used the tranquil motion of the swing to create a gentle, rhythmic friction.

There was no hurry. No pounding race to the finish. No frenzy to find the pleasure they both knew the other was capable of providing.

Nothing else to be done and nowhere else to be.

Their fucking became a slow dance to which they both knew the simple steps. Their breaths created the metronome. Their bodies the movement. The music belonged to the tops of the towering trees and the way in which the elements danced across the earth.

Ethan could see nothing but Darby.

His lips parted slightly while hers puckered to a pretty bow on her flushed face. Eyes wide, pupils dilated, she locked gazes with him, the color in her cheeks brilliant and fevered.

Five days.

Her body wrapped around him like a velvet sheath as he drowned in her eyes. Every slow, deep, eternal thrust into her seemed to unlock something inside of him. A new need. A quiet hope. An alarming word. Then another.

Yes.

This.

Mine.

Stay.

Ethan froze. His muscles locked down again as the word hit him like an ACME anvil. Parts of him revolted. Other parts rejoiced.

His man parts protested the interruption.

Stay?

No. *Nope.* That wasn't what this was...

Leaning in closer, he allowed adrenaline to inject gravel into his voice. "Let go," he ordered her.

She blinked at him through pleasure-glazed eyes. "What?"

"Let go of the rope," he said, gathering her ass in his hands and standing. "I'm in control now."

* * *

I'm in control now.

Control.

The whole damn problem, when Darby thought about it.

Had he truly been referring to dominance over her, she'd have been ready to throw a party. Organize a parade. Call out the band. Rent a crop duster to write it in the sky.

Ethan Townsend found his inner dom.

But no.

As she was a veteran of many a bad relationship, Darby's hypervigilance bordered on an art form. Searching the smallest shift in tone or twitch of a facial muscle for unspoken thoughts.

She had felt the exact second when he'd disconnected. When the small window on his soul slammed shut, leaving only the impenetrable veneer he maintained as fastidiously as everything else in his life.

He wanted her.

That much was abundantly evident, throbbing away inside her in pulses that sent electric shocks skittering through her veins.

But he didn't *want* to want her.

And it stung.

Which pissed her right the hell off.

"Let go," he urged again, a whisper against her ear.

You first.

Maybe it had been the revelation of Ethan's connection to the land. Maybe his attempt at a thoughtful gesture to redeem himself after the woodshop. Whatever the reason, Darby elected to relent.

Or to let him think she had.

Held aloft by Ethan's powerful hands, she relinquished her grip on the rope. And with it, her leverage. His grip on her tightened as Darby slid down his body. She paused for a moment to take it in, savoring the sensation of his being as physically close as he was emotionally distant.

She cupped the smooth, hard expense of his jaw, tracing down the sandpapery skin over the raised tendons of his neck. She let her hands play outward on the slope of his bare shoulders. His knotted trapezius muscles flexed beneath her fingertips, bearing the weight of the world, even now. A burden he'd likely taken on too young.

Her heart ached for him. He was strong, so strong, and yet there was a fragility to him that she couldn't quite put her finger on.

But she wanted to. She wanted to peel back every layer of his being until she knew him inside and out. She wanted to tell him that she understood.

That she knew how heavy heritage could be. To make him see her as a harbor, a haven, even if just for a moment.

Ethan was already pulling away.

The air around them seemed suddenly heavier with anticipation as he spun her around to face the swing.

No accident, she knew, that he didn't want to look her in the eye.

His big hands braced her ribcage, moving down to her waist and sliding around to the small of her back. With one hand planted in the dip at the base of her spine, he guided her torso down so the swing notched itself against her lower belly.

"I was wondering why you mounted it so high," Darby teased, glancing at Ethan over her shoulder.

His face remained stony. Serious. The look of a man who had traveled deep within himself. Circling her wrists, he drew her arms back and anchored her hand on the rope. When she had steadied herself, he lifted her legs wheelbarrow style and hooked her ankles over the crooks of his elbows. Her knees bent and widened as he gripped the sides of the swing's wooden seat on either side of her hips.

She doubted whether Ethan knew the name magazines like *Cosmo* had assigned to this position—flying doggy—but felt a grudging jolt of pride for the unexpected burst of creativity on his part.

The silky wood bit into the crease of her hips as he drew the swing backward. She felt him notched against her, this silky heat of his head probing gently, maddeningly, as he gave her the barest taste of his full length.

And all at once, Darby knew.

He was taking this slowly to prove to himself that he could.

To prove that even now, he could tighten the iron cables of his self-control.

She felt a pang of sadness as he rocked the swing back and forth in a gentle rhythm. Building, but slowly. Carefully. Not a hint of the wild abandon they'd known when he put the border of a country between him and the town that shared his name.

Fuck that.

Darby shifted her weight and leaned forward, elevating her hips to enhance his view. His breath caught in his throat, and she felt him tense behind her as he gripped the swing's wooden seat until his knuckles turned white.

Before Ethan could catch on to what Darby intended, she slipped her ankles from his arms and hooked them behind his hips, using her heels to drive him deeper.

"Darby," he warned, his voice thick with warring desire and restraint.

"I know," she whispered, craning to look back at him.

"No," he groaned. "No, you don't."

"Yes, I do," she insisted. "I know what you're afraid of, because I'm afraid of it too."

And that was the truth. The whole truth.

"I know this is the worst possible idea in the history of terrible fucking ideas. I know that you want me off this land and out of your town. I know that I shouldn't want you, but I do. I want you, Ethan Townsend. I want *all* of you."

Ethan's eyes darkened, his gaze burning straight through to her soul. The swing creaked as he pulled back, sliding out of her, and for one terrible moment, Darby thought he was going to leave her there, suspended and wanting. Weak with desire.

But then he surged forward, gripping her hips as he drove into her with a force that tore an ecstatic cry from her throat.

"Like that?" he growled.

He didn't give her time to answer. Instead, he set a brutal rhythm, punctuated by the rapid slap of his hips against her ass.

"More."

He obliged, powering into her again and again, filling her with his heat, his desire.

His frustration.

Darby yielded to it all, arching back into him as she met him thrust for thrust. Need for need.

"Christ, Darby. I can't—" Ethan gasped, his movements growing erratic as he twitched inside her.

"You can," she panted, squeezing her thighs to tighten around him in silent plea.

Bend me. Break me. Make me yours.

Ethan's rhythm grew frantic, a frenzied, primal pounding that left Darby's vision spangled with bursts of color as vibrant as fireworks over the Hudson River.

It was too much and not nearly enough. All she could do was surrender.

To let it take her. To let it claim her.

"Ethan," she whimpered, and the sound of his name on her lips only spurred him in time with the wild, reckless beating of her heart.

And then she was disintegrating into pure pleasure again, a long, drawn-out shudder that didn't end until her lungs were burning and her whole body shook.

The muscles in Ethan's arms, his chest, his shoulders, strained taut. He threw his head back on a strangled roar as he lost himself inside her. His torso folded forward, and his forearms wrapped beneath her sternum. His heart beat like a jackhammer between her shoulder blades as their breath slowed.

Ethan lifted himself off her and collapsed to the grass, his arms flung out wide. Darby sank down beside him, the dew-damp blades cool against their fevered skin. She allowed herself to revel in the simple pleasure of the backs of their hands kissing. The precious handful of seconds before the chip reassembled itself on her shoulder.

"I'm sorry," he murmured into her hair.

Darby shook her head, a faint smile curving her lips. Already with the apologies. "For what?"

The swing creaked in the silence, interrupted only by the night wind through the trees.

A tremor ran through him, and Ethan stilled before turning to meet her gaze.

"Trespassing."

Darby propped herself up on elbow. "You planning on turning yourself in?"

The ghost of a smile flickered at one corner of his lips. "To whom?"

She grazed her fingertips on his chest, playing over the dip of his sternum. "I could call Deputy McGarvey on you. He'd be here in a hot second," she said with a teasing smile. "He asked me to dinner, in fact."

The moment the words were out of her mouth, she knew it had been a mistake. All humor evaporated from Ethan's face as his gaze turned stony and he pushed himself up to a sitting position. Darby wanted to say something, anything that would ease the tension emanating from him in waves, but no words came. Instead, she just sat there, watching the walls that had been crumbling around him just moments before reassembling themselves with record speed.

"Hey," she said softly, lightly resting a hand on his shoulder. "I was kidding."

But Ethan had already retreated, withdrawing from her touch like a cat. He was silent as he quickly rearranged his boxers and zipped his jeans.

"I should get going," he said gruffly as he pushed himself off the ground.

Darby reached for her discarded sleep shorts and shimmied into them before hugging her arms over her bare breasts. "Ethan. Look at me."

He only bent and retrieved her t-shirt, tossing it toward her before beginning to gather his tools.

"*Ethan.*"

He finally turned to her, his expression unreadable in the darkness.

"What the hell crawled up your ass in the last two minutes?"

Ethan's jaw tightened, but he didn't respond.

"Is this about McGarvey wanting to take me out?"

"It's not," he said a little too quickly.

"Then what's the deal?" Darby asked in exasperation. "Because whatever this is, it needs to stop right now. I'm not a toy you can just set on a shelf when you're finished playing."

Ethan whipped around to face her. "Look, it's none of my business who you talk to—"

"You're right," she said, parking her hand on her hip and narrowing her eyes at him. "It's not."

"But Trent is...is—"

"Is? The suspense is killing me, truly."

The muscles in Ethan's jaw bunched. "Never mind."

Darby stepped on the length of extra rope with the callused sole of her bare foot. "Oh no you don't."

"I really need to get going."

"You really need to tell me what you were going to say."

Ethan's eyes sank to the gnarled roots of the tree. "McGarvey is a new hire."

"And?"

Ethan's Adam's apple bobbed on a swallow. "And he's still earning the town's trust. Learning how things work around here."

Darby felt the corner of her eye begin to twitch. The way everyone talked about Townsend Harbor like it was someone's maiden aunt in need of sheltering from life's seedier details drove her absolutely batshit.

"And you're afraid that his fraternizing with the local slattern would impede his gradual transformation into a close-minded Townsendite?"

The sole of Ethan's boot scuffed at a patch of grass they'd gouged during the course of their senseless frenzy. "That's not what I mean."

"Then what do you mean?"

He glanced over his shoulder, toward the road that led to the hamlet in question. "There's a certain distance I like to keep between my private life and my civic responsibility. Deputy McGarvey is part of the civic responsibility. If you're going to see him socially, I only ask that what's between us stays between us."

Darby blinked at him, her mouth in imminent danger of becoming a moth cave if she didn't remember how the hinge of her jaw worked.

"I literally have your DNA drying on my ass cheek, and you've got your testes in a twist thinking that I'm going to out you to your own deputy over a bowl of cioppino?"

Ethan's ears had turned the color of a ripe tomato, effectively answering her question.

"Jesus, Ethan." Darby shook her head, turning away from him and running a hand through her passion-tangled hair. Treacherous tears welled behind her eyelids, threatening to spill down her cheeks. She needed to get rid of him, and fast.

"This isn't why I—"

"Get off my property," she said through gritted teeth.

Ethan didn't need to be told twice. He scooped his tools into the wooden box and made for his truck. As the taillights disappeared through trees, Darby kicked at a nearby rock with such force that it ricocheted off a tree trunk with an audible thud before disappearing into the darkness of the night. She wanted to scream. She wanted to throw something.

She wanted...

She wanted to rewind the last five minutes and slap a piece of duct tape across his mouth before he could ruin a perfectly good postcoital cuddle.

Despite her simmering rage, Darby could still feel the imprint of his body against hers, could sense the heat of their passionate embrace still lingering on her skin.

Son of a bitch.

Darby had come to Townsend Harbor hoping for nothing more than a little peace and quiet. A place where she could spend her days in her cozy, coffee-scented camper and her nights doing whatever—and whoever—she felt like. A place to recover from sickening heartbreak and betrayal. A place to catch a break.

Instead, she was catching feels.

TWELVE
Extraction

USING WATER THAT IS "JUST OFF THE BOIL" TO DRAW FLAVOR FROM COFFEE GROUNDS

FOUR DAYS.

The words ricocheted through Darby's head like shrapnel as her taxi passed the *Get Knotty in Townsend Harbor* sign she now knew Ethan Townsend had made with his own hands.

Hands that hauled her bicycle into town to be fixed. Hands that had repaired her shoe and hung a swing from the beautiful old oak tree on her property. Hands that had brought indescribable pleasure to her body and commensurate fuckery to her doorstep.

The sweat hadn't even dried on their bodies, and he'd already been anticipating who else might get to touch her.

Once upon a time, she might've slept with Deputy Trent McGarvey to make a very valid point. Show Ethan and the entire damn town she could do what she pleased, *whom* she pleased, when she pleased.

But...

But.

From her present vantage, revenge boning seemed like a lot of work.

The primping, the shaving, the seduction. The pushing, and

sweating, and post-pasta jostling. The very idea of the whole production made her feel dog tired and dryer than a popcorn fart.

Nevertheless, as Sister Mary Mildred had been so fond of saying, Darby would not—*could not*—be controlled. Not by guilt, shame, societal pressure, and certainly the fuck not by the likes of Ethan Townsend.

Jesus.

Even thinking his name began to make her heart pound as the taxi whizzed past the shipyards.

The late-afternoon sunlight glinted off the rippling water beyond the bobbing boats, creating a sparkling tapestry against the shoreline. A rare clear day with a cornflower-blue sky that the sheriff could be anywhere under. Waiting around the corner of every historic building, ready to pop out and commit some act of unsolicited chivalry that might weaken her resolve.

"This okay?" the taxi driver asked, slowing as they approached the corner of Water Street and Maple.

"Fine," she said, punching up the pay app and parting with a sum that made both sets of her cheeks clench. Worth it, she told herself, to avoid potentially being T-boned by another forest creature or buffing her muffin raw with the ride into town on a bike bearing a set of gleaming handlebars courtesy of Roy the recluse.

Roy, she thought with a furious pulse of joy.

Yes. At last, the lady-boner-killing reminder she needed.

Exiting the cab, she stepped out onto the street to get on with her mission.

In peep-toe wedge platforms whose structural integrity Darby had checked no less than six times before leaving her camper, she walked the half block to her target.

Bazaar Girls.

Darby pushed through the front door, somewhat perplexed by the sound of a sheep enthusiastically bleating her arrival.

Glancing around for the source, she spotted a small black box fixed on the wall above the door, the small red eye of a motion sensor trained on the entryway.

"It also has a cow, a goat, and three different guard dogs." Gemma McKendrick stood atop an ancient wooden ladder, easing an armload of wool knots in a deep emerald green onto a shelf high on the wall behind the cash register. The relic of wood and rusted metal wobbled precariously as she began to descend. "I know it's ridiculous, but I love it."

"Please," Darby said, shooting Gemma a conspiratorial smile. "You're talking to the woman who owns a pink toaster oven. Ridiculous is my middle name. Well, it's actually Leighton, but I prefer not to think about the fact that my misogynistic steel tycoon grandfather's crusty moniker is stamped on every piece of paperwork in my life."

Every piece of paperwork including the one signed by a healthy cross section of the townsfolk. The triple espresso Darby had mainlined after she closed Brewbies early that afternoon turned to acid in her stomach.

"I see your misogynistic grandfather and raise you a circa 1990s phone psychic." The ladder emitted an unearthly shriek of protest as Gemma folded it and shoved it behind a curtain behind the register. "Gemini Cleo McKendrick, at your service," she said with a curtsy that flared her mustard-yellow and burgundy plaid skirt.

Today, it was paired with opaque tights in an oxblood mauve that picked up thin lines in the plaid, a short-sleeved blouse with a collar that looked to have hand-tatted lace edging, and a knitted vest embroidered with frolicking kittens.

An ensemble that clearly advertised the impressive array of her skills.

Other examples were displayed throughout the cozy, sunlit shop. Hats. Scarves. Socks. Gloves. G-strings?

"We ended up playing truth or dare at the last meeting of the Stitch n' Bitch Club, and it got a little out of hand," Gemma said, catching the direction of Darby's gaze.

"And what are these?" Darby asked, lifting a small sleeve that looked like nothing so much as a knitted condom from a basket on the counter.

"Oh! I'm making a new line of dildo covers for Vee's shop. We're calling them *cooz*-ies," Gemma said, bracketing the word with air quotes. "I happen to have a hot-pink one in a lovely merino wool if you're in the market." She arched a dark eyebrow at Darby, a smirk lifting one corner of her bright red lips.

"I'm always in the market." Darby began pawing through the pile. Hell, maybe an aesthetic upgrade of her sexual artillery would make her more likely to reach for her vibrator like a responsible-ass adult instead of swing-shagging the sheriff.

Bareback, her lethargic conscience laconically pointed out.

A single bead of sweat crawled down Darby's ribs beneath the fabric of her Barbie-pink sundress.

She could practically hear Sister Mary Mildred's voice in the back of her head, a stern and disapproving reminder that those who "sin in haste, repent at leisure." Or, as Darby and her classmates had put it, *wrap the rod or spawn the wad.*

Granted, Buckingham Palace's guard could set their pocket watches by Darby's cycle, and it was completely the wrong time of the month for anything to happen, but thirteen years of Catholic school had left her with the lingering impression that smiting women who had sex for fun was the heavenly host's answer to craps or roulette.

"Here we are." Gemma produced the promised penis-shaped handicraft and held it out to Darby. "On the house."

"No way," Darby said. "After everything you guys are doing for me, buying this is the least I can do."

"Suit yourself." Gemma walked back to the register, where she began unpacking a box of sewing notions. "Is there anything you're looking for in particular?"

"Actually, yes." Reaching into the messenger bag strapped across her chest, Darby pulled out the bustier she had been feverishly working on to distract herself from thoughts of Ethan. "I need some lace trim for this. Do you have anything in a dark purple or black?"

Gemma's gold-green eyes lit up. "Does Raggedy Ann have a cotton crotch?" She disappeared behind the curtain, leaving Darby alone to peruse the other items in the shop.

"Amazing place you have here," Darby called through the curtain. Despite her mostly selfish reasons for coming, she meant the compliment sincerely. Yarn in every color of the rainbow adorned the walls and shelves, forming a Technicolor landscape that dazzled her eye. Jewel tones, pastels, and neons mingled together in a wild and beautiful display.

"It's been a labor of love," Gemma called back. "Meaning I do all the labor and my dad loves to remind me that crafting isn't likely to be a stable market long term."

"Sounds like your dad and mine would get along swimmingly." Darby reached out to touch the buttery fibers of a mint-green shawl draped over an antique dressmaker's bust. "Mine was less then enthused when I informed him I was dropping out of law school to become an aerialist in a burlesque troupe."

And by "less than enthused," Darby meant he had pretty much stopped talking to her altogether.

Gemma pushed the curtain aside and dumped several spools of lace onto the counter in front of Darby. "I mean, I can't be too mad at him, seeing as owns this building and he still put up the seed loan that got me started."

Ah.

This answered one point of Darby's personal curiosity.

More than once, she'd wondered how two women in their early twenties had ended up as the proprietresses of shops she knew the value of from her obsessive real estate stalking prior to her purchase of the land just outside town.

In her early twenties, Darby still had brown hair and a trust fund that trickled just enough money into her bank account every month to keep her from selling term papers online.

"Do your parents live around here?" She picked up one of the spools of lace and held it to the edge of the bustier to get a visual.

"From May to September," Gemma said. "Winters, they spend in Arizona near my twin sister Lyra and her chode-boil of a fiancé."

"Twin?" Darby asked, deciding to gloss over the potentially sensitive subject.

"Identical," Gemma replied. "Except when it comes to our taste in men."

With this second mention of her sister's fiancé, Darby finally twigged to the fact that this was obviously something Gemma *wanted* to talk about.

Shit, she was rusty.

But then, walking into your best friend's dressing room to find your own fiancé buried nose deep in her twat tended to sour you on trust-based intrapersonal connections.

"And what do we hate about the bastard?" Darby asked, reaching for the electric-purple lace next.

"Well," Gemma began, and promptly launched into a tirade that lasted long enough for Darby to settle on the roll of witchy black lace with batwing edges. Not her usual aesthetic, but it suited her vengeful mood.

"...doesn't deserve to scrape gutter gum from the red soles of her Louboutins with his stupid, horsey teeth," Gemma finished, the freckles standing out against her glowing cheeks.

After hearing a thorough assessment of Lyra's fiancé, Darby was inclined to agree. And yet the frequent mention of their upcoming nuptials at a Sedona resort inclined Darby to suspect the roots of Gemma's ire sank deeper than her sister's intended constantly tugging at his foreskin through his golf shorts or the assertion that the color Lyra had chosen for her bridesmaids made Gemma look like a consumption victim.

Setting the lace next to her pert pink dildo cardigan, Darby leaned a hip against the counter while Gemma rang up her purchases. "That's got to be hard. Both your sister and best friend engaged when you're not currently coupled up."

"*Tell* me about it. I'm so happy for Cady, I really am, but here I am watching reruns of *Golden Girls* and knitting slipcovers for sex toys while listening to her gush about Fawkes' donkey dick and lizard tongue or all the ridiculously thoughtful things he does for her, and basically I want to throw myself in front of a steamroller."

"No prospects on the horizon?" Darby asked.

"Please. There are spit bubbles deeper than the Townsend Harbor dating pool." Gemma shook her head in disgust. "That'll be seventeen twenty-two."

"You know," Darby began, digging her debit card out of her bag, "I have it on good authority that there will be some eligible bachelors coming into town for the carnival."

"Oh!" Gemma took Darby's card and plugged it into the appropriate slot. "That reminds me. I have your permits. I had to promise Judy at the county clerk's office a front-row seat to that rope performer guy you were telling us about, but I've got them." She waited until the receipt finished printing before tearing it off and handing it to Darby along with her card. "How's the rest of the talent looking?"

"In a word, fabulous." And for once in Darby's recent past, this was true. Every invitation she'd sent out to the colorful crop of characters she'd amassed before her career shift to caffeinated beverages had been enthusiastically accepted. Plane tickets had been booked. Carnival rides rented. The whole of her colorful, seductive underworld ready to lift its skirts and scandalize Townsend Harbor.

Especially its hypocritical hunk of a sheriff.

"Yay!" Gemma chirped, bouncing on the soles of her Mary Janes. "I'm so freaking excited I can't even feel my face."

"Well, you better prepare yourself, because that face is going to have the hetero half of the entertainment drooling down their dick slings."

"Right." Gemma snorted. "Your fabulously interesting, urbane performer friends will take one look at this and fall madly in love." She waved her hands over a body Darby suspected was curved in all the right places beneath her cat-centric granny-core couture.

"Why not?"

"And, of course, they'll want to leave the big city lights behind in favor of a boring little town full of retirees who think prune juice cocktails and canasta represents a wild night," Gemma added.

"I think you're vastly underestimating the allure of both the town and its resident city counsel spy/knitting maven."

Gemma's flush deepened as she handed Darby's bag over. "Speaking of spying, I heard a certain sheriff was involved in a very public spat right there on the sidewalk in front of God and his gardener after rhody-fest yesterday afternoon."

Now, it was Darby's turn to flush. "You did?"

"Mmhmm," Gemma said, tapping a nail against her chin. "Seems multiple parties witnessed a *very* heated discussion."

Darby swallowed sand. "You don't say."

"All I know is, the rumor mill is going nuts, and my voicemail box was full this morning, and I haven't even made it through all the text messages."

Fuckity fecking fuck.

"That's...unfortunate," Darby said, her mind already preparing an elaborate denial of whatever it was Gemma had heard.

"Right? And super weird, because I didn't think Ethan and his mother were even speaking."

His...*mother*?

Oh, thank God. Or whomever.

The relief Darby felt was immediate and intense. Of all the shit-awful luck that had befallen her in the past several days, at least her dirty dalliance with Townsend Harbor's favorite son remained a secret.

"So," Gemma said, bringing a cuticle to her teeth. "How long have you and Ethan been fucking?"

Had Darby been sipping a relaxing beverage at that precise moment, Gemma would have been treated to a full-on spit take.

"Excuse me?" she sputtered.

"You. Ethan. Tapping ass. Shaking sheets. Planting the parsnip. Bam-bam in the ham. Squat thrusts in the cucumber patch. Amorous congress of a carnal nature. You follow?"

"I do, but—"

"There's no use denying it." Gemma's grin broadened. "I've known Ethan since I was basically a zygote, and he's about as hard to read as a billboard. Might was well tell me everything, seeing as I basically run this town and you definitely need my help."

And to her utter surprise, Darby told her.

About meeting Ethan in the Canadian bar. Their first run-in at her coffee camper. Her talk with Roy. The woodshop. The swing. All of it.

When she was finished, Gemma stared straight ahead as if in a trance. Eyes glossy. Pupils dilated. Lips lightly parted on shallow breaths as she fanned her flushed cheeks with a dog-eared copy of *Crochet Today*.

"Do you have a cigarette?" she asked. "Because I don't even smoke, but I really feel like a need a cigarette."

"Sorry," Darby said. "Gave it up during radiation."

Blowing out a long breath, Gemma sagged onto the wooden stool behind the register and gulped water from a bottle covered with various knitting-related stickers.

"Okay," she said, the hectic color finally receding from her cheeks. "What's our plan?"

Our plan.

Until that precise moment, Darby hadn't realized just how much she'd missed this.

She'd spent so much self-imposed time alone since she'd left Boston that she'd forgotten what it felt like to just talk—really talk—to someone, anyone, without worrying what they wanted from her, what might hide behind their kindness.

How long had it been since she had an ally? A confidante.

Sure, when she was been in Boston, she'd occasionally whined to Tony Two Toes and Gabe Kelly, both of them frequently offering to "take care of" her problems in ways she suspected might involve bone chips in Miami apartment blocks.

Not exactly ideal, given the current situation.

Darby placed her elbows on the counter and leaned in toward her new friend. "I need everything you've got on Caryn Townsend."

THIRTEEN

Hand Pump

FIVE DAYS LATER

A SQUAWKING RADIO BROKE ETHAN FROM HIS exhausted stupor.

It wasn't that he awoke driving his car through the uptown Victorian mansion thoroughfare, but he couldn't exactly remember how he got there.

A handful of sleepless nights would do that to a guy.

Not only had he been haunted in the dark by the memory of having Darby in his arms, but his goddamned radio had been jumping since four a.m.

The day began when a call pulled him out of a fitful sleep to check on an escaped alpaca from the Amber Lights B&B that was terrorizing the goats on the *Fromage de Chèvre* farm a couple miles out of town.

Things just got weirder from there.

What the fuck was with people today? Had he missed a full moon? Was Mercury in retrograde? Solar flares? Amphetamines in the water supply?

Something was off, and just as soon as he took this call, he intended to leave the wild goose chases to his deputies and figure out the crux of the fuckery.

"Say again, Judy?" Ethan tilted his chin toward his radio, paying close attention this time so the dispatcher didn't sound like some grownup in a Charlie Brown special.

"Report of a 10-52 with possible 208 on Water Street, Townsend Harbor. TH Police requesting 510 from 1J-33." Judy blew an against-regulation gum bubble and popped it loudly.

A burglary with possible suspect on scene. Code 510 was an officer in need of assistance.

1J-33? That was Ethan's call sign.

Which officer from Townsend Harbor would be requesting his assistance, specifically?

"1J-33 responding. ETA two minutes." Flicking on his sirens, Ethan made a quick U-turn and ran one of the town's five red lights as Judy rattled off the Water Street address between audible clicks of her knitting needles.

Other than the B+E scare at Nevermore Bookstore the prior autumn—shamefully perpetrated by his own mother and her unlikely cohort—Water Street was considered the safest street in the state.

Property crimes compounded the bulk of violations in Townsend Harbor, followed closely by the usual small-town nonsense. Tourist issues, shoplifting, a bar brawl at a local watering hole or the yacht club, domestic disturbances, dog bites, and vehicle infractions. Occasionally the heir to a deceased retiree called to try to make a murder out of a molehill in order to control the will.

But a downtown burglary in broad daylight?

Unheard of in the town's almost-two-hundred-year history.

Ethan did *not* count the KIKI FORRESTER FOR SHERIFF signs he passed on the way (eleven) and double-parked in front of Vee's Lady Garden. Keeping his lights alternately flashing and his head on a swivel, he leapt from his vehicle and dove into the open door of the shop with his hand on his duty weapon.

Two familiar heads turned toward him, wearing comically identical expressions of relief at his appearance.

The first? Townsend Harbor Police Sergeant Dan Eccles, a deeply religious Episcopalian minister who fellowshipped at the soup kitchen he shared with his best friend and worst fishing enemy, Rabbi Moskowitz. Eccles was a good cop and a terrible prude, which made his current predicament more than a little amusing.

Feet planted wide in front of the beet-red sergeant, was Vivian "Vee" Prescott, a British waif of a woman with steel-gray hair and a backbone of titanium. Both literally and figuratively in her case, after a few recent surgeries had fused together a crumbling spine.

Blinking the daylight out of his eyes, Ethan quickly realized the three of them were alone in the store.

"There you are, sheriff, just in the nick of time." Vee's several silk scarves flowed from her like billowing tentacles as she rushed Ethan. "This Philistine refuses to believe I've been burgled and won't take down a report for insurance." Her gnarled fingers, tipped by unbelievable inches of claw-shaped acrylics, dug into Ethan's forearm as she clutched him.

"She doesn't have the receipts to match what she claims is missing," Eccles said with biblical amounts of patience as he consulted his notes. In his plump, square hand, an iPhone looked like a doll toy. "Complainant did not witness the alleged robbery, can only identify three of the four missing items, and is claiming in excess of twenty-five thousand dollars of lost merchandise."

"And is also standing right here, you absolute dullard."

Ethan lifted his brows at Vee, whose talon-like grip relaxed when he patted her hand. "The shelves look stocked, Vee." He gestured to her little storefront, replete with oils, nightgowns, bottles of supplements, nipple creams, warming and cooling gels, remedies for everything from hot flashes and stretch marks, to period cramps and body-hair removal. Feeling his own ears warm, he kept his demeanor soft and calm. "Wanna tell me what's going on?"

"Wanna get rid of Porky Pig first?" She hitched a thumb at Sergeant Eccles, a stout, round-shouldered man whose stomach was expanding further over his belt with every year he inched closer to retirement.

"Hey, that was uncalled for, ma'am," Eccles complained, rubbing at his solar plexus as if she'd struck it.

"So is your presence, and yet here you still are." Vee motioned to the door.

"You called the police," Eccles reminded her.

Ethan stepped in. "Damn, Vee, Myrtle is really rubbing off on you."

The woman unfurled her dentures in a self-satisfied grin. "Were that the case, sheriff, I'd have said something about his mother."

Ethan pinched the bridge of his nose. "You have any pressing need to pull the jurisdiction card and keep this one, sergeant?"

Eccles moved faster than a man his size ought to on his way to the door. "Nope. It's all yours, sheriff. Have a good—"

The door closed on the word *day*, leaving the perfume of Eccles' favorite Chinese takeout in his wake.

Welp, *this* might as well be happening.

"Okay, Vee," Ethan said, white-knuckle-gripping his mild-mannered small-town sheriff persona. The one he used to coach little league rather than break up bar fights. "Tell me what happened. Start with the moment you realized a burglary had occurred, and if there was any evidence of a break-in, such as broken locks or windows."

The woman's rheumy blue eyes melted into pools of gratitude as she tugged his arm toward a beaded curtain covering *another* velvet curtain that hung from an archway at the back of the shop. "Oh, it was terrible! I came to open up the shop and found the door unlocked! I thought it strange, but I'm turning fifty-nine in a few months, you see, and my memory isn't what it used to be. So, I thought, maybe I didn't lock up correctly."

Ethan bit his tongue.

He'd pulled Vee over not three years ago, and her driver's license had declared her sixty-eight years old. Mentioning this at the moment wouldn't only be counterproductive, it was against every survival instinct his ancestors had passed down through the ages.

The Brits were famous ear twisters, and his were sensitive.

Slapping the curtains aside with a jangle, she tugged him into a room twice as big as the one they'd only just occupied. "When checking on my inventory to see if anything was, indeed, missing... I discovered this!"

She swept a hand to an empty, four-tiered display case that rotated at a melancholy pace.

Ethan's jaw hit the carpet.

Not because of the display case and its missing contents, but because of everything else crowded into the room.

Cocks, mostly.

So. Many. Cocks.

Shelves and shelves and more shelves were lined with phallic objects, dildos and vibrators and butt plugs, jeweled cocks, polished cocks, cocks that glowed in the dark, cocks that sang, cocks that vibrated, cocks that were curved like carrots, cocks smooth as carvings by Michelangelo himself, cocks with openings large enough to fit a fist into, and cocks small enough to fit in the palm of your hand or in a pocket.

The far wall boasted an endless array of leather, lace, and lingerie, and the one adjacent displayed erotic art, movies, and books.

Ethan fought the urge to tug on the collar of his shirt or wipe at the mist on his upper lip, knowing the canny woman would immediately sense his unease.

And crucify him for it.

"What—" Were those nut sac clamps under the table? Who in their right mind—? "Uh, what is missing from the display case?" he asked. "Jewelry?" Judging by the price tag she'd put on the missing items, it was the only thing that made sense.

"After a fashion," she said with a trembling wink. "This case is on loan to me as one of the only physical U.S. vendors of the Lillith LUXE line of exclusive pleasure products."

"The what now?" Ethan gulped at the thought of the report he was going to have to write.

If he wasn't imagining things, her eyes went somewhat dreamy, hands moving as if she were presenting the Crown Jewels. "Five items handcrafted in Milan and Antwerp by the most indulgent of artisans. Each implement takes thirty days to manufacture to customer specifications."

Ethan swallowed once again, which didn't work, so he was forced to clear the cobwebs from his throat before asking, "You're telling me someone stole five high-end luxury—er— dildos from you?"

She burst into a throaty laugh that ended on a wheeze. "No, you simple man, I'm telling you someone pilfered a g-spot stimulator, a butt plug, a clitoral vibrator, a cock ring, and a dick sleeve that could only be defined by the decadence in the lavish twenty-four-karat gold plating!"

"Ohhhh. Kaaaay." Whatever warmth that started in his ears spilled down his neck and surged into his cheeks. "Someone stole five gold-plated—er—objects from your inventory."

"Sex toys, yes."

"And this...inventory you have no receipts for?"

"That's what I was trying to tell your pompous predecessor," she snapped. "They're on loan for display. I have paperwork, somewhere, but I need to fish it out of storage."

"Someone loaned you twenty-five thousand dollars' worth of gold-plated...adult—um, and you're not certain where you left the paperwork?"

Vee brushed a bit of hair off her forehead and tucked it behind her ear as she narrowed suspicious eyes at him. "Oh, sheriff, please don't tell me you can't say the words."

"I say plenty of words," he muttered, searching for spiders on the carpet so he didn't have to make eye contact with exactly a thousand dicks.

"Darling boy, if you can't bring yourself to talk about it, how do you ever expect to have good sex?"

"I don't have any issues in that area, thank you for mentioning," he grumbled, casting a level look at the woman. "Now when was the last time you remember seeing the—um—? Or let me ask you this. Do you have a description of the missing—er..."

Dammit, he could *so* say the words! He was a goddamned adult. And had fantastic sex.

Sometimes even with pink-haired sexpots who didn't like him.

It was just... Vee looked like every adorable grandmother since the beginning of time, and he couldn't bring himself to say anything sexual in her proximity.

He'd rather just hand over the 25k.

"I'm the most worried about the Lillith LUXE clitoral stimulator." She bustled over to the nearest wall and took something from a display that looked like a feather quill pen made out of soft blue silicone. "Even though only the handle is plated in gold, the tip looks something like this." She brandished the silicone feather at him like a sword. "It's worth almost ten thousand on its own."

"Why?" He scowled, angry that he'd allowed the question to escape.

"Because this!" She clicked on a button with her thumb.

Nothing happened.

"Oh, ballocks." She held it up to her ear, shook it a little, turned it on and off several times to no effect. "Well." She shrugged. "Doesn't matter. What you do is put it on the clitoris like this." Gently, she ran it across his jawbone. "And when it's on she can feel it go, *Blitdlelelelelelele,*" she trilled as she manually vibrated it against his face with little wiggles of her liver-spotted hand.

Dear God! He flinched away and ducked around the glass display table.

And here he was without "be a human clitoris" on his bingo card for this rando Thursday.

"Then there's the bejeweled LUXE g-spot smooth glide," she said, pausing for him to make note. "It's the most popular one, though I can't figure out why... All those cut gems would needlessly upbraid the meat curtains, if you catch my meaning." Just in case, she circled her hand around the region of her hips and...

Never. Ethan never in his entire life wanted to understand Vivian Prescott's reference to—*bwark*—her—*barf*—meat curtains.

"So." Ethan's strangled word precluded a round of throat clearing to cover up the actual gagging. "H-how many people knew the...inventory was on site? How many knew the price?" He did his level best to direct the conversation back to the actual crime while mentally flipping through which detective pissed him off lately enough to assign this to.

McGarvey's handsome face floated into his mind's view.

That motherfucker had too many nights off.

"No one but Myrtle and my one employee, Dax," she said, her eyes wide beneath enormous false lashes.

"Dax who?" he asked, not recognizing the name.

"Used to be Maria Quinto's boy Daniel, but they are now Dax and work here part time."

"You trust Dax?"

"With my life," she said, pushing her jaw forward in defiance. "They didn't do this."

He'd come back to that later. "Any unusual people hanging about?"

Vee eyed him as if he'd lost his mind. "The only ubiquitous thing about Townsend Harbor is the unusual people. You know that as well as anyone."

"Sure I just meant—"

"You know who probably saw them leaving?" Her eyes lit as if she had a great idea. Ethan realized immediately that Vee was many things, but among them was a terrible actress. "Um.

Captain Butterfield on the old *Red Head*. You should go question him about it! I think he's a smuggler. Could fence those pieces for a pretty penny on the black market."

Ethan cocked his head. "You think Eugene Butterfield—the whale-watching guide—is going to fence a few golden dongs for 25k?" he asked. Okay. Now something was really off. "You realize his first tour leaves before seven a.m. and no one is stirring on Water Street by then."

"Yes, but I think I saw him peeking in here—er—last night." Her eyes kept floating to the clock above the door as if it had some importance. "That's right. It certainly could have been him."

"You *think* you saw him, or you did see him?"

Captain Butterfield perpetually dressed like a sailor in the navy circa whenever Elvis made movies. Bell bottoms and all. You didn't *think* you sighted the thin, red-bearded man who stood six foot seven. You couldn't look the fuck away.

Ethan's eyes narrowed. "You hate Captain Butterfield."

"Myrtle hates him. I'm ambivalent," she said airily. "But he would be the kind of man to fence something so precious. I really think you should go to the docks and question him. Probably right now. Who knows if he's looking to abscond across the border to Canada?"

Wouldn't get far with a bunch of shiny dicks. Or twenty-five grand. Not in this economy.

"The docks on the other side of the peninsula?" Ethan asked. "By the lighthouse."

She nodded, now shoving him toward the door. "That drive would probably take you at least fifteen minutes. Then you'll have to talk Captain Butterfield out of his boat, which could be... weeeeeeell, longer. Best get to it. No matter how long it takes."

"Knowing Butterfield? All fucking day," he guessed, folding his arms over his chest. "What is going on here, Vee?" Ethan asked, certain now that he was enmeshed in someone's messy lie.

"Nothing!" she said, batting her eyes a little too quickly. "Nothing except the theft of a few incredibly expensive gold-plated sex toys. Probably by a modern-day pirate. Now. Off you go! I'm missing... I need to be somewhere."

Where was she going after such a theft? Most people would need to chase a benzo with a vodka after missing 25k.

Ethan was searching his beleaguered brain for something to say when the vibration of his cell rescued him.

"What's up, McGarvey?" he answered when the deputy's name came up on the screen.

"Sheriff?" The anxious voice filtered through what sounded like a riot.

Instantly alert, Ethan stood. "What's happened?"

"Sheriff, you need to meet me at Brewbies," McGarvey's garbled voice declared.

"Why? What's going on?"

A long pause gave Ethan time to dash outside and rip his driver's door open.

"I don't even know how to describe this," the deputy said with ball-shriveling gravitas. "You'll have to see it for yourself."

FOURTEEN

Body

THE PERCEIVED THICKNESS, RICHNESS, OR VISCOSITY OF BREWED COFFEE. A FULL-BODIED COFFEE IS ONE WITH A HEAVY MOUTHFEEL

As Thursdays went, today had been a pretty damn good one, all things considered.

The sun was shining, Ethan Townsend was miserable, and preparations for *Cirque du Café* were coming along beautifully.

Darby swept an appreciative eye over the clearing beyond her coffee camper, dazzled by the transformation that had taken place virtually overnight.

Colorful lights zigzagged across the main entry path off the highway turnout, leading to orderly rows of striped tents housing everything from tattoo artists to tarot card readers. A kind of makeshift carnival midway buzzing with a cheerfully chaotic commotion that lent a distinct festival air to the proceedings.

Games. Booths. Candy apples. Carousels.

And friends.

In her single-minded campaign to make sure her plan went off without a hitch, Darby had spent virtually no time thinking about the reality of reuniting with her colorful contacts from the bohemian demimonde.

Or how well they may or may not mesh with her small but loyal Townsend Harbor social circle.

As she stood there surveying the scene, Darby could feel a profound sense of satisfaction flood through her pleasantly exhausted body. She had always been drawn to the creative, the eclectic, the unconventional. But as a child choked by the cold grip of her parents' propriety, she'd always longed for places witchy and wild as well.

Some-fucking-how, on the outskirts of Townsend Harbor, she'd managed to merge them both.

Nowhere was this more apparent than in the three sets of eyes fixed on the main attraction: a very impressive man hanging from hot-pink aerial silks affixed to an equally impressive two-story pipe rig dead center of the action.

"Whoa."

"Damn."

"Does he even gravity?"

Gemma, Cady, Myrtle, and Vee watched in abject awe as Gabe Kelly of the Boston Kellys executed a series of jaw-dropping aerial acrobatics that gave the stiff middle finger to the laws of physics.

And a stiff lady boner to half the population that had showed up to help with the Brewbies benefit carnival.

To Darby, Gabe would remain the Peter Pan-like, somewhat scrawny sixteen-year-old he'd been when she first met him. The kid brother she'd never had. Had never wanted, if she was being honest.

But he'd been so damn pugnacious, so intolerably and insistently charming, that she'd eventually adopted him like a scrappy stray.

Now, at the ripe age of twenty-three, he'd added twenty pounds of brawn, an impressive collection of ink, and a two-year stint at Deer Island Correctional to his resumé.

As was the Kelly way.

"Where'd he learn to move like that?" Gemma wondered

aloud, a matted puff of cotton candy melting in her fingers as she stared.

"Chippendales would be my guess." Myrtle's mouth missed the straw of her elaborate coconut tiki bar cocktail the first couple tries, smearing fuchsia lipstick on her recyclable bamboo straw.

"The way those hips move, I'd bet he could shag you from around the corner," Vee observed.

"But then you'd miss the view."

All four heads tilted to the left as Gabe did some sort of Magic Mike-esque pelvic thrust that flipped his legs over his head.

"That's amazing," Cady breathed.

"*He's* amazing," Gemma added, leaning back against the camper.

The muscles of Gabe's shirtless back rippled with each movement, making the tattoos on his wide, winged back muscles dance.

"What was he in prison for again?" Cady asked, flicking a pointed glance at Gemma.

"Grand theft auto." Darby knew this as she'd been one of his regular correspondents during his incarceration, frequently providing the emotional support his family was too busy helping restaurant equipment fall off delivery trucks to offer.

"Like a real-life GTA character," Gemma said with a sigh.

"Like a real-life felon," Cady reminded her.

Darby knew it had been said from a place of protectiveness on Cady's part, but she felt a twinge of defensiveness even so.

Which—like her post-boning temper tantrum—was unexpected. All the ties she'd tried so hard to cut, fate seemed determined to mend, resulting in strange knots of her past and present.

Edgy and parched, Darby took a bottled water from the pastel-pink cooler she'd set out for all the volunteers who'd showed up to help with the carnival prep while Vee et al. distracted Ethan.

Darby's heart swelled with manic glee as she remembered

Vee's account of Ethan turning pre-stroke purple when she took him into the back room.

It was the little things.

"I'd bet I could help him graduate to breaking and entering," Myrtle said, dentures sinking into her lower lip.

Vee gave her partner a long-suffering look. "Have you any idea the training he'd need? He's a puppy. I'll bet he's not even housebroken."

"You only need to train what you intend to keep," Myrtle pointed out. "I'm just talking about a foster."

A breeze heavy with the scent of cotton candy lifted the silvery-blonde wings of Vee's chin-length hair. "Need I remind you of what happened last time you requested to open our relationship?"

Darby glanced at Cady and Gemma, who looked just as dumbfounded. This was new information for them as well, apparently.

"Oh, please." Myrtle snorted. "It's not like I didn't warn you about the rug burn, and anyway, if we *hadn't* let those folk singers stay with us for the summer, you might never have had the idea for the Lady Garden in the first place."

Vee's eyes narrowed. "Because I spent an entire month welded to the stove brewing tinctures for antibiotic-resistant UTIs."

"How did you say that you know him?" Cady asked in an obvious bid to change the subject.

"He's the son of that Irish mob guy who owned the restaurant next door to Darby's coffee shop in Boston," Gemma explained, obviously building from a previous conversation they'd had. "He used to run off the guys who came in just to jerk off under the table."

"Since when does your gossip network extend to Boston?" Cady asked, elbowing Gemma in the ribs.

Was it Darby's imagination, or had a ripple of concern shadowed the bookstore owner's dreamy features?

"Since Darby moved to Townsend Harbor," Gemma said, shooting Darby a quick wink.

"I stopped by Bazaar Girls the other day to grab the permits," Darby explained, knowing that it was less about justifying her presence in Gemma's shop, and more about reassuring Cady that she had no intentions of insinuating herself into their friendship. She was all too familiar with the delicate dynamics that cemented such bonds in place. Too versed in their inadvertent destruction.

"He ought to have a permit for those guns," Myrtle said as Gabe powered himself to the top of the silks using his upper arm strength alone.

Knowing what was coming next, Darby shifted her gaze to watch their reactions.

Gabe suddenly let go of the fabric and plummeted toward the ground in a free-fall, eliciting a gasp from the various vendors and performers hurrying through their last-minute preparations. Five feet from the ground, the hidden knots around his powerful thighs engaged, abruptly halting his momentum as he struck a final pose.

The stunned silence erupted in a spatter of applause as Gabe caught Darby's eye and grinned.

Still a show-off.

He gracefully dismounted, swinging his legs out from the silks with a flourish before sauntering toward them.

"Is he coming over here?" The edge of panic in Gemma's voice caused a ripple of alarm in Darby's bustier-compressed chest.

"It...looks like it," Darby said, somewhat confused.

"She struggles in social interactions with very attractive people," Cady explained patiently.

"Very attractive?" Gemma repeated, her eyes wide enough to show an intact ring of white sclera around the green irises. "*Very attractive*? The man is hot enough to melt Satan's butt plug."

"Gemma," Cady tried again.

"We have visible V muscles. I repeat, *visible motherfucking V muscles.*" Gemma's cheeks had paled while spots of red bloomed across her neck and chest. "You know I can't make my face do the right things in the presence of visible V muscles. Oh God, I'm going to look at his crotch. I just know it."

Darby stepped toward her, ready to provide support if needed, but Cady spoke up first.

"You're not going to look at his crotch," Cady said gently, laying a hand over Gemma's forearm. "Remember the three Bs?"

"Breath. Brevity," Gemma recited. A crease appeared in her forehead as she glanced toward the crowd, where Gabe was closing fast. "I can't remember the third B." Her fingers curled into the sleeves of Cady's flannel shirt as panic iced over her gaze. "Cady, help me. I can't remember the third B!"

"Be gone."

"Yes!" Gemma nodded. "That's it. I've got to go. I'm going. Here I go." She stalked off toward the fortune-teller tent without another word, her cotton-candy-pink plaid skirt flouncing in her wake.

"What was that about?" Darby asked.

"The ADHD sometimes affects her impulse control," Vee explained. "Her brain likes to feed her a detailed list of the worst possible things she could say at any given moment."

"I mean, whose brain doesn't?" Darby asked, having wondered for some time if she might have been part of the legion of women in their early thirties who had escaped the attention of professionals handing out the diagnosis.

"The trouble is, Gemma will actually *say* them sometimes," Myrtle reported before pausing to slurp the last of her drink from the coconut husk. "Usually when some stud muffin short-circuits her ability to mask."

Well, that was one box Darby couldn't tick.

She had never much bothered with masks. Had never had much patience for arbitrary social rituals or pointless niceties.

Which, she supposed, had greatly contributed to her current mess.

A simple "what do you do?" as a preamble to her leap into Ethan Townsend's lap could have saved them both an assload of pain.

Woulda, shoulda, coulda.

Darby glanced up just in time to see Gabe approach them, his hands tucked into the pockets of his low-slung jeans, a smile tugging at the corners of his mouth.

Upon closer investigation, she could almost understand Cady's vigilance.

Gabe Kelly *looked* like trouble.

The chiseled features, the wild shock of dark hair stuck to his forehead in boyish tufts and closely cropped into a *Peaky Blinders*-esque fade. The full tattoo sleeves and intricate Celtic spirals climbing up his neck.

Good thing Gemma hadn't been close enough to see the dimples, lest she go into apoplectic shock.

"Looking pretty good, kiddo."

Gabe accepted the towel Darby tossed to him and mopped the sweat from his bare chest.

"You think?" he asked in a voice several octaves deeper than she remembered. "I'm rustier than an Oldsmobile 324."

"*You're* rusty?" Darby laughed. "I haven't hung upside down like that since—" *Last Saturday?* her brain helpfully filled in. *Probably Ethan's swimmers are just as duty dedicated as he is, and gravity gave them a perfect conveyor belt straight to the—*

"Since?" Gabe prodded.

"Since...um, forever." A hot wave of nausea rolled through her, redoubling her panic.

Please, please, please, don't let that be a symptom, she begged the universe at large.

"Seemed like you did pretty okay to me." Gabe's amber-brown gaze shifted to the ladies, Darby's official cue to make the introductions.

"Gabe Kelly, meet Cady Bloomquist, Myrtle LeGrande, and Vee Prescott. They're the ones who helped me put all this together. Along with Gemma McKendrick, who owns the yarn shop I was telling you about? She wanted to be here, but—"

"Decided to hide behind your camper instead?" Gabe finished for her with a devastatingly mischievous sideways smirk.

Darby glanced toward the end of the camper just in time to see a flash of pink skirt disappear.

Poor Gemma.

"She wasn't feeling so hot earlier," Darby quickly cut in. "Didn't want to risk infecting our star performer and all."

A quick glance at Cady confirmed that Darby hadn't over-stepped, to her infinite relief.

"Star performer," Gabe scoffed. "We both know you invited me because you knew I needed the work. Nice to meet you, ladies," he said, offering his hand to each of them in turn. "Darby here has told me all about you, and I just want you to know that if you need anything at all while I'm in town, I'm happy to be of service."

The ghost of a distinctive Southie accent haunted his words, blindsiding Darby with a wave of unexpected homesickness.

Since when had that been a thing?

Boston hadn't even been her home.

Not that the East Hamptons estate where she'd grown up had felt like much of one either.

Aside from the camper, the closest thing Darby had ever known to a place that felt like hers would be the brownstone in Back Bay she'd shared with Aidan.

It had been a prewar money pit patched within an inch of its life, but she had loved it. One rogue thought of the morning sun pouring through her bay window and crawling across the parquet floor, and the ache in her chest deepened.

"What kind of services we talking about, exactly?" Myrtle asked, gratefully drawing Darby back from the edge of a self-pity suck hole. "Because I'm sure I could think of a few things we could use some help with around the farm." She waggled her penciled-in eyebrows suggestively, causing Vee to roll her eyes and Cady to stifle a snort.

Gabe's dimples deepened as he grinned. "Well, I was thinking more along the lines of lifting heavy shit, but if you have something else needs doing, I'm all ears."

Something about the way he said this made Darby wonder if he'd done more than gyrate for bachelorettes at the club he'd worked at while on parole.

Myrtle beamed, clearly enjoying the attention, but before she could respond with a wildly inappropriate suggestion, a commotion drew their attention to the entrance of the carnival.

"Holy shitballs," Cady muttered.

Following her gaze, Darby couldn't even find the words.

Protestors.

While they'd been distracted by Gabe, a swarming phalanx of shouting, sign-waving, angry-faced zealots had assembled across the 101.

Darby felt her stomach flip as the sheer force of their anger hit her like a physical blow. She could almost taste the bitterness, hatred, and contempt as it rolled over her like a cloying wave of smoke. Her heart began to race, and she felt a telltale heat in her fingertips as panic bubbled up from some deep well inside of her.

She scanned the line, reaching the end just as a familiar vehicle pulled up, its lights strobing an official red-blue warning.

The tires screeched to a halt, and Ethan Townsend got out, his face a mask of grim determination as he took in the scene before him. As he approached, the dull roar of the protestors' chant ratcheted up in volume, their signs and banners jerking and shaking with renewed vigor. Darby felt a cold trickle of fear slide through her middle as Ethan faced the mob.

But then the *really* weird shit happened.

Ethan began to speak, his voice low and calm. Darby strained to hear what he was saying, but his words were carried away on a mingled stream of carnival and highway traffic. All she could see was the way he held himself, strong and unyielding even in the face of hostility.

The protestors' voices grew quieter as Ethan gestured toward the carnival. Darby watched as some of the rabble turned to look, their expressions softening as they took in the colorful lights and the sound of laughter and music.

Time slowed as Ethan's piercing blue eyes locked with hers across the crowd, his gaze moving down her body as if they were the only two people left in the world, and all the time in it belonged to them alone. He lingered on her breasts, her corset-cinched waist, her hips and legs in her rhinestone-bedazzled panties and fishnet stockings.

Despite everything that had unfolded over the last several days, Darby couldn't help but feel a flutter of excitement deep within her.

Probably implantation pains, her conscience conjectured.

She banished the thought from her mind.

Ethan, on the other hand, looked less than enthused. His mouth tightened. His jaw set. His fingers flexed into fists at his side.

When Gabe spoke close to her ear, she understood why. "That the stiff?"

Darby raised her hand and gave Ethan a little finger wave. "Yep."

"Showtime?" Gabe asked, resting a hand at her waist.

"Definitely."

FIFTEEN
Natural Conditioning

A SECONDARY FERMENTATION MATURATION
THAT OCCURS DURING AGING

WELL, IF IT ISN'T THE CONSEQUENCES OF MY OWN actions, Ethan thought as he broke from the Townsend Harbor tree tunnel into a Category Eleven Shit Storm.

On one side of Highway 101 was the Raven Creek property, where a— Wait. What the fuck?

His eyes widened as far as they could go at the sight of a whole-ass tent city right on *his* creek! Other canopies came into view as he crested the hill. A circus tent the size of a man o' war. Two long aisles of artisans setting up display booths and unpacking their wares.

Across the highway from the chaos of the circus was—in a word—a *nightmare*.

Or, at least, a nightmare for most officers of the law.

Protestors.

Stringing together a line of profanity he'd be immediately canceled for, he swerved toward the demonstrators and parked perilously close, partially blocking the road. Praying for patience, he jerked open the door and unfolded into what was supposed to have been a lovely late-spring afternoon dappled by sunshine and the restless shadows of deciduous leaves.

Instead, he was greeted by the chant some fucking Shakespeare had started among the protestors. "We're not mean. We keep it clean. Don't want our kiddies to see your titties!"

Holy Christ. It was worse than he thought.

Ethan scanned the throng, estimating their number at about a hundred, and then the crowd for any sign of weapons, disturbing the peace, or criminal activity. He had seen enough protests in his lifetime to know how quickly things could turn violent, but these folks seemed content to just stand there with their signs and chant their rhymes. Besides, the median age of the group was very likely in the high fifties.

And that was being kind.

Still, though the day was fading, it was a Thursday, which meant whatever was going on over on his—er Darby's—er—the Raven Creek property was winding up to be a weekend affair.

Well. Fuck.

Finally, Ethan found himself face to face with the ringleader of the protest. Pamela Christiansen, a woman with a shock of white hair and a face like a prune.

He'd rather come face to face with Sasquatch... *Who probably has fewer chin hairs,* he thought unkindly.

Pamela was one of the county's premier protesters. She could be found on the wrong side of history at about every place people gathered to be grumpy. Women's wellness clinics, book burnings, drag shows, places with unisex bathrooms—anywhere people were fighting for human rights, basically, she was there with a reason to deny them, usually with a helpful scripture quote as to why.

"What's going on here, Pam?" Ethan demanded, trying to keep his voice calm and level.

"Thank the Good Lord you're here!" the old woman screeched, shaking a red, angry sign in his face. "This erotic circus is a den of sin and debauchery! And it's right in our backyard! Just what do you intend to do about it, sheriff?"

Ethan sighed, looking across the street to see a scruffy teenager standing on his grandpa's swing, riding it way too high for safety.

Didn't like that. He did *not* like that. One. Fucking. Bit.

Lashed to one of the oak's many gnarled branches was a huge vinyl sign advertising Cirque du Café with the tag line: Save Brewbies and Save Boobies.

When the actual fuck did Ms. Dunwell have the time to organize something of this magnitude? Only a week ago he'd informed her she'd be shut down, and that went into effect just yesterday.

Which had nothing at all to do with why he and his pink-haired adversary-with-benefits had been avoiding each other since they'd made it weird for minors to touch that swing.

Ethan had imprisoned himself in Townsend Harbor proper, so he didn't pop a semi every time he drove to the highway.

One of Pamela's minions, Janet Something-or-other, waddled over in her violet housecoat. A tall wooden cross was her only sign, and she pumped it up and down so hard, the extra flab beneath her arms threatened to knock over anyone who ventured too close.

"What are you planning to do about this, sheriff?" Janet shrilled a second time. "George and I donate good money to your election campaign because the Townsends have always been so good at keeping out the rabble who bring filth and smut to our town!" She spat twice on the ground—to ward away sex demons, probably.

Frowning, Ethan considered how to answer. *Rabble? Didn't people stop saying that after they guillotined a bunch of nobles two hundred years ago?* "Ma'am, I can't keep anyone from entering or exiting Townsend Harbor unless they break a law. That's part of living in a free country."

"Then what good are you?" a man said from somewhere at his elbow. "You're just going to watch the morality of this town go to shit? What am I supposed to tell my children when they ask why no one is wearing underpants beneath their chaps?" He pointed at a pair of pink-leather-framed ass cheeks attached to a statuesque woman with a very prominent Adam's apple.

"Tell them what you like," Ethan answered. "Another advantage of living in a free country."

The man—who apparently only knew how to buzz-cut every hair on his body—wiped the sweat from his brow with an American flag bandana and got right in Ethan's face. "I shouldn't have to. They aren't even out of diapers yet."

Ethan had learned long ago not to give inflammatory men credence. They always had something to prove and were more than willing to turn the heat up until violence exploded.

That violence lived in him, as well, but he couldn't pull the pin on his grenade.

Not with his job.

"If they're that young, they probably have some very healthy feelings toward breasts, in general, unless you're formula folks." Stepping around the man, he spotted McGarvey at the edge of the demonstrators, crinkling his forehead at a sign that'd misspelled the word *offensive*.

Janet recovered from her bristle at Ethan and shadowed him through the crowd. "We have a right to protest, young man! And we won't stop until this circus of sin is shut down!"

"Like I said, can't stop you. Just here to keep an eye on things."

"We all thought that petition you circulated would be enough, but this bitch is burrowed in like a tick!" Janet's voice rose to a level that had him checking his eardrums for leaking fluid. "Can't tell when she's not wanted!"

Ethan's blood pressure rose twenty points as he whirled on the woman. "Listen here, *ma'am*." He leaned on the word, to emphasize any number of things he'd opted not to call her. "Think what you want about the woman, but Darby Dunwell and her business are very much wanted here, or there'd be more people on this side of the street." He motioned across to where more and more travelers pulled off the highway to peek in at what was happening. Townsend Harbor locals. Coastal road-trippers.

Seattleites away from the city for the weekend. Bikers and RVs. Subarus of every age and flavor.

Pamela joined her friend, and they stood against him like steel-haired sentinels. "You fallen under the influence, sheriff? I thought you were on the *right* side." She eyed him with over-wrought suspicion.

Ethan's sound of irritation was swallowed in the chant that had morphed to *If you love your town, keep it clean. Shut this down, it's too obscene!* "I take no sides, Pam. Everyone is within their rights to do what they're doing," he repeated. "My hands are tied."

"OMG! So are mine!" Daniel—er—Dax Quinto sashayed across the street on four-inch-heels, their leg hairs crisply poking out of caramel silk stockings. Up top, they were in a fitted gray blazer and paisley ascot, whereas below they sported volleyball shorts over said stockings. *"Mama, necesito mis medicamentos, por favor."*

Ethan's jaw went slack as the tall Latinx kid—who'd had to have dislocated their shoulders to fit them in such tight, intricate knots—bent down to receive two cheek kisses from a stout, dark-eyed protester.

The chanting died down as the crowd patiently waited for the woman to set down her sign, dig an inhaler from her purse, and hold the mouthpiece toward the tall performer.

"Here you are, *mijo*," she said, patiently pressing twice so her child could inhale. *"¡Que todo salga bien!"*

"Gracias, mama. Ciao." They kissed each other, and the woman patted the retreating performer on the bum like she'd changed it a million times.

Quietly, she gathered her sign—*Dios ama a todos! (incluso a estos pendejos)*—met the very confused eyes of her fellow demon-strators—none of whom read Spanish, apparently—and made a face. "What? I'm only here because Father O'Leary said protesting would count as penance." Hitching a thumb in her kid's direction, she finished, "After sunset I'm going over to watch them suspend Dax from the ropes."

A couple murmurs of assent rose from the Catholic contingency.

The Latinx woman leaned closer to Ethan, crossing herself. "I heard one of the men from the Magic Mikes is here." She thrust her chin toward Officer McGarvey. "You think that's him?"

He opened his mouth to deny it, then changed his mind. "Can't remember," he lied. "You should go ask."

"Ah, *gracias, jefe.*" She patted his shoulder and waddled off.

Ethan glanced across the highway, scanning the colorful crowd for a strawberry swirl of hair.

The air tasted like a barbecue, not just the smoke but the sweet sauce and the tang of a little vinegar to hold it all together. Pots of coffee brewed at several stations, and the scent mingled with fudge cooking, pastries baking, and burgers sizzling.

A few of the gathered artists stopped to antagonize the demonstrators by flipping the bird or doing something needlessly crude, but by and large they were ignored.

Ethan gazed at the community of outsiders, then back at the demonstrators.

This was wrong.

He was standing on the *wrong* side of the street with the *wrong* people, who apparently thought he'd summoned them.

This entire time, he'd been so sure it was the other way around. That he was doing his job for the constituents. Keeping his town happy. Safe. Wholesome. Economically sound.

Not to mention your emotional and coital conflicts of interest, his conscience reminded him.

Fuck.

"Did the devil woman procure the proper permits?" Janet asked. "If not, you have to shut this circus down, don't you? It's your job."

Ethan scowled at the woman. Mostly because she was right.

These days...he was really starting to hate his job.

Ethan looked over to see Darby in the clutches of a young, handsome, muscular man with a WWI haircut and dimples he could see from the across the street.

Should he be trusted to have to watch some absolute soul-shriveling bullshit like that and also responsibly carry a gun?

To be *fucking* determined.

Curling both hands into fists, he waited for the traffic to make a space and marched across the highway.

It wasn't that he was a jealous man, per se. In the handful of relationships he'd considered for the long term, his partners had varied from faithful to clingy to file-a-protective-order obsessed.

Women liked him. Were attracted to him. They appreciated his looks, his body, his money, his dick, his manners, and his mouth. He'd not pieced this information together like some delusional incel, either. Women told him so. Embarrassingly often.

He was today years old when he realized it was weird that he'd never encountered a situation like this in his personal life.

He was friends with his exes, or at least friendly. He shook hands with their new partners. Exclaimed over their babies, etc. When something came to its necessary and unavoidable conclusion, he shrugged with regret and moved the fuck on.

Like a goddamned grownup.

So why in the name of Newton's nut sac did the sight of some tattooed toddler coaxing smiles from Darby's lips with a whisper make him want to hang the kid upside down from the silk and take his time flaying the skin from the overbuilt body?

Who was this asshole who thought he could enjoy the perfume of her neck? The silk of her vibrant hair against his cheek. The favor of her fond winks and the laugh that made every hair on his body prickle.

Her...ass in *his hand*?

Sure, it was just to give her a boost up to her own aerial silk, but still...

He had an ax in the truck that'd take the offending hand off with one swing. Just who the fuck did this *Fast & Furious* reject think he—

"Sheriff Townsend. Hold up," called a remarkably tall Salish-style raven's headdress. The "wings" of the onyx shawl flapped in the ocean breeze as Kiki Forrester ducked under a canopy and jogged toward him with a rhythmic jangle of bells and beads.

Behind her, other local Natives donned the astonishing effigies of whale, salmon, stag, fox, eagle, wolf, coyote, and otter, representing their tribe's sacred totems in dances that awed, humbled, and inspired their audiences.

The statuesque woman cut him off before he could stride past the old oak and swing, lifting the massive headdress from her plaited hair. "Hey," she greeted him with a curt, I-mean-business toss of her strong jaw, then buttered him up with her kind, dark eyes. "I've been trying to get a hold of you, but can't catch you in the office this week." She glanced toward the protesters, her expression tightening. "I wanted to warn you about my campaign, but I guess it's too late for that. Still. I'd like to clear the air between us before the election."

The eldest of the prolific Forrester kids, Kiki had graduated high school before Ethan started his freshman year, which put her at fortyish. She was a good peer, a great cop, and one *hell* of a single mom.

Were Darby not being mauled by a moron, he'd love to stand with her and shoot the shit or bury the hatchet or whatever the fuck. However, right now that shirtless beefcake bastard had finished climbing his own silk and reached for Darby's silk to pull her close with a move that could have been interpreted as *protective*.

"Yeah, we're good, Forrester," he said, managing to relax his lips into a semblance of a welcome smile, though he kept one eye over her shoulder at where the Water Street mavens all gaped at what was going on in the silks above them. "You support this?" he asked, waving his hand at the...everything. "Enough to perform?"

She made a face at him. "You don't?" Opening her shawl, she

uncovered the tank top that sported the Brewbies logo in gigantic pink letters, beneath which said, *Have the breast day!* "My favorite drink is the Filthy Earl Grey. Basically a London Fog has a lovechild with a dirty chai. It doesn't matter. You have a second later this weekend to chat?"

"Yeah? Um. Yeah." He was listening. *Honestly.* This conversation mattered. Kiki's respect and friendship were important. But how the fuck was he supposed to follow a conversation when Darby was bent almost in half backward, one bare, smooth, long, sexy leg wrapped in the spiral of her silk, and the other wrapped around the torso of a dead man?

"I heard you were the one who shut her down." Kiki crinkled her brow as if waiting for him to deny it.

"Wasn't my idea." *Initially,* he finished to himself. Fucking hell. The kid had to stabilize her in that position, *but did he have to put his hands there?*

That's it. He was going to cut off every finger with dull garden shears.

"What statute did you use?" Kiki asked idly, glancing over her shoulder as if to ascertain whatever was keeping his attention.

He rattled off the statute numbers he'd memorized, and she took out her phone and tapped something into it. It allowed him to watch Darby unroll from her partner and catch herself in the splits to a smattering of applause from those who lingered around the practice.

Fuuuuuuuuuuuuk... He could remember the exact moment he realized she could do that in Canada when she'd stretched her leg up over—

Kiki snapped her fingers.

"Um. Sorry. What?" He dragged his notice back to her.

"I found the statute." She wriggled her phone in his face. "What the hell, Ethan?"

It seemed less lame before he was forced to explain it to a perfectly reasonable woman who lived outside the wonky boundaries of Townsend Harbor. "I know that law is a bit obscure—"

"Obscure?" She regarded him as if he'd just whispered the word *moist.* "What it is, is bullshit. I mean, most small towns have shitty, bigoted laws on the books—I think even my town has something against sodomy or whatever, but when has that stopped people from taking it up the ass whenever they want? Only a back-asswards dumb fuck would even bother to enforce such an archaic and awful law."

Ethan always appreciated Kiki's directness, especially when relying on her experience and wisdom to help with his own job. But when she crossed her arms and gave him a *What now, you bigoted, dumb fuck?* glare, he didn't feel like less of a man taking a step in retreat.

"Means to an end, Kiki," was all he felt like explaining, seeing as how everything else made him feel about as likable as the sharp end of a catheter.

"I've heard women loooooooove being a means to an end," she said as she turned to stand shoulder to shoulder with him to see what was happening. "If you want to get them really hot, you should use your authority to harass them and make their lives difficult because you're pissed they bought the land your mother sold out from under you."

That brought his head around sharply, and Kiki lifted her hands in a placating gesture, "Not common knowledge, but Cy has been working closely with Myrtle to fertilize the back pasture and fruit orchards."

Of course. Her younger brother, Cypress Forrester, was the premier arborist in town. Not known as a gossip, but there was no accounting for what you said to family.

"It's..." He had to swallow his heart when it appeared that Darby was falling from her silk, only to have her catch at the bottom like a yo-yo and strike a stunning pose.

Yeesh. He wasn't going to survive this.

"It's complicated."

Kiki slid him the side-eye and shook her head. "Christ, sheriff, when life hands you lemonade, you're not supposed to turn it *back* into lemons." She chucked him on the shoulder with the strength of a man before setting her ginormous raven totem head back on her crown.

"Family trait, I think," he muttered. His dad had left him a fucking lemon orchard.

"Yeah, well, don't be too hard on yourself. You Townsends are okay...you know...for colonizers." She winked good-naturedly. "Well, good luck with your pink lemonade. I'll contact your office next week for a parley?"

"Sure thing." He nodded, setting off toward the net beneath the arial and trapeze displays, mostly because it seemed like the thing to do. It stretched like a helpful spider's web behind the now-closed Airstream to catch any plummeting acrobats. If they missed the net, they could just dive into Gemma, Myrtle, Vee, and Cady's open mouths.

As he stepped closer, his feet muffled by mossy earth, he heard his name just in time to duck around the Airstream out of their line of sight.

"Ethan's going to shit an entire brick house when he sees this," Cady marveled before giving a little *wooo!* at their next trick, clapping happily. "That Gabe sure is *foine* for a felon, isn't he?"

A cold dread coiled through Ethan's gut.

Felon?

Casting her best friend a somewhat salty look, Gemma adjusted the ties on her knitted bikini halter and lifted her heavy, dark hair to allow the breeze to kiss her back. "Should you be looking? I don't see Fox anywhere..." She made a show of searching in a 360-degree range that Ethan almost didn't move fast enough to evade.

Cady's mischievous grin shone in her reply. "I'm engaged, not dead." She laughed. "Besides, Fox doesn't care where I get my naughty inspiration, so long as I bring it home to try on him."

Ethan highly suspected that even retired marine Captain Roman Fawkes would remain ambivalent to his lady's salivary glands activated by an ex-con/aerial ass-nugget with too many show-off muscles and not enough body hair.

Kid barely looked old enough to have graduated from juvie, and walked with a don't-fuck-with-me gait learned very specifically by the incarcerated. Not so much the I *might have drugs or razorblades hidden up my butthole* look, more the *I've killed a man but that's not what they arrested me for* look.

Ethan didn't like it. Didn't like any single part of it.

Didn't like his fucking hands on Darby.

Nope. Not there.

Or there.

Or like that...or—

The kid moved beneath Darby so her ass fit into the arch of his motherfucking foot...and she sat there...leaning back to kick out her lovely legs.

Ethan was going to be sick. Just barf up his BLT-with-olive-oil-mayo lunch all over her potted petunias.

Mostly because she'd just wrapped her leg around the guy's shoulders to lift into another pose.

My shoulders, his inner caveman protested. *Only my shoulders go between her thighs.*

To add insult to injury, Darby crawled up his body, and they shared a look of fondness that sent Ethan rearing backward, knocking something from the discarded pile in a box on her steps. Acting quickly, he caught it before it shattered on the ground. A small fishbowl decorated with stickers of several pairs of breasts and writing that said: *Just put in the tip, see how it feels.*

Her gratuity jar.

Discarding it with a grimace, he rubbed his hands on his shirt and went back to watching the torture porn.

Only to shrink back around the corner as Vee returned with her gnarled fingers wrapped around four drinks.

Better for all involved if he stopped trying to watch.

"I hoped I didn't miss the opening ceremonies while keeping Ethan busy," Vee said.

"Nope," Myrtle said after a loud smooch. "We're lucky they're just warming up still. Probably got about an hour. That what you're wearing?"

"Why, you don't like it?" Vee asked. Ethan could no longer see the group without being discovered, but he could hear the dismay beneath the brusque British accent.

"No!" Myrtle squawked two octaves too high. "No. You look...um...festive! Downright stunning, I'd say. Couldn't lose you in a crowd...even if we wanted to." Apparently, Myrtle worked in bullshit, as well as the regular stuff, and agreed with Ethan's estimation of Vee's questionable couture. "Speaking of, I saw the sheriff pull up. He's around here somewhere, but there's no brakes on this train now!"

"Had he not been summoned here by a deputy, I might have kept him in the store a while longer," Vee lamented.

"Solid gold sex toys," Myrtle marveled. "I couldn't even bring myself to touch one before I stashed them in the old cupboard where I keep the magic mushrooms. Too fancy for my blood. Sheriff'll never think to look there, and we'll 'find' them in a few days."

"He didn't seem like he wanted to look for them at all," Vee groused. "I was certain to make him categorically aware of the expense. Granted, it's harder to cry wolf these days when everyone has so many cameras everywhere... Just as easy to prove something didn't happen as to prove it did."

Ethan scrubbed at his temples for a few moments. One of these days, those biddies were going to be arrested for one of their numerous infractions. So help him, he was sorely tempted. All day, *all day*, he'd been chasing wild geese, led around by two of the most mischievous boomers alive, who deep-faked a gilded dildo theft to keep him away from a sexy circus.

For fuck's sake.

"Did he buy anything?" Myrtle asked.

After a pregnant pause, every single woman dissolved into a fit of giggles.

"OMG, can you imagine?" Cady snorted. "Did he even know what was *in* there?"

"I'd say not, judging by the several colors he turned when he took a glance at the wall of wankers," said Vee. "I've never seen a grown man blush that color."

Well, if they found him now, she would see the color twice in one day.

"I'd have paid money to witness that." Gemma's laugh-warmed voice still sounded somewhat distracted. "He's just such a... Well, I don't know the word for it, but it'd be like taking your grandpa into a sex shop."

Ethan grimaced. *Ouch.*

Myrtle cleared her throat. "Well he's a...you know..." Her voice dropped off ominously.

No, he didn't fucking know.

"A what?" Cady prompted.

Long pause.

"A pervert?" Gemma guessed.

Hey!

"A public masturbator?"

What the fuck?

"No!" An exasperated Myrtle snapped. "Pay attention!"

"We are, my dear," Vee soothed patiently, "but no one seems to figure out why do you keep reaching your hands down your pants."

"He's a shirt tucker. I'm tucking in my shirt!" Myrtle scoffed. "I know who I'm *not* taking to charades. This group."

"Oh, yeah," Gemma said. "I've never heard it put like that, but yes. Ethan is a consummate shirt-tucker. Makes absolute sense."

It did? To whom? And why?

He looked down at his neatly tucked blue shirt and shiny belt. He had to tuck. It was protocol. Besides, it looked nice. What, was he supposed to walk around looking like he'd wrestled a bear like

184

all these other windbreaker-wearing doofs with their open flannel shirts and pants that hung down to their—

Oh. Yep. He heard it now... The grandpa. Wow. When did that happen?

"Hey, guys!" Darby's breath sounded sort of like it did when they'd finished fucking. Short and satisfied. "Whatcha laughing at?"

"Sheriff Shirt-tucker," Myrtle crowed.

Oh sheeeit. That was going to catch on.

"I saw him across the street," Darby said through her panting. "But lost him in the crowd when we practiced our routine."

"Which was incredible, by the way!" Gemma gushed.

"Thank you!" Darby stopped to take a drink. "But this is nothing. Just wait until you see the program for tomorrow night. I pulled belly dancers from Oakland, sword swallowers from Albuquerque, drag queens from Tennessee, and an amazing contortionist act from here in Seattle."

"I can't believe they'd be willing to come all this way," Cady said reverently.

"Hell, I think getting them to go home will be the hard part," Darby said breathlessly. "You wouldn't believe how many of them are already batshit crazy about this place. Can you believe they want to build a brand-new bohemian commune right here by Townsend Harbor?"

"How amazing would that be?" Gemma asked.

"Right?" Darby agreed. "Not like I don't have the land for it."

A violent twitch took up in Ethan's left eye.

"Think they'll still feel so warm about the place even after the protesters?" Cady chimed in.

An unfamiliar masculine snort intervened. "Folks like us are protested wherever we try to be. Or worse. That's why we stick together... Look out for each other, right, Darbs?"

Darbs? Fucking *Darbs*? With his lazy tongue, the nickname came out sounding like "Dahbs."

"Abso-fucking-lutely," Darby agreed. "We run from no one."

She was brave. Whatever else she was...courage was her superpower.

Brave. Resourceful. Intelligent. Hot AF. And could do the splits in the air?

Ethan bit down on his fist. Trouble. He'd known it from the beginning.

"What about the Boy Scout sheriff you told me about?" the guy asked with more gravel than someone in his twenties should be able to throw from their voice. "Seems like someone you don't want to antagonize."

"That walking dad joke? He's harmless," Myrtle replied.

Ethan's brows slammed together. Not that he meant anyone harm.

But harmless? *Come on!*

Principled wasn't harmless. Self-contained didn't mean useless.

"If he was harmless, Darby wouldn't have to be putting on this fundraiser to fight the sanctions," Cady reminded them.

"Yeah, but we've proven we can rely on his Dudley Do-Right attitude to keep him distracted when we need," Myrtle commented with an inappropriate amount of glee, if they were asking him. "All they'd have to do is steam the crease out of his khakis and he'd be down for the count."

Jaw dropping open, Ethan barely kept an incensed gasp to himself. Everyone knew if you didn't crease your slacks, they made your thighs look feminine. Or fat.

No one on either side of the war of the sexes liked their thighs to look fatter than absolutely necessary—he didn't care who the fuck you were.

"That man will break hearts and melt the panties off a snowman until his future is realized and he gives in to the clarion call of tube socks, Velcro sneakers, orthotics, and ensure," Myrtle said.

And here he'd thought they were friends.

"Vanilla flavored." Vee cackled like the Wicked Witch of the West Coast. "He'll tuck his tie into his belt, as well."

"Which will cinch right below his nipples!" Myrtle crowed.

Oh man. Ethan slumped against the Airstream with a beleaguered exhale given by one just lucky enough to survive enemy fire and who was waiting for insurgents to reload.

Fucking roasted by septuagenarians.

Was this what people thought of him? When they called him the town hero, had they been smiling behind their hands the entire time?

What made him a hero, exactly? He'd saved several lives, delivered a few babies in the nick of time, kept angry drunks from killing each other, donated to struggling small businesses after the pandemic...

He was a good man. He did good things.

But was he right?

Glancing across the street, he watched the faces beneath the signs. Angry. Pinched. Loud.

For what?

Decency? A virtue that became less and less quantifiable as society demanded equality and privilege for people other than men like him.

What exactly was indecent about these people? Here they were, showing up from all corners of the country to help out a friend who was in need.

In need because of him.

Fuck this. Ethan set his jaw, pulled up his pants (not too high), and marched in front of the firing squad. He had a few things to set straight.

SIXTEEN
Grinding

REDUCE COFFEE TO FINE PARTICLES, AS BY POUNDING OR CRUSHING; BRAY, TRITURATE, OR PULVERIZE

IF THE COMBINATION OF CORSET-CONSTRICTED LUNGS and more vigorous athletic activity than she'd done in an embarrassing length of time wasn't enough to steal her breath, seeing Ethan Townsend emerge from behind her camper would have.

Sometimes, her plans worked a little *too* well.

She'd only meant to season this triumphant affair with the merest hint of jealousy, followed by a sprinkle of good-natured ribbing at Ethan's expense.

Myrtle's off-script salvos had hit closer to the sheriff's spleen, if his stormy expression was any indication. He greeted them with a face in full scowl and his eyes cold enough to leave frostbite.

For a moment, they just stared at each other, the tension between them palpable. Darby felt her heart rate increasing, and sweat coated her palms as she worked to slow her breathing.

Despite looking like he could chew granite, Ethan cleared his throat and spoke with a polite, if slightly frosty, tone. "I need a word with you, Miss Dunwell."

"Well, good evening to you, too, Sheriff Townsend," she said, fishing water out of the cooler and passing one to Gabe. "So nice of you to *swing* by."

The knot of Ethan's Adam's apple bobbed on a swallow.

"I don't think you've met Gabe. Gabe Kelly, this is Sheriff Ethan Townsend. Sheriff Townsend, this Gabe. He was kind enough to come all the way from Boston to support our little fundraiser."

"Pleasure." Gabe stuck his hand out.

Now, this was an interesting test.

Manners versus masculine pride.

Ethan looked like he'd prefer to tear off Gabe's inked-up arm and jam the wet end down the man's throat, but with half of Townsend Harbor looking on, such a display of temper would surely prove poor optics in light of the upcoming election.

Ethan's hand closed over Gabe's, and both their knuckles went white as they gripped each other's palms.

Gabe released first, twisting open his water bottle and chugging a few sips before sloshing it over his head and neck. He emitted a moan just on the edge of decency as the droplets sluiced down the ridges of his rippling abdominals, soaking into the waistband of his jeans. "I'm wicked hot after all that back and forth."

A walnut-sized lump appeared at the hinge of Ethan's jaw. "Hose is over there if you didn't want to waste drinking water."

"Thanks," Gabe said, "but Darby said I could grab a shower in her camper when we were all done for the night. Isn't that right, Darbs?"

At this, Gabe shook his head like a dog, sending droplets flying from his hair to speckle Ethan's pristine dress shirt. "Oh, geez. Sorry about that, brother," he said, his accent rounding the *er* into an *uh*. "You want a towel or something? I could nip into the camper and—"

"No." Cady, Myrtle and Vee all jumped at the force of the single syllable. Ethan cleared his throat. "No," he said again more mildly. "But I do need to speak with you." His eyes moved from Gabe to Darby. "In private."

"Private?" Darby batted her feathery false lashes at him.

"What could you possibly have to say to me that you can't say right here in front of my friends?"

Cady, Myrtle, and Vee all lifted their chins an inch, taking up her challenge with a readiness that warmed Darby's leathery heart.

Ethan's eyes moved from the ladies to Darby and back again. A silent challenge passed between them, each daring the other to make the first move. A duel of wills with no clear victor.

Eventually, he inclined his head and took a step back, but not before Darby caught the glint of admiration in his eye.

"You wouldn't happen to have your permits for this gathering handy, would you?"

"This outfit doesn't exactly leave room for pockets." Darby swept her hands down her body, inviting his eyes to do the same.

Ethan kept them stubbornly trained on her face. "I'm going to need you to get them for me," he said. "Assuming they're on the premises."

"Oh, they're on the premises," she said, taking a step toward him. "Right there in my camper."

"May I see them?"

"So you can find some loophole that will force me to shut the carnival down too?"

"So I can show them to Pam and Janet in hopes that they'll take their boycott back to town."

Darby arched an eyebrow at him. "You *want* to get rid of the protestors?"

"Their median age is sixty, which is also the speed limit. Not that anyone actually obeys it." With this, he aimed a meaningful glance at Myrtle, who Darby had personally seen motoring her old convertible along at speeds approaching the triple digits on several occasions. "I have no desire to rake any titanium knees or porcelain teeth from the asphalt."

Their staring contest entered its second heat.

"As I believe I already mentioned, they're in the camper."

"Fine." The gravel crunched as Ethan turned on his boot heel and gestured for her to lead the way.

Darby traded a pointed look with Gabe, Cady, Myrtle, and Vee before trailing after Ethan, all too aware of the gawking onlookers tracking their progress.

As they reached the camper, Ethan paused, standing to one side of the aluminum steps as Darby ascended them. "Wait here," she ordered him.

Only, Ethan didn't.

She barely had time to register his presence behind her before the heavy camper door slammed shut, leaving her wide-eyed as Ethan backed her into it.

His hips pinned hers, and his ribcage expanded on hectic breaths as he stared down into her face. Despite the steady throb already beginning to gather behind the Lycra crotch of her glittery briefs, she forced herself to hold his gaze.

"The permits are on the bottom shelf of the pantry between the Fruity Pebbles and peanut butter Cap'n Crunch. If you—"

"Fuck the permits." Ethan lowered his mouth to hers, tracing the seam of her lips until they parted on a sigh as soft as his kiss was bruising.

Ethan *devoured* her.

His hunger made her clutch his shoulders to keep from sliding to the floor of the camper. One of his hands tangled in her hair, angling her head to deepen the onslaught as the other pressed between her shoulder blades, holding her against him.

She was drowning. Losing her breath. Her balance.

Her mind.

"Wait," Darby rasped, tearing her mouth away from his. "Wait. You can't just—"

"Who is he?" Ethan asked, dipping his head to trail wet kisses along the length of her throat.

"Who?" Darby asked, only half aware of the floor beneath her feet as she arched into him.

In one fluid motion, Ethan lifted her, wrapping her legs around his hips and pressing his erection against her. "The guy you performed with."

"I told you," she said. "His name is Gabe. He—"

"I know his name." Ethan curled his hips, branding her belly with the ridge of his arousal. "Who is he to *you*?"

Darby fixed a bratty smile on her already swollen lips as she worked a hand between them to mold her hand to his steely length. "No one that will blur the lines between your private and civic life."

Ethan captured her wrists and pinned them above her head. "You want everyone to know? Is that it?"

What *did* she want, exactly? No sooner had the question been introduced did the answer come to her.

"I want *you* to know, Ethan."

He drew back, and their eyes met for a moment on which the gravity of the entire planet seemed to hang.

"I want you to not be ashamed of the part of you that wants me," she said, rocking her hips against his.

"Darby—"

"I want you to see me on the street and not flinch." She laced her fingers into his hair, tipping his head back so she could meet his eyes. "I want you to want me, Ethan. Regardless of where we meet or who happens to be watching."

Ethan's eyes blazed the electric blue of a pilot light. "I want you, Darby. I want you so much I don't even know who the fuck I am anymore."

Darby gasped as the elastic fabric of her fishnets and costume bottoms tore with a brief hiss of protest. The sudden draft felt delicious over her heated skin, cool where she was already wet.

"Do you have—"

Ethan lifted a foil packet that he'd produced from somewhere on his person and tore it with his teeth.

"Where was this the other night?" Darby asked, quickly unbuckling his belt and freeing his erection.

Ethan's lips twitched as he angled himself between her thighs.

"Oh, f—" Darby's words dissolved into a moan as Ethan buried himself inside her.

He rocked into her, his hips thrusting as he—quite literally—drove her up the wall.

He moved his hands to the corset at her chest, entwining his fingers in the satin ribbons that held it together. With one swift tug, Ethan freed Darby's breasts.

When he saw the pasties over her nipples, his eyes met hers in a rare moment of understanding.

She was wearing them because she'd be removing her corset as part of her performance with Gabe. Because people would look at the breasts that he'd had his hands, his lips, his tongue on.

Because she intended to show her body to every person on the other side of these camper walls.

Walls that were beginning to list ever so slightly in time with Ethan's punishing thrusts. Thrusts that were beginning to make the ancient axles of the camper's wheel wells emit cheerful squeaks. Squeaks that were slowly being drowned out by Ethan's raw, rhythmic grunts.

Heat flooded into Darby's cheeks and spilled down her chest.

There was not one chance in hell that every single soul didn't know what they were doing.

"Ethan," she said, both warning and plea as the first coiled tendrils of her release unfurled within her.

"I know." He followed her over the brink with a roar that could likely be heard at least as far as the ferry.

Ethan collapsed over her in the aftermath. His scent filled her nostrils, and she closed her eyes, breathing him in. Letting the warmth of his body seep into hers until every inch of her skin was humming.

Darby's lids fluttered open to find his face hovering a hairsbreadth away from hers, his eyes burning an unspoken question. With a single nod, Darby answered it, pressing her lips to his in an all-consuming kiss that left no doubt as to what was coming next.

She melted into him, savoring the feel of his muscular arms wrapped around her waist as he drew her closer.

When they finally untangled their limbs, their breathing had slowed.

"Now about those permits?" Ethan asked.

Darby smiled up at him, gaining her feet with some effort and crossing the short distance to her pantry on wobbling legs. Finding the stack, she rolled them into a scroll and tucked them into the waistband of his still-unbuttoned pants.

"Happy now?" she asked as she stepped into a pair of shorts to cover the mess he'd created.

Ethan tucked the papers under his arm and began to zip up. "I will be when you agree to go out with me."

Darby choked on her watery sip of the iced mocha she'd abandoned in her hurry this morning. "Excuse me?"

Ethan turned to face her. "A date, Darby. You and me. Talking. Eating food."

Darby's mouth dropped open. "You mean, in public?"

"Yep."

"Within the presence of other humans?" she asked.

"That's the idea." He held out his hand. "Ready for our walk of shame?"

Darby took it, running a hand through her hair as the door creaked open.

That would have to count as preparation enough for Myrtle, Cady, and any other curious stares that were aimed her way.

What she hadn't prepared for was the large white van parked ten feet away from her camper. On its roof, a large antenna spiraled toward the heavens, beaming the signal down to electronic devices the world over.

On its side, bold black letters explained the presence of the polished blonde news anchor and the large camera aimed directly at Darby's van behind the padded shoulders of her hot-pink blazer.

KIRO 7.

Seattle News.

SEVENTEEN

Shade Grown

COFFEE GROWN UNDER THE SHADE CANOPY OF NATIVE TREES WHICH REDUCES THE NEED FOR PESTICIDE SINCE BIRDS ACT AS NATURAL INSECT CONTROL AGENTS

THE SOLES OF DARBY'S STRAPPY SANDALS FELT LIKE they didn't quite touch the sidewalk as she made her way toward Olive or Twist, one of Townsend Harbor's upscale pubs. Even the burn in her thighs from her hike up Townsend Harbor's famous hillside staircase seemed sweet.

And she'd said at least thirty-seven percent less swear words in her head as she'd puffed up the final flight.

A date with Ethan Townsend.

Like, officially.

He'd even asked—well, told her—out loud in front of other humans. The conclusion of a series of events she still couldn't quite process.

But Lord, had she tried. Had scraped her memory for every single second of their camper clinch and replayed it again and again until she was in danger of swooning dead away.

His mouth crushing to hers the instant her camper door closed. Their words clashing as their bodies merged and battled for dominance. The feel of him inside her, filling her, claiming her.

Darby shook her head, trying to clear the deliciously dizzying memories from her mind. She was on a mission. She had to focus. To concentrate. To keep her head clear and her panties dry.

The muffled hum of sultry jazz reached her through the heavy wood door. A small metal panel slid open as she approached, revealing a set of vaguely familiar eyes. Masculine, but kind and wide-set on either side of a prominent nose.

"Password?"

Darby's heart raced.

She'd been so busy head-humping the town sheriff, she completely blanked on whether a password had been part of Gemma's download on Caryn Townsend.

"Umm..." Darby said, dredging her hormone-addled memory. *D. There is definitely a D.*

Or several Ds? "Dumbwaiter?"

"Nope."

"Diphthong?"

"Uh-uh."

"Doggerel?" she guessed. "Dingleberry?"

"Negative."

"D...d...do you accept bribes?"

The eyes lifted from view and a mouth appeared, the corner of the lips cracking open on a furtive whisper. "Dizzy dames don't drop dimes."

"Dizzy dames don't drop dimes," Darby repeated, loud enough for anyone lingering behind the door attendant to hear.

Something clicked within the bowels of the heavy brass handle plate, and the door swung open, bathing Darby in a whoosh of air scented with the leather and spice of cigar smoke.

"For the record, that's a pass *phrase*," she said, slipping inside.

Cy Forrester's mouth stretched in a wide grin. "For the record, I'm not really the door attendant. Gemma asked me to keep an eye out for you. This way," he said, gesturing down a small, dark hallway to the main bar.

Dimly lit sconces threw shadows against the plush velvet wallpaper as they passed, the light dancing over vintage photographs of 1920s partygoers in their finest flapper attire, getting up to the dickens.

"Those were taken right here in this building," Cy reported. "Back then, it was owned by Lou Graham."

"Wasn't she one of Seattle's wealthiest women?" Darby asked, hoping to score points with her exceedingly limited knowledge of Puget Sound social history.

"Yep," Cy confirmed. "And a notorious madam."

"No shit." A curious warmth flooded Darby's chest as she glanced back at the photograph. Hers was not a new fight.

"Not a crumb."

At the end of the hallway, Cy produced a key from the pocket of his jeans and plugged it into the lock of yet another heavy oak door.

"After you," he invited, swinging it open.

Darby stepped over the threshold, and into another time.

The speakeasy was a chic, dimly lit affair. Luxurious oriental rugs, tasseled lamps, bookshelves, and dark booths. At the center of the room, a small platform housed a stand-up bass, drums, and an old but beautiful black-lacquered piano. Waiting, perhaps, for their musicians to return from a break.

It was over-the-top kitsch at its finest, and Darby fell immediately and wholeheartedly in love.

"Welcome to Olive or Twist!" declared a costumed barkeep, her voice tempered by years of whisky fumes and cigar smoke. She slid a smoking cocktail across the counter in Darby's direction.

"Oh," Darby said, eyeing the drink. "I haven't ordered yet."

"That's the bees' knees." The bartender winked at her. "On the house."

Darby gave the woman a tentative smile and nodded, taking a sip of the smoky-sweet concoction.

If nothing else, it gave her something to do with her sweaty hands and twitchy face while she covertly looked for Caryn.

And where had these nerves come from, exactly?

From the quiet understanding that you're about to go talk to a woman who practically owns this town and has likely already heard about your banging her son in your camper of iniquity.

Oh. That.

"You need anything, you let me know," Cy said, as if sensing her unease. "I'll be right here at the bar."

"Thanks," Darby said.

Drawing in a deep breath, she scanned the tables.

At five p.m. on a Friday, there were a surprising number of patrons scattered around the room, drinking and talking in small groups, their conversations punctuated by the occasional staccato burst of laughter or clink of glassware.

Here uptown, there were fewer tourists and pass-through traffic. The assortment appeared to be comprised of locals looking to offload their Friday workday and unwind with a cocktail or six at the official start of their weekend.

Darby could relate.

Once upon a time, she'd been one of them.

A lowly first-year law student with a summer internship at her father's law firm: Dunwell, McKendall & Starkes.

She'd spent a grueling summer of shuffling paperwork and answering phones when Starkes had taken one too many nips from his desk flask and decided to get grab-assy whileshe working late on a deposition. When she'd told her father about it, he frowned, then reminded her how much pressure the team had been under.

At which point, she'd asked her father if she could expect to receive the same accommodation if she up and decided to palm Starkes' shriveled plums while he was making his opening argument.

Smack in the middle of the firm's summer barbecue might not have been the opportune moment to ask this question, but Darby had thought it a valid point.

The lawn-full of lawyers hadn't agreed.

Darby downed the rest of her drink in two swallows, wishing for something stronger.

Ancient history.

She had a job to do.

Slipping her vintage compact from her also vintage purse, she dusted translucent powder on her nose and used the small, circular mirror to scan the back of the room.

There in the corner booth, holding court like a queen, was Caryn Townsend.

Her sleek platinum bob gleamed in the amber lamplight, and the soft hue made her peaches-and-cream complexion glow.

Or was that the musicians?

Despite belonging to a generation with an entirely different letter (or two), they flocked around her like attentive moths. Offering drink refills. Promising to play any special requests she might have. Inquiring as to her plans for the remainder of the evening.

Inspiration hit Darby in a sudden flash.

Was Caryn Townsend...a cougar?

A woman shamelessly using her superior experience and sophistication to seduce unsuspecting conquests decades her junior for the purposes of wild, sweaty, uninhibited sex?

Darby could respect that.

Closing the compact with a snap, she tucked it in her bag and rose. She attempted to swallow the lump in her throat, pasting a neutral expression on her face before weaving her way through the haze.

Before Darby was within view, Caryn's lips thinned, and the subtle lines next to her eyes smoothed as her smile melted. Her head swiveled, and eyes the exact same shade as Ethan's ice blue locked on Darby's.

The room seemed to be narrowing around Darby as the conversations and music faded into the background. She was no longer approaching a booth, but the headmistress's desk with a backpack full of cigarettes purchased from her bake sale's ill-gotten gains.

The same pounding heart, dry mouth, and damp palms. Same feeling of generalized dread mingled with irritation at herself for being intimidated.

One by one, the musicians turned to see what Caryn was looking at.

When they spotted Darby, their eyes quickly flicked over her body before immediately shifting to mirror Caryn's.

Damn.

The woman was *good*.

"Guess we better get back to it," the hot hipster with a pony-tail and pierced nose said, scooting toward the edge of the booth bench.

His bandmates followed suit, grabbing their beers—coasters and all—and making their way back to the stage.

"Hi," Darby said when her attention returned to the table. "Mind if I sit?"

Caryn took her time exacting a measured once-over, inclining her head slightly as if she was trying to work out Darby's intentions. Diamonds winked from her fingers as she gestured to the tufted velvet banquette across from her.

Darby slid in and set her bag on the table. "Bass player?" she asked, somehow knowing that Caryn would understand what she was implying.

Caryn's cool blue gaze shifted to the stage where Ponytail tipped his fedora to her and winked. "Maybe," she said breezily. "Depends on how well he plays 'Moonlight Serenade.'"

"But Glenn Miller isn't jazz."

Caryn angled an assessing look at Darby. "I know."

Scratch that. The woman was very, *very* good.

The first mellow strains of the song began as a woman wearing the tasseled dress of a flapper sashayed over to them. Her charcoal-smoked eyes flicked from Caryn's fresh martini to Darby's empty glass. "Bring you anything, doll?"

Darby stole a glance at Caryn to gauge how she might feel about the idea of Darby's squatting at her table for a drink. The former first lady only gazed toward the stage, a strange smile lifting the corners of her lips and a faraway expression in her eyes.

"Dirty gin martini," she said. "Three olives, please."

"Sure thing," the server said, and moved off.

When Caryn turned her attention back to the table, Darby cleared her throat. "I gather from the stink-eye that I don't need to introduce myself."

Caryn twirled the slim stem of her martini glass in perfectly manicured fingers. "You gather correctly."

"So you're familiar with Brewbies, then?"

Lifting her glass, Caryn took a sip of her drink. "I'm familiar with the seven o'clock news."

Shit.

Darby dearly wished she could slither under the table like a slug.

It wasn't that she was ashamed of her and Ethan's heated tryst in her camper. It was that she'd have preferred it not be broadcast to the greater Seattle area and subsequently made into thousands of TikTok videos and Facebook reels by amateur videographers who artfully assembled clips of the camper rocking followed by Darby and Ethan emerging hand in hand to an endless variety of sounds featuring Cardi B and/or Marvin Gaye.

And then, there were the hashtags. #sheriffzaddy #sexysheriff #sheriffsnack

Saints be praised, the server chose that precise moment to arrive with Darby's drink. "Thanks," she said, then took a healthy slug and set it on the table. "Where was I?"

"You were going to explain how you managed to completely destroy the reputation it took my son decades to build in a period of fifteen minutes," Caryn replied coolly.

Had it only been fifteen minutes?

To Darby, the memory had taken on a timeless quality previously reserved for core memories. Like weddings, or the annual spring clearance at Bergdorf Goodman.

"Well, you see," she began. "It's sort of a long story."

Caryn glanced down at the Cartier watch circling her wrist. "You have exactly ten minutes to tell it."

"And then?" Darby asked, attempting to keep herself from visibly bristling at the ultimatum.

"And then I leave for my UV therapy green-tea sea-salt bath at Soak on the Sound."

"That sounds fucking amazing, actually."

"It is." Caryn locked eyes with the bass player during a lull in the music. "So kindly get on with it."

How to put this? Was there any good way to inform a mother that her son routinely drove to Canada in search of anonymous, illicit sex? Unlikely.

You don't need to make her like you. You just need to get her to talk to Roy.

From her present vantage, Darby wasn't sure which one sounded more difficult. *Everybody's got an angle, darlin',* she heard Tony Two Toes say in a voice made gravelly by decades of vice.

As quickly and expediently as she could, Darby summarized the circumstances of her and Ethan's meeting. Heavily edited, of course. Caryn was silent for a moment when she'd finished, slowly and methodically smoothing the damp ring her cocktail had left on the art deco napkin.

"You met my son at a bar in Canada," she repeated.

"That's right," Darby said.

"And he had no idea you were the owner of the business the petition targeted?"

"Correct," Darby said. "It's actually sort of funny when you think about it."

"How so?" Caryn asked, her face completely free of anything resembling amusement.

"Well, here you are attempting to pick up a musician from

out of town, and Ethan goes out of town and accidentally picks up somebody from Townsend Harbor."

"Being *from* Townsend Harbor is very different than living *in* Townsend Harbor," Caryn said carefully.

"So I hear," Darby said, unable to keep the trace of bitterness out of her voice. "When I bought the property from your real estate agent, I anticipated potential pushback, but damned if I thought it would create enough drama to necessitate an entire protest."

Caryn drained the last of her nearly empty drink. "Talk to me when you start receiving burning bags of dog feces on your doorstep."

Darby had been so wound up about not incurring Caryn's wrath that she'd nearly forgotten Caryn had once been the target of the town's ire.

"I mean, the least they could do is come up with something original," Darby said.

Caryn's snort almost sounded like solidarity. "The cradle of originality, Townsend Harbor is not."

"Did you know that someone actually climbed onto the top of my camper and placed a custom-made black censorship bar over my ti—er—logo?"

Caryn rolled her eyes on a gusty sigh. "Ridiculous."

"How much you want to bet that if it were male-owned establishment objectifying women as opposed to a woman voluntarily displaying her own body, half of those protesters would have been home sipping decaf and watching *Jeopardy*?"

Caryn's perfectly matte lips tightened for a moment, and Darby thought she might have blown it.

"Amazing how ready the public is to forgive men with money. So long as they mumble the lamest of apologies and carry out their indiscretions quietly."

"It's almost like you met my weasel of an ex," Darby said.

"If you've met one philanderer, you've met them all." Their server appeared, and Darby felt an odd surge of satisfaction when Caryn ordered another drink as opposed to asking for her check.

She debated reminding Caryn of her appointment but held off in the end, afraid to break their exceedingly tenuous connection.

"You too?' she asked, before finishing the last of her drink in preparation for the next.

Caryn nodded. "It wasn't as if I didn't know better. Before he cheated on me, he cheated *with* me. And I was foolish enough to think that I was different. I believe they call that karma."

"I believe they call that being human," Darby said.

"A naïve human, maybe. Ethan's father was a decade older. A good deal more sophisticated."

Looking at the woman seated across the table from her, Darby felt it hard to believe that anybody could be more sophisticated than Caryn Townsend.

"How did you meet?" she asked before pausing to consider whether it would be a painful question to answer.

"A political fundraiser. He had his sights set on Congress before he became the mayor."

Darby could see it all in a blink. Ethan's father, a good-looking young man from a well-connected, wealthy family, expecting to coast into his seat of power. Outraged and confused when it disappeared right from beneath his ass. Downsizing his dream. Ethan Townsend senior had made one call right: Caryn Townsend would have made an exquisite first lady in any office.

"I put my MBA on hold to help with his campaign, but then we married and I got pregnant with Ethan, and there just didn't seem to be much point in finishing it." She shrugged.

"It's not too late, you know," Darby said, then took a sip of the fresh drink that had arrived while Caryn spoke.

Caryn lifted hers as well. "I'm afraid that ship has sailed, as they say."

"When I was in law school, one of my classmates was a sixty-year-old former housewife with five grown children. She's a DA in Chicago now."

Something flickered behind Caryn's eyes. "To what point?"

"Does there have to be a point?" Darby asked.

"Everyone would think I'd lost my mind."

"Why do they get to have an opinion about what you do with the rest of your time here on earth?" The question hung in the air between them, and Darby felt her heart begin to beat faster as a rush of adrenaline coursed through her veins. "You sacrificed your time so your husband could achieve his dream. Sacrificed your body for a child who's now fully grown and amply capable of making his own decisions."

Probably a terrible example, but Darby kept rolling anyway.

"You silently supported your husband even after he cheated on you, which, let's be honest, is probably why he was able to hold on to his office until he passed. And he maintained his image even after that. I mean, yeah. What you did to Cady was pretty fucked up. But you never would have resorted to that if your cheat of a husband hadn't gifted the building out from under you and left you to find out about it at the reading of the will. You ask me, this town doesn't just owe you an apology, it owes you a pension.

"Sorry," Darby said when she saw Caryn gaping at her, her cocktail hovering halfway to her mouth. "I get a little hot about this stuff."

Looking at her second martini, Darby was shocked to find it more than three-quarters of the way gone. *Oops*.

Another one appeared before her.

"Oh," she began. "I shouldn't. I have to—"

"Don't pretend on my account," Caryn said. "I know WASP genetics when I see them."

"Takes one to know one?" Darby asked.

Caryn raised her cocktail, and they clinked glasses. "Indeed."

"How much does Ethan know?"

Caryn rolled her glass's slim stem in her fingers. "Enough to resent me, but not enough hate his father."

A lump formed in Darby's throat, choking off her swallow of icy gin. "Hate him for what?"

Caryn's chest deflated on a heavy sigh. "His father had big ideas but never the drive and discipline to see them through. His true love was gambling. So much so, he burned through a significant chunk of the Townsend fortunes. By the time he passed, I had no option but to sell off enough property to settle what was owed. If there had been any way to keep the land in the family—" Her eyes shone like sapphires as a scrim of tears glazed them.

How many fathers and sons went into the ground wearing the same name without knowing each other in the slightest?

"You should tell him."

Shut up, Darby. This is not why you came.

Caryn's perfectly stenciled brows shot toward her sleek hairline. "I couldn't. He's barely speaking to me as it is."

"Oh, he'd pitch a fit, all right. Probably piss and moan a good deal about how betrayed he felt, how you had no right to withhold this information from him, blah blah blah, but let's face it— if men didn't want us to lie to them, they shouldn't have made a world where we're burned for our truths."

The band finished the song, dropping the room into sudden silence. Caryn stared at her for several beats before remembering to clap. The bass player appeared somewhat crestfallen.

"I appreciate and even agree with your impassioned soliloquy," she said, toying with the garnish in her drink. "But I suspect a motivational speech isn't the purpose for your coming."

"I wouldn't insult you by pretending otherwise." Darby sat up straighter on her plush bench. "It's about Roy, actually."

Caryn's expression darkened. Not a good sign.

"Roy?" she repeated. "What on earth for?"

"Because he promised me some juicy gossip that's meant to help me get this ridiculous petition thrown out, and getting you to talk to him was the price he named."

What the hell was it about this goddamn town that had the unvarnished truth falling from Darby's mouth left and right?

"If deep, dark secrets were what you were after, you ought to have come to me first." Caryn slid a sly glance at Darby over the rim of her cocktail glass.

"Had I known that was an option, I probably would have," Darby answered honestly. "You're not exactly at the top of people's lists in terms of approachability."

"Thank God," Caryn said. "After decades of playing hostess, therapist, homemaker, decorator, nurse, muse, chauffeur, and wardrobe consultant, I must admit that it's rather refreshing."

Darby could scarcely argue with that logic.

"I'll talk to Roy," Caryn said in a measured tone. "But I will need a favor in return."

By the time this was over, Darby was going to owe the whole county.

"And that would be?"

Caryn stared into her condensation-kissed glass as if it were the Oracle of Delphi. "Once upon a time, Ethan had plans for the land you bought." When her eyes lifted to Darby's, they almost looked sad. "I'd like to know what those plans were."

Darby hesitated for approximately a millisecond before holding out her hand. "Caryn Townsend, you have a deal."

EIGHTEEN

Heat Exchanger

EQUIPMENT USED TO HEAT THE MIX RAPIDLY

ETHAN ARRIVED AT THE CIRQUE DU CAFÉ AT PRECISELY 6:56 p.m., so he sat in his truck for exactly five minutes fucking around on his phone.

At 7:01 p.m., he got out and walked into the shadows of the old oak grove past which her trailer sat dark, except for the lights glowing behind the drawn curtains. Even the strings of patio lights had been turned off in deference to the sexy, slapdash circus behind it.

When he knocked on her door, she took as much time to answer as if she lived in a five-story mansion.

Not that he knew what that was like.

He would have thought of something amazing to say if she wasn't standing there looking like a desperate housewife circa 1949, except for the pink hair and sex-kitten makeup.

Her turquoise polka-dot dress made her look like a birthday present waiting to be unwrapped.

Ethan opened his mouth to tell her so, but she beat him to it.

"Lavender *and* African daisies? Is this a peace bouquet?" She snatched the carefully wrapped flowers and buried her entire face in them before taking a huge whiff. "Come on in, I'm just freshening up. I didn't expect you early."

He scowled and checked his watch. "I'm not early. I'm a minute...two minutes late," he amended as the dial flipped over.

"Oh my God, you're the cutest. Follow me." She bustled in, laying the flowers on the counter on the way to the back hall.

"It's the bouquet I thought looked most like it belonged to you," he confessed as the entire Airstream tilted slightly to accommodate his weight. "I only know lavender because the color and flower match."

A smile toyed with the corners of her pink mouth as she applied gloss in her tiny hallway that doubled as an armoire. "Maybe you're the kind of guy who just knows things. Listens to intuition."

Christ, he'd already dicked this woman down several times—hell, a few hours ago in the very spot he stood—so why were his palms sweating like this was his first date ever? "Nah. I'm your regular, oblivious, straight white male who can't tell his ass from a hole in the ground."

The smile appeared in full force, accompanied by a wink that did something funny to his insides. "It's okay. I'd know your ass anywhere," she teased. "Between you and me, we'll keep track."

"Don't flirt with me inside your trailer," he grumbled.

She looked over from where she teased her curls into a victory roll. "Why not?"

"Because we're not having sex tonight."

She froze mid-stick with a bobby pin, and skewered him with her glare. "Excuse me?"

It was Ethan's turn to smirk. "I hope you're wearing a chastity belt, because my hands, mouth, and other parts are staying north of the waist."

Her pout was enough to shake his resolve, but instead of arguing, she said, "Okay, then. I'll be right back." Ethan didn't think he'd made a face until she clarified, "I have to put on panties."

His every muscle turned into gritty stone before he wheezed. "I'm leaving."

"Already?" The pout turned into a sultry invitation that turned his frown into a scowl.

"Lady, I have fucked you ninety-nine-point-*always*-percent of the times I've been in this trailer, and I'm about to keep that percentage whole, so..." He jammed his finger toward the door. "I'mma wait outside, if you don't mind."

She snorted. "Suit yourself, but that KIRO cameraman is lingering around somewhere. Lurking all weekend." A pair of panties sailed over his head. Pink, like her hair. Then another black scrap of lace that would cover exactly nothing.

Retreating, he placed his hand on the latch. "After Thursday, I'm a social pariah who had sex hair and a half-tucked shirt on the local news, so...what can the cameraman do to me now?" His mortification still stained his Nordic skin several shades pinker than the sun ever could.

"They'll catch you returning to the scene of the crime, so just stay in the kitchen. I'll only be a sec."

"Fine. Wear ugly underwear," he reminded her.

"I don't own ugly underwear."

"And I don't fucking need to know that."

While he waited, he unwrapped the discarded bouquet, searching in her surprisingly neat cupboards for a vase. Finding one, he filled it with water, poured in the contents of the flower food package, and then snipped off the stems diagonally. The lavender filled the room with a sweet, but not overpowering, aroma that mingled nicely with the constant undertone of coffee beans and buttery vanilla.

After giving the flowers one final floofing, he turned to check her progress.

Darby stood in the hallway, gazing at him with a look he couldn't identify. "Where the hell did you come from, Ethan Townsend?"

"I've been here the whole time."

The atmosphere in the trailer shifted as Ethan stepped back. The air was filled with her perfume, creating an intoxicating and inviting mood that was broken only by a husky whisper. "Ethan?"

He froze, eyes drawn to a single point of focus. Darby's bed at the end of the hall. It looked far more inviting than it should have, considering he'd made it his mission to stay away from anything considered horizontal.

She moved closer, reaching out to touch his face. He didn't flinch or move away, instead leaning into her palm as she stroked his cheek softly.

His breathing had grown shallow and fast from standing so close to her, and he could feel his heart thudding against his ribcage like an unrelenting drumbeat in this moment of heavy silence.

With a desperate move, Ethan nearly pulled the door off its hinges as he escaped into the cool kiss of the evening air.

He was grateful she didn't balk at taking his one-handed offer to help her down the two steps, and she didn't make like his chivalry wasn't appreciated.

Once the night enveloped them, their easy teasing from inside stayed there, leaving them with a protracted silence neither of them seemed to know how to fill.

Should he ask about her family? Nah, she'd mentioned that before, and it seemed a sore topic.

Maybe ask about her favorite place she'd lived? Or would that sound like he still wanted her to go?

Did he still want her to go?

Was she planning to eventually?

Were they crazy for even trying this?

"So you've never lived anywhere other than Townsend Harbor?" It was Darby who threw him the proverbial bone as she ran a finger across a feathered fan on display at an Asian imports booth.

"I lived on campus when I did my undergrad degree at UCLA," he said.

"Yeah?"

"Yeah. Then a master's...also in California." Grimacing, he hoped she didn't notice the flub.

"Not UCLA?" Of course she noticed.

"Close enough."

Her eyes narrowed. "Where?"

"Does it matter?"

"It does when you're being weird."

Puffing his cheeks out, he mumbled. "Stanford."

"What the shit? You have a master's degree from Stanford?" she shrilled, causing several scarf-buying customers to glance in their direction.

"I mean, it was kind of a legacy situation." As in, all the Ethan Townsends received matching MBAs. "Got a partial sports scholarship, and the rest was tuition. A lot of tuition."

One pink penciled eyebrow lifted. "Poly-sci major?"

"How'd you know?"

"Smell it all over you, Sheriff Townsend."

"You can call me Ethan," he grumbled again. "I'm off duty."

"Okay, off-duty Sheriff Townsend. You puddle-jumped to California. That's as far as you ventured from home? Two states?"

He took a blood-red dress that she held up in front of a mirror and replaced it with a teal/silver number that made her hair look like frosting against an ocean. A fashion suggestion of which she approved. "Worked a few college summers in Alaska on fishing/crab boats. My grandpa thought it would help to build character."

"Helped build these, I bet." Reaching out, she squeezed his biceps, eliciting another blush.

"I like to be busy." Jesus, he was spending more time looking at his own shoes than the face she'd painted so prettily just for him.

But damned if he didn't feel like the class nerd taking out the beauty queen in all those terrible eighties movies.

What was he supposed to do with his hands? All he wanted

was to put them on her in all the ways. But once that started... where would he stop?

"So, you've ventured up and down the West Coast..." she finished, waving to some friends who laughed and made obscene gestures at the two of them.

Fucking springs on the fucking Airstream.

"I've seen more than you would think and have visited every continent that doesn't host a pole. We used to vacation all the time when Dad was alive," he remembered out loud. "Iceland, the Maldives, Himalayas, Bali, etc. If my parents had one thing in common, it was their mutual hatred of big cities, so we always went somewhere out of the way. I did love the glass igloos in Norway. The Northern Lights are ridiculous—Darby?"

It took him several more steps down the aisle of diminishing crowds to realize she was no longer following him. He turned to find her frozen to the grass beneath her feet, eyes wide as she stared up at him. "You never saw *any* place in *all* that time that called to you to come back? I mean, you're telling me you've been all over most of the world and ended up a sheriff in the bumfuck town you were born in?"

He looked toward the tree tunnel, wishing her question didn't scratch at something tender inside of him. A defensiveness that reared its head in her presence every damn time. "I've been awestruck in Dubai. I've fallen in love for one night in Paris. I... experimented...in the red-light district of Amsterdam."

She looked around as if to see who else might have captured that bit of pure bullshit. "You? Amsterdam?"

Ethan grunted. "Okay, I was the designated driver...which is weird on a bicycle, so I spent most of my night playing sherpa to my drunk/high buddies and making sure they made it back to the hotel alive."

She broke into a warm laugh halfway through his explanation. "There's the Ethan I know. You didn't even get to be with one hooker?"

"Excuse me, I think they're called sex workers," he corrected her in a nasally voice.

She smirked at him. "Touché. So...was it family that called you back here to stay?"

Ethan looked around at the grass trampled by people. At the lights and energy and gleaming faces. People eating, playing, spectating, clapping.

This was right. It was good. It didn't disrespect his grandfather's land or memory. It brought Raven Creek to life.

"There isn't a place in the world like Townsend Harbor," he murmured.

"I can attest to that."

As he spoke, Ethan's chest expanded with real feeling. "I feel like I know every tree and hollow. Every shop and keeper. The tide schedules. The seasons. The festivals. Hell, even the criminals. I know the names of people's dogs and grandkids. And they know me and mine. They say it takes a village to raise a child, and this one raised me."

"Probably why you're so weird."

That evoked a snort of laughter. "Oh, it's exactly why I'm so weird. And protective. And involved. And—"

"Overbearing? Controlling? Closed-minded?"

Okay, he deserved that, but she didn't need to know. "Keep it up and you're paying for your own deep-fried stick of butter."

They laughed as they paused at a crossroads. One way was the stage where Kiki and her family gave their final performance, and the other way stood a friendly half-circle of food trucks.

"I had raw butter for lunch," she teased, holding her hand over a pretend-full stomach. "Maybe something...healthier?"

They stared at each other for a second, each of them thinking about devouring the other.

"Meat?" he finally suggested.

"Meat," she agreed.

They wandered over to the food trucks, too absorbed in each

other to see Cady and Fox until they were almost wearing the basket of fries they were sharing.

Welp, guess they were eating at the Humble Pie Cafe, table for one shirt-tucker where the soup of the day was cream of awkward.

Cady and Darby shared exclamations as if they hadn't been together all day. Fox and Ethan, on the other hand, quietly mad-dogged as if it would take the twitch of an eyelash to kick nine shades of shit out of the other.

"Cady talked you into a crowd today, huh?" Darby chucked Fox on the shoulder as if they were old war buddies.

Hmmmm...

"She likes it when I break stuff and throw things." Fox shrugged.

"Look what he won me!" Cady reached into a backpack and pulled out an adorable stuffed bear...

Dressed in a black leather harness, numerous buckles, and a bright red ball gag cinched in his little teddy bear mouth.

"I love it!" Darby squeezed the bear. "You guys are too cute. A match made in...well, in Townsend Harbor."

Cady flipped a long blonde strand over her shoulder and adjusted her beanie. "You guys getting food?"

Ethan sent Darby a silent message: *Don't invite them to eat with us. Don't invite them to eat with us. Don't invite them to eat with us.*

"We are. You want to join us?"

Cady took one look at both men and immediately said, "No thanks! We ate already. Just sort of making our goodbyes."

"And getting dessert," Fawkes reminded her, tugging her gently toward a booth painted to look like a vintage ice cream truck that sold frozen yogurt boobs and dong popsicles.

"I have to tell Darby something really quick—do you mind grabbing us something?" Cady blinked her moon-cow eyes at Fox, and Ethan remembered how devastating they could be.

"Of course—what do you want?"

"Make it a surprise."

"One surprise coming right up."

Her eyes lit as she had an idea. "Can you make that surprise a doughnut?"

Fox's face melted with tenderness, and if he didn't give a Westley-ish *as you wish*, then Ethan was imagining things.

Cady turned to them, her hands imprisoning both their wrists with surprising strength for someone with her autoimmune disorder. "Okay, you two. I have been asked exactly twenty million times if you guys hate-banged your way into a relationship. What do I tell everyone? Is this a thing? *Please tell me this is a thiii-iiinguh.*"

Even Darby sputtered at her effusiveness. "Um. This is...it's..."

"It's a date," Ethan clarified.

"You're *dating*?" Cady appeared this close to apoplexy.

"We are on a date. Singular. Currently. *Or trying to be.*" He shot his sort-of-ex a get-the-fuck-out-of-here look. But in the nicest way possible.

"Gotcha. Loud and clear." She saluted him before turning to Darby. "OMG. Message me later. Or in the morning. Or if he leaves after breakfast."

"He said we're not going to bone tonight," Darby lamented.

"What?" Crossing her arms, Cady made a sound between a laugh and a groan. "That's sort of closing the barn door after letting the horse out. Did he say why?"

"*He* is right the fuck here," Ethan pointed out.

"I think he's trying to figure out if he can stand the other things I can do with my mouth. Like talking." Darby's pat on the shoulder turned him all the rest of the way the color of steamed beets.

"How is it going so far?" Cady inquired, not skipping a beat. "What do you think of our Darby, Ethan?"

"I think she's..." *Extraordinary. Overwhelming. Exquisite. Sexy. Complicated.* "I think she's one of the smartest, strongest, most independent women I've ever met."

"Oh, *great*." Darby rolled her eyes. "Everyone *loves* smart, strong, independent women...except men and most other women."

"Maybe that's because what we've been taught to see as *trouble* is really just power we're afraid of you all using on us."

Both women shot him an approving look he'd not at all expected.

When he was thinking of a polite way to get the fuck out of there, Vee, of all people, goosed him from behind before shoving her way into the middle of the gathering. Her silver-blue hair stuck up like she'd been kissing light sockets.

"You'll never guess what," she slurred, splashing a bit of her gin and tonic on Darby's shoe. "I was just offered seventy-five quid for the use of my body!"

Ethan didn't have a chance to remind anyone that solicitation was a crime before Myrtle shouldered in just in time to catch Vee's insubstantial weight before she flung herself on the grass.

"That isn't a lot of money, honey. Let's get you home."

Vee jerked her arm out of Myrtle's grasp. "It was when I was in my twenties. Why can't you let me have this?"

"Because it wasn't for your body, my love, it was Mayor Stewart offering you money to abandon the pea-shooting booth so you'd stop taking all the good prizes from his thirteen-year-old nephew," Vee reminded her.

"That walking vasectomy advertisement? Who cares? Probably off rubbing knobs in Henry's Hardware instead of doing his job."

After much shushing, Myrtle turned to the group. "Sorry, everyone in town knows not to give her gin, but no one told the newbies."

"It's good to see you are being the mature one for once." Ethan chuckled.

"Yeah! I'm being the mature one," Myrtle agreed, eyeing him like he wasn't from around these parts. "Now, what are you doing harassing Darby, you big, hairy twat face?"

"They're on a date," Cady answered for him.

Myrtle jumped back, almost upsetting a dangerously green Vee in the process. "They don't look like they're on a date."

"He brought me flowers and everything," Darby said, looping her arm through his.

This, he liked. This he could get used to.

The fertilizer maven snorted. "He'd better buy you dinner and a new set of shocks after what he did to you earlier."

Ethan cleared his throat loudly, smothering some very choice words.

"Oh, don't be embarrassed—most people here have seen your schmeeckle at some point or other."

"What? No they haven't."

Myrtle lifted her elbow. "Raise your hand if you've seen the sheriff's no-no parts."

Every hand but one went up.

Darby didn't *not* notice that Cady's arms were *very carefully* adhered to her sides.

"When the hell, Myrtle?" Ethan demanded. She hadn't been there when Kiki pantsed him.

"I changed your diaper exactly thirty-three years ago." She lifted her hand to say aside to Darby, "Don't let this one tell you he has bad aim—little fucker pissed right up my nose."

"I'm leaving," Ethan announced. If his skin got any hotter, it would peel right off.

"Oh, come on..." Vee cut in. "It isn't like Caryn is going to break out naked baby pictures of little Ethan—someone has to humiliate you on dates."

"Well, mission fucking accomplished, you two," he groused before spinning on his heel and taking off in a random direction.

Girlish giggles followed him, and Ethan caught himself wondering if he might find this funny when he finished dying of mortification.

A small, cool hand slid into his, and suddenly the night wasn't so bright and loud. Darby filled every corner of his thoughts, all of his senses, and his entire concept of time, crowding out the chaos of everything that didn't matter.

"It's starting to make sense why you fled all the way to Canada for a shag," she said, tugging him toward the shadows of the meadow beyond, at the end of which the brook burbled lazily.

"They're harmless." He waved a hand back toward the people who'd known him the longest. "Just seemed like...the right thing to do, not to pull a woman from a bar that I might pull over the next day." He smiled down at her, maneuvering their hands until her fingers were laced through his.

Click.

Just like puzzle pieces. Or perfectly fitted cedar joints.

No one could think of a reason they should ever be separated again.

Wait. What?

"You always try to do the right thing, don't you? To do what is expected of you?" Her voice had lowered two octaves in the hush beyond the meadow, as the night seemed to muffle the carnival behind them.

Ethan picked a flower that'd closed blossoms to the night, and started to unfurl the petals. "I always try to do the *good* thing."

She made a derisive sound. "I envy people who see the world as binary sometimes. Must be nice, being so certain of what's right and wrong."

Ethan maneuvered them around two large roots raised in the middle of the path, careful that she didn't trip in the dark. "I used to think the right thing was simple."

"What changed your mind?"

"You."

Ethan caught her around the middle when she stumbled, liking that he threw her off her axis for a minute.

Felt a little like the universe balancing itself.

Lacing her arm back through his, she allowed him to help her down the bank to the stream, trusting that he knew just about every rock, divot, and root on their path. "How did you become sheriff?" she asked suddenly.

"Talk about a boring story," he said, kicking a limb out of the way.

"Make it as interesting as possible."

"Okay. Um…" He did his best to annotate in his mind before speaking up. "Sheriff Turnstalk was the county sheriff for a handful of decades. As long as I was alive, at least. His mother was Salish, so he held a lot of weight on the rez and kept things between their town and ours prosperous and peaceful. When he died in office, they held a special election and, even though I'd only been a deputy for a handful of years, the other officers and deputies talked me into running. So here we are. Two unopposed terms under my belt. One boring story."

"Helps that the town is your namesake," she said, bending down to extract a white feather drifting through the tall grasses on the riverbank.

"Doesn't hurt. But it's not why I ran."

"Why did you?"

"Someone needed to. The town council was out of control, establishing insane zoning and business laws. The police were overrun with tourist issues, noise complaints, and bar fights, and the people in the outlying rural areas were being overlooked because of a deputy shortage. We didn't have enough firefighters or EMTs. Turnstalk was a good man, but he did things his way. He didn't listen to people. To the people he served. That's what I promised I would do."

"Which is why you shut me down?" she asked, keeping her voice even.

"Partly." He winced, regretting the entire situation like hell. "I'm realizing…that those who bark the loudest don't necessarily speak for the rest of the pack." He ran an uneasy hand over his hair.

"Meaning what?"

"The world out there is so full of everything. Fear, mostly.

Hatred. Division. Marginalization. One of the things that kept Townsend Harbor so special was the fact that all that bullshit seemed to leave itself at the tree tunnel."

Noticing a slight shiver and goosepimples on her moonlit flesh, he wrapped his jacket around her shoulders, pleased when she nestled into it as he continued.

"For a while, it seemed like the place was truly frozen in time, and I guess I believed the illusion that the outside world didn't need to...dilute it. Water Street barely survived the pandemic, and our town was almost brought to its knees by supply shortages and the loss of tourist dollars. Then something magic happened. Everyone pooled together to keep this town alive. In every way. The citizens here were generous with funds. With volunteer work. They were careful with each other's health and safety and comfort levels. So many people who give their hearts and souls to this place are terrified it'll give over to strip malls and Walmart. That the magic of this community will disappear into the depressing isolation we've become accustomed to these days. I guess some felt as though your shop was a portent of other things..."

She nodded, chewing on her lip. "I can understand that."

"I realize now how myopic that was... Because change, though uncomfortable, is inevitable, and people in this town need to be dumped on their heads more often." He paused at a bend in the river, catching at her hand and drawing her into the heat of his body. "Especially me."

Ethan moved her to a large, flat stone slab shaped like an altar. He would sun himself here as a boy after fishing in the creek. "This is maybe my favorite place in the world."

A liminal place. One neither here nor there.

A place in between. Just for them.

Music and laughter and lights were far over there, and couldn't compete with the laughter of the water over stones and moss.

"Can I ask you something?" She tilted her head back, and her skin gleamed like the center of a moonstone. "You've never said a thing about *wanting* to be sheriff. I mean, you have a Stanford education and then you became a deputy?"

He shrugged. "What else would I be?"

"A trust fund douche?"

Perching on the rock, he opened his thighs, and she moved between them, pressing their bodies together more intimately than sexually. "I tried that for a week," he said against her hair. "Got really bored. I'm not good at video games, and fishing is only relaxing if you're *not* relaxing from your relaxing life. If I'm not useful, I don't feel like anything at all."

"That's sad." She pulled her head back to regard him with melancholy eyes.

He cocked his head in puzzlement. "Why? It's good to be useful."

"Yeah, but you don't want your worth to only be tied up into what you can do for others."

"You don't—er, I don't?"

Elegant fingers charted a course down his jaw line to cup it in her hands. "What would you do for yourself? If you had no impediment to your dreams, what did little Ethan the fourth dream about on this rock?"

"Beer." At her laugh, he said, "No. Seriously. When I was nine, my grandpa gave me my first sip of beer as a deterrent. I loved it so much, I snuck a whole glass and broke my toe on this very rock. Since then, he taught me about the mainstays of ale. How to brew it. The ingredients. How to grow your own hops and barley. The fermentation process. Even the history of it. Did you know that the earliest evidence of brewing beer dates back to about 3500-2900 BC? In ancient Iran, of all places. That's just wild. I'd have loved to taste it."

"I was not aware," she breathed quietly.

"I lost you already." He pulled her tighter.

"No you didn't..." Still, something he'd said had sent her far away.

With him sitting on the rock and her standing in the circle of his arms and legs, they were level, eye to eye.

Her gaze held a million tender phrases. Her lips slightly parted in anticipation.

Ethan lowered his head slowly until their mouths touched, gentle and soft at first, then deepening as the kiss became more passionate. He moved his hands up her back to cup her face and pull her closer still.

The air around them heated, and they were lost in the moment, lost in each other. She tasted like wine and honey, and he couldn't get enough of her.

As they pulled back, breathless, he couldn't help but smile. "I remember what else little Ethan the fourth dreamed about on this rock."

She grinned back, her eyes shining. "Working your wood?"

"No. I mean...not that there wasn't plenty of that." He smirked and shook his head, trailing his fingers down her arms. "Being here with you. Kissing you. Making memories that will meld with the ones I already have of this place."

She leaned in for another kiss, tangling her hands in his hair. They stayed there, on that rock in the middle of the river, lost in each other, until the moon had risen high in the sky.

He hoped that she felt the way he did.

That, to this woman who was equal parts wild heart and wanderlust, this wasn't a kiss goodbye.

Because he could kiss Darby Dunwell forever.

NINETEEN
Taint

A NEGATIVE TASTE, FRAGRANCE OR AROMA OCCURRING ANYWHERE IN THE COFFEE CHAIN

DARBY WOKE WITH THE SUN WARMING HER CHEEKS AND a profound sense of disorientation swirling behind the darkness of her sleep-sealed eyes.

A body—large, warm, and definitely male—was in her bed.

Hair-roughened legs tangled with hers, a heavy, muscular arm was thrown over her torso, warm breath feathered the nape of her neck, and one hell of a hard-on branded her ass cheek.

Cautiously peeling open one gritty lid, Darby was struck by a miraculous sight.

Sheriff Ethan Townsend, sleeping in her bed.

His deep chest rose and fell in a steady rhythm, and his sandy hair was tousled against his forehead. His normally stern face was peaceful—boyish, innocent, and so damn vulnerable it made her heart lurch and a strange, unfamiliar ache grow in her chest.

Danger, Will Robinson.

Darby's gaze strayed downward, and she drank in his naked torso. Her fingers itched to trace the planes of his abdomen, the ridges of his chest, the lightly furred lines of the powerful arms she'd fallen asleep in last night.

True to his word, sleep was all they'd done.

In her camper.

The carnival, on the other hand, had basically been a foreplay free-for-all.

They'd gotten handsy in the haunted castle. Grappled and groped their way through the funhouse. Bumped bits in the adult bounce castle—which she still couldn't believe Ethan had shucked his boots to crawl into.

And now, his nearly naked body was in her bed. Nearly naked Ethan Townsend with a nearly naked erection branding her nearly naked ass.

Maybe it was the early-morning hour, or the potent concentration of Ethan's sexy sleep scent in her sleep cubby. Maybe it was the birds filling the morning air with Disney-esque song.

Darby's throat closed. Her heart squeezed in her chest.

He was here.

Ethan was *here*.

In her camper. In her bed.

In her life?

Oh, shit.

She needed to move before she pulled up Redfin and started browsing for ramblers in Townsend Harbor's suburban outskirts.

With the care of a bomb technician, she began the painstaking process of sneaking out of bed. Limb by limb, inch by inch, she disentangled herself until all that remained was her ankle trapped beneath Ethan's muscular calf.

"Easy," she whispered to herself. "Eeeasy—"

"Mmmm."

She felt the low rumble of a moan vibrate the mattress as Ethan's arm snaked around her waist, pulling her back into the crook of his arm and trapping her leg between his.

"Where do you think you're going?"

Darby's heart fluttered in her chest as she felt the evidence of Ethan's desire pressing into her backside.

"I...uh... I just thought..." She trailed off helplessly, unable to form a coherent sentence with Ethan pressed so close behind her. "I should get coffee started."

"I have a better idea." He dragged his hand over her hip, splaying his fingers over the sensitive skin of her belly. Gooseflesh spilled down her neck and arms as Ethan's lips brushed against the spot just below her ear. "Stay in bed with me."

"Can't," she breathed. "I have so much to do today."

His fingers trailed lower, toying with the edge of the compromise panties she'd slipped into while he watched. "You can start by doing me."

Son of a bitch.

Not even a quasi-sleep-delirious, terrible come-on line was enough to dampen her revving libido. "Ethan…"

He moved his hand back up to her waist, sliding it over her ribs until his thumb brushed against the underside of her breast. "Hmm?"

She arched into him, nipples peaking beneath the buttery-soft fabric of his undershirt she'd stolen to sleep in.

"I thought we weren't having sex," she reminded him.

"I said we weren't having sex last night." Ethan's arm tightened around her waist, pulling her closer to him. His breath was hot against her neck, and she shivered despite the warmth of the morning sun. "I didn't say dick about this morning."

Speaking of…

Ethan's cock twitched against Darby's lower back, and damned if a sympathetic rush of moisture didn't dampen her panties.

Well, this was going to be a problem.

"I have to get started on cleanup," she protested halfheartedly. "I'm scared to even look out that front door."

"All the more reason to stay here." Ethan's lips curved into a smile against her skin, making her insides flip-flop.

"Sheriff Ethan Townsend suggesting that I neglect my custodial duties in favor of sexual gratification?" she asked with exaggerated disbelief.

"Not neglect," he murmured against her. "Delay."

"How about we delay this until after I have a shower and a

cup of coffee?" she suggested, already wishing she'd at least rinsed off before she crawled into bed last night. She could practically feel their date on her skin.

"Because I like how you taste now."

Darby was briefly distracted by the feel of his tongue tracing the shell of her ear. Her eyelids fluttered. "Like tequila sweat and gossip fodder?"

"Like...cotton candy." He nipped at her lobe. "And gossip fodder."

Darby's breath caught in her throat as Ethan skimmed his palm over her ribcage to cup her breast, brushing his thumb over her scar before jerking away as if burned.

"It's okay," she said quietly. "We can talk about it."

"You don't have to tell me anything you don't want to," he said.

But strangely, Darby *wanted* to talk about it. She wanted to give him this piece of her personal history that knitted together the disparate threads of her life.

"It was the summer after my first year of law school. I'd quit an internship at my father's firm after his letch of a partner made a pass at me and I started bartending at this Irish dive in Boston."

Darby drew in a deep breath, grounding herself by the steady thrum of Ethan's heart between her shoulder blades.

"A couple of the waitresses also did burlesque, and I'd always been curious, so I gave it a shot."

"And you were amazing at it?"

Darby's cheeks warmed at the compliment. "Hardly. I spent the first month covered in bruises and rope burn, but I was hooked."

Ethan's large, warm foot pressed against Darby's like the punctuation to her admission.

"It was the first time in my life I felt...free. Free from the expectations of my parents and their money. Free to wear what I wanted and move how I wanted without judgment or criticism. Free to be myself without apology."

Darby closed her eyes, tracing the calluses on his hand. "Needless to say, fall rolled around, and I didn't want to go back to Boston College. Which was"—she paused, searching for the correct words—"an unpopular decision with my parents."

"I could see that."

"But," she continued, "I'd already met Aidan by that point and was thoroughly entrenched in the neurochemically stupid phase of a new relationship."

Ethan's stomach tensed against her back at the mention of another man's name, but Darby rolled on, too far down the road now to stop.

"We were on the couch Netflix and chilling one night"— much like she and Ethan were doing now, Darby thought but didn't say—"and he felt it."

Her heart skipped as the moment returned to her in a rush. The screen's glow flickering on the ceiling and walls of the apartment they'd just moved into together, their boxes not even fully unpacked. Darby's lungs refusing to inflate as his fingers guided hers to the spot.

What's this?

This was a frag bomb that divided her life into two distinct periods.

Before, and after.

The during, she preferred not to think about even on a spring morning beneath sun-dappled sheets and lunatic birds calling for mates outside her camper window.

"I knew what it was," she said. "Even before the doctor confirmed it. I'd lost my insurance when I dropped out of BC, and my parents and I weren't exactly on speaking terms."

Ethan's chin shifted atop her snuggle-smashed hair, and Darby could practically feel his jaw tightening.

"I honestly had no idea what I was going to do, but all my performer friends banded together to raise money for my treatments." Her throat ached as tears threatened to well over her eyelids. "One of them even let people staple money to his skin."

"That seems...extreme," Ethan said.

"Not really," Darby replied. "Usually it was lollipop wrappers. It was sort of his thing. Performance art and all that."

Ethan gave a noncommittal grunt.

"That's what I wish people in Townsend Harbor understood." Rolling onto her side, Darby faced Ethan across her rumpled pillow. "These artists, these performers that they're so quick to judge and label? They're the same people who had next to nothing themselves, but moved heaven and earth to help me. Someone they knew only a few months, and they took turns coming with me to appointments, organizing benefit shows. And here they are again," she said, gesturing toward her camper window. "They hear Brewbies is in trouble, and boom. They're here with bells on."

"Are you talking about the guy who was wandering around with the cowbell hooked through his scrotum?"

Darby rudely nudged her hips backward, making Ethan grunt. "You know what I mean. Townsend Harbor isn't a tight-knit community because its residents are close. It's because they're *closed*. Closed-minded. Closed-hearted. And Lord help anyone who tries to infiltrate those ranks."

Ethan studied her with an intensity that made her feel simultaneously vulnerable and real. "I wouldn't say *anyone*."

"Just sex positive, boob-themed coffee campers that donate a portion of their proceeds to breast cancer research?"

He looked thoughtful for a moment. "In all fairness, had more people realized the cancer research part, I doubt you'd have garnered the same reaction."

"But that's the whole fucking point," she insisted, her pulse beginning to thunder in her ears. "I'm not interested in having to wear my status as a breast cancer survivor like some kind of shield against social judgment. Women shouldn't have to almost die to live life on their terms."

A crease appeared in Ethan's lightly freckled forehead.

"On a related topic, I'd trade my vintage Swarovski crystal

pasties to know who started the petition in the first place." Darby flopped over onto her back and stared at the rainbow shards bobbing along her camper's ceiling from the prism in the window. "Someone has some serious comeuppance coming their way."

Heavy silence thickened the air.

Ethan shifted away from her and sat up in bed, and the sheets slipped down his bare chest as he stared toward the front of the camper.

A powerful wave of déjà vu rocked her as her body experienced a sudden and involuntary onslaught.

Tunneling vision. Damp palms. Racing heart. Metallic saliva gathering beneath her tongue.

Ethan looked at her then—really looked at her—his eyes appearing impossibly blue next to the sleep-reddened whites.

"I did."

Darby's heart lurched as if she'd sustained a physical blow. She tried to find her voice but only managed one stuttered syllable. "You?"

"Yes," Ethan confirmed, his face contorting with what looked an awful lot like guilt. "I started the petition."

The world tipped on its axis as she looked at him, trying to process the implications of what he'd just said. "You?" she asked again.

"Yes."

Pushing against the bed, Darby turned to face him. "So, were you just never going to tell me before I brought it up?"

Ethan shifted slightly, adjusting himself on the bed before he answered her. "I honestly thought you might have assumed it anyway."

"But when you came to serve the notice, you said, and I quote, 'This isn't coming from me.'"

"Because it wasn't."

Darby folded her arms over her chest, wishing she'd at least bothered to wear a sports bra before she turned in for the night. "I'm going to need you to make that make sense."

On a heavy sigh, Ethan whipped back the sheet, awkwardly crab-scooting to the end of the bed.

One major downside to camper living—not enough real estate to properly retreat to your separate corners during a disagreement.

Snatching his jeans from the hook by her full-body mirror, he jammed his legs into them. "I started the petition because everyone and their goddamned dogs were lighting up the departments' lines around the clock. If they hadn't had somewhere constructive for their objections to go, you'd have had protestors camped across the highway a hell of a lot sooner."

"So it had absolutely nothing to do with your own personal objections to a sex- and body-positive bikini coffee camper?" she asked.

It was a tripwire, and they both knew it.

There was no way Ethan could answer in the negative without lying. And while Ethan Townsend was many things—the list grew longer every minute—a liar wasn't one of them.

"As sheriff of Townsend Harbor, my first duty was to this town and its residents. I couldn't ignore the fact that a very vocal faction of those residents didn't want a business of this kind on the outskirts of town." His jaw tightened as he spoke, and his eyes flickered with a mix of emotions that Darby couldn't quite read. "I thought I was doing the right thing."

"Of course you did," she scoffed, not even attempting to keep the bitterness from her voice. "Because you always know what the right thing is, don't you?"

She waited for an answer that never came.

"Did you ever, even for a second, stop to think that the town itself might be the problem?"

Ethan blinked at her, his jaw still welded shut.

"You said it yourself with you served me with that bullshit

order," Darby said. "*Clique-ish* and *myopic* were the words you used, I believe. I mean, Jesus. The simple fact that you felt you had to drive to a whole-ass other country to get laid ought to give you pause."

"It did," he ground out. "It does. Did you not see me out attempting to get rid of the protestors?" he asked, stabbing a finger toward the highway-facing side of the camper. "I never intended for things to snowball into an out-and-out shitshow. I thought whoever owned Brewbies would do what everyone else who's tried to make a business work here would do."

"Fuck off so you could have your land back?"

Ethan's eyes darkened as his face drained of color. "That's not what this was about, Darby."

She swallowed hard and blinked to clear the treacherous tears blurring her vision. "Isn't it, though?"

"No," he said, but with considerably less conviction.

She dashed a hot, salty track from her cheek and seized hard on the sudden gust of anger that blew through her. Not because Ethan had been the one to initiate the petition. Not even because he'd actively wanted her to leave.

Because he had the power to make her cry.

"You showed up with a chickenshit petition because you can't face that you were too much of a coward to own what you really wanted to do with your life."

She wanted the words back as soon as they were out of her mouth, but it was too late. Darby watched as he ran a hand through his messy hair, his eyes downcast. Hurt was written in bold type all over his face.

"You're right," he said. "I did want my land back. I wanted to start my brewery and honor my grandpa and claim the life I might deserve after giving so much of myself to this town. This got too big." His eyes met hers, and the intensity of his gaze seared straight through to her soul. Even from across the room, she could feel the strength of his conviction and the sincerity of the longing in his words. "You belong everywhere," he continued. "You belong to this entire world. This was just my corner of it. I was angry that you wouldn't just let me have my tiny corner of it when you could own this entire thing."

Silence.

"I'm sorry, Darby," he finally said, his voice low and ragged. "I never wanted it to end up like this."

Her wrath collapsed into a crushing wave of sadness. "Me neither," she said. "But here we are."

"No." Ethan's expression softened, and he stepped forward, cupping her face. "Here *you* are." He brushed her lips as tenderly as he had her scar, this part of her that had wounded him so deeply. "This isn't my place anymore."

It was a goodbye and a blessing, all at once. Darby's eyes fluttered closed as he kissed her forehead before pulling away.

Ethan gathered his things in silence, the air between them heavy with regret. He pulled open the door to the camper and stepped outside into the sunlight, pausing for a moment on the threshold. Darby waited for him to say something—anything— but he just stood there until finally, without another word, he turned and walked away.

When he was gone, Darby felt something inside of her unravel and give way. She let herself dissolve, hugging a pillow to her chest as if it could somehow cushion the ache in her chest.

Some immeasurable span of time later, a sharp rap on her camper door woke Darby from a thick nap. She shot out of bed, her heart knocking a glad rhythm against her ribs as she sprinted the short distance to fling it wide to Ethan's—hopefully remorseful—face.

Only, it wasn't Ethan.

It was Gabe.

Flanked by a small army of men who looked like they'd been dumped directly off local fishing boats.

Gabe's features underwent a radical transformation when he saw her, melting from his standard perma-smolder to something like shock.

"Holy Christ." A low whistle issued from his pursed lips.

233

"What the hell happened to you?"

A night at the carnival, sleeping sans skincare routine, a morning make-out session, an epic crying jag, a lobotomy nap...

And a broken heart.

Breaking every mirror in her camper might be the thing to do now.

Gabe's amber eyes narrowed. "Did that sheriff do this? Did he hurt you?"

"I'm okay. Really," Darby lied. "I just haven't had my coffee yet."

Cords stood out on Gabe's neck, making the Celtic knots covering his throat appear to tighten. "Because you give me the word, and I'll break Flannel Flanders goddamn legs. I don't care if he *did* hire these guys to help with cleanup."

Darby glanced behind her friend to the dozen or so men standing in a semicircle, eyeing the dumpster fire of carnival aftermath.

She wasn't sure which thought was more devastating.

The possibility that Ethan had planned to surprise her had their morning gone differently, or that he'd wanted to make sure she'd be okay even though she'd verbally ripped his spleen from his ass.

"There will be no breaking of legs, arms, or any other appendages," she said, gathering her hair into a pile atop her head. "No maiming of any kind, in fact."

Gabe kicked the bleached shell gravel with his motorcycle boot like a disappointed boy.

"What d'you want I should do with them?" he asked, jerking his angular chin over his shoulder.

"Put them to work," Darby said, already shuffling toward her coffee counter. "I need to get this place cleaned up as soon as possible."

"Because the city is coming to inspect the grounds?"

Darby dumped a double shot of earth-dark grounds into her behemoth of an espresso maker. "Because I'm leaving."

TWENTY

Hot Break

THE PRECIPITATION OF PROTEIN AND TANNIC MATTER WHEN HOPS ARE ADDED TO BOILING MIX

"BEEN TRYING TO GET A HOLD OF YOU ALL DAY, sheriff," said a businesslike woman on the other end of the line. "You're a tough man to find."

Maybe a guy who is hard to find doesn't wanna be found, was the retort he bit back as he threw his wood driver chisel on the bench of his lathe. He wasn't fit for human consumption at the moment, so he was doing things that made him feel better. Like chopping and shaping wood. Bending it to his will. Hammering. Nailing. Pounding.

Jesus Christ, did ninety-eight-and-a-half percent of sex euphemisms come from contracting nomenclature?

"What can I do for you, Gwen?"

Gwendolyn Baadsgaard's family had stones in the graveyard next to the Townsends. The Viking-sized woman had turned a legacy of pillaging land into subdividing and selling it.

"Please tell me I'm the first real estate broker to inform you that the Raven Creek property hit the market about an hour ago. I have here on a huge pink sticky note dated that in no uncertain terms should anyone be shown the Raven Creek property without first allowing you to offer."

Ethan choked on thin air in his haste to gasp, "What?"

"Yeah, seller is very motivated to buy, though people thought you and she were..." Gwen let the thought trail off, waiting for him to pick up the conversational thread she dropped.

His heart pumped with such violence, Ethan couldn't produce a reply.

"Tell you what," she said when the silence stretched a beat too long. "I'm going to miss her Titty-Twisted Iced Tea."

Shock gave way to alarm that escaped as anger. "Is she remaining on the property until it sells?" he demanded, louder than he'd meant.

"Dunno, sheriff, she used an out-of-town agent. Can't say as I blame her. But everyone is so sad to see her go."

"Are they?" he asked.

"Of course. I mean, there's always that contingent with the big truck wheels and Confederate flags who will protest just about any-damn-thing. That Venn diagram intersects with the old 'traditional values' people, but they're a dying—if entitled and wealthy—breed out here. But yeah, the scuttlebutt around town is that most folks are real salty about her leaving. That Cirque du Café was certainly fun, and several people made B&B and vacation home reservations in case it's coming back next year."

They did?

"Do you think Caryn drove her off?" Gwen's question cut through a thousand thoughts and emotions trying to crowd into him at once.

"Caryn, my mom Caryn?"

"Yeah, I saw them drinking at Olive or Twist on Friday night. I was going to say hi, but the conversation sounded serious. I bet your mother *loves* that your...lady friend has pink hair." She snort-laughed.

It occurred to Ethan that in a normal situation—in a normal town where the head real estate agent didn't pants you in eighth grade—her question would be wildly inappropriate.

He grunted something that sounded like an excuse and ended

the call, realizing belatedly he'd never answered her question, nor did he tell her to hold the Raven Creek property.

Because it wasn't his. He'd given it up. Given over to her.

Hell, he'd spent the past couple of weeks trying to figure out just how the hell to fix this. How to win back a woman who didn't really want to be won.

Ethan stared at the chair he'd been wrestling with all morning, wondering why nothing would fit together like it should. The measurements were right. The components of the highest quality. The tools well kept. It was part of a fucking set he'd made from the same batch of wood.

Get off my property. The look in her eyes as she spewed those words at him haunted every goddamn minute.

Because when it came to ownership, Darby had stolen the one thing he'd always wanted to give to someone.

And even he was surprised that thing wasn't Raven Creek.

Picking up the sledgehammer in the corner, he decided a little smash therapy was in order.

It felt good to create things. But sometimes, it felt better to demolish them. Shatter into a thousand pieces.

Because his tragedy was that he got everything he'd set out to achieve, and it left him emptier and angrier than he'd ever been.

She was leaving, which had been his aim all along.

So why did it feel like the world was ending? Why did the thought of Raven Creek without her kitschy little trailer on the corner by the swing seem like just an empty plot of dirt?

Nostrils flaring, muscles full of blood and rage, and surging with a primal violence he'd flirted with but never allowed himself to feel, Ethan lifted the hammer over his head and prepared to bring it down like Hephaestus.

A movement in the shadows stayed his hand, but when he turned to where the scroll saw sat, the corner was empty.

Except for the memory that lived there.

Grandpa Townsend retrieving pieces of a writing desk Ethan had thrown in the corner in a fifteen-year-old tantrum at his own mistakes.

"You know, Tove's father's family used to have a saying. Træet ønsker ikke at blive en båd. *The tree doesn't want to be a boat."*

Ethan scowled up at his grandpa, the metaphor not sinking into his thick head. "We're not working on boats, dur. And I just can't do it. I'm not as good as you are."

When other men might have cuffed him for his back talk, his grandpa only squatted down, set the discarded block on his own woodpile, and hugged him. "This happens to everyone," he soothed with a shake of his silver-gold head. "It isn't the woodworker that is in the wrong. But neither is it the piece of wood. Sometimes, it's just not supposed to be what you're trying to make it. It already knows its fate. It already decided, and you can't exert your will on it."

Grandpa Townsend smiled, flashing the same dimple in his left cheek that Ethan claimed as a Townsend birthright.

"Kinda like women, in a way...but you'll learn that later."

"Ew, Grandpa."

The memory blurred through a skein of moisture as Ethan dropped the axe, picked up his phone, and tapped out a text.

I'm coming over.

Three dots appeared. Disappeared. Then appeared again.

I know.

* * *

Ethan always took the stairs at the Townsend manse two at a time. They were cut for Victorian feet, which were famously smaller than the descendants of Danes (the tallest people in the world) now fed an American diet.

His mother generally existed on the third floor of the Highclere-meets-*Charmed* mansion, being very busy and very important. So, when he followed his ears to the den at the back of the main floor to catch her watching *House Hunters International*, surrounded by caramel wrappers and day-drinking the prosecco his father had spent a fortune on in Italy, he almost gave birth to an entire cow.

"What did you say to her?" he greeted his mom.

Pausing a tiff between two finicky gays squabbling over an apartment in the South of France, Caryn Townsend looked up as if his question hadn't been the one she'd expected.

"Ethan." She unfolded her legs from beneath her and drained her glass before she stood to face him.

"What did you say to Darby? Did you threaten her with something?"

His mother tucked her ever-ready hair behind her ear as she narrowed assessing eyes at him. "I know why you would assume I—"

"Did you or Roy have anything to do with her putting the Raven Creek property up for sale?"

His mother turned on him, her silken, smooth demeanor replaced with something softer, and harsher. She looked her age, for once...and younger. Younger because of the vulnerability floating in eyes that matched his own. Older because of a soul-weariness she'd apparently been very good at masking.

"That was all your fault, Ethan," she informed him gently.

Suddenly he wished she were a man, so he could brace for a punch in the face. He'd prefer a good right hook to the quiet expression of pitying disappointment that made it impossible to look at her for too long.

"You two were seen having drinks together," he accused, though what he was accusing her of, he wasn't sure. "What did you say?"

"I like Darby." Caryn set her wine glass down and drifted to the sideboard to pour water from a crystal-cut pitcher, silently expressing how much of his business it *wasn't*. "She's witty, and, despite her vocation, she has class. She's the kind of clever that can't be taught, and she knows her own mind..." She took a sip and made a face as though the water was bitter, rather than her next thought. "I wish I could have claimed the same at her age. So much trouble could have been avoided."

Ethan blinked, taken aback. "What do you mean?"

After an inhale that lasted several concerning seconds too long, his mother said, "The money is gone." At his shocked expression, she said, "Fortunately, I put so much of it in a trust for you before your father passed, and that couldn't be touched. *Your* money is safe."

"How?"

His mother paused. Chewed her lip. Started to say something. Stopped. Then, "Your grandfather made some terrible investments, and what was left, your father gambled or...fucking gave away." She slammed the glass down on the table, which was tantamount to an all-out tantrum from his mom.

Holy shit, that was maybe the first time he'd ever heard her curse. He didn't know whether to laugh or be terrified.

When she approached him, she took his large hands into her small, gnarled fingers. "I should have told you how difficult I found being an outsider in this town. In my own marriage. I should have shared with and educated you, so you wouldn't grow up to make the same mistakes your father did."

At that, Ethan jerked out of her hold, incensed. "I'm nothing like him," he snarled. "I don't gamble. I don't cheat. I don't think of myself and my needs over my family and responsibilities, I—"

"You made that kind, strong, beautiful, *vital* woman feel unworthy, and Ethan, I'm standing here telling you that comes from the same place as did all father's misdeeds. That place your father, your grandfather, your inheritance, and even *I* mistakenly installed and encouraged inside of you. The one that tries to contain the illusion that life isn't messy and laden with mistakes and regret. Who holds everyone to an impossible standard of conduct, yourself most of all."

Ethan stood stock-still in the center of a room he could fit his entire condo into and gazed at the wall. Powerful emotion glued his boots to the ground.

"I fucked it up, Mom," he said, voice cracking like it had when he was a heartbroken young man losing his beloved grandpa.

With a foreign sound of sympathy, she opened her arms and enfolded him in an embrace that felt warm and big and enveloping, even though she stood eight inches shorter and a hundred pounds lighter than him.

"Ethan. You've always been a good boy. A darling boy," she said against his chest, before pulling back to look up at him. "You've never required much in the way of parenting because you were born with a moral compass so completely well-adjusted that you could be relied upon to be good. And above all, to protect the *appearance* of being good, which was what we were all trained to do. But if recent events have taught me anything, it's this..."

Reaching up, she smoothed a forelock away from his forehead.

"You can't spend one more second worrying what other people think about your choices... At the end of the day, it's you who has to live with them."

TWENTY-ONE

Pulping

PROCESS OF REMOVING THE OUTERMOST SKIN OF THE COFFEE CHERRY OR FRUIT

"ARE YOU SURE THERE ISN'T ANYTHING WE CAN DO TO convince you to stay?"

Cady's big blue eyes bored into Darby's, and the pleading expression on her face was powerful enough to produce a quasi-maternal twinge in Darby's middle.

Hopefully her last.

She and Gemma stood opposite Darby in the entryway of Nevermore Bookstore negotiating their way through the third round of goodbye hugs.

"I'm positive," Darby said.

As positive as her pregnancy test had been negative, thank whomever. She'd been in such an awful funk for the last two weeks that she'd damn near convinced herself it *had* to be the hormonal warmup act of her having conceived a love child.

A child she had one hundred percent never imagined having large icy-blue eyes and a tiny cleft in its tiny chin.

Just like she had never imagined dressing it in a crisp flannel onesie and itty-bitty khaki overalls. That was the thing about onesies—they kind of always had to be tucked in.

And here she'd thought the whole biological clock thing had been a crock of shit.

Ethan Townsend *had* to have altered her brain chemistry in some unimaginable way. A fact she intended to move about a thousand Mai-Tais as soon as her camper was safely parked in the long-term storage facility in Seattle, where she would catch her flight to Hawaii.

Sunshine, cocoa butter rub-downs, and perfectly roasted Kona coffee beans, here I come, she promised herself.

If only she could figure out how to be excited about that promise.

"But who's gonna keep me in ill-advised iced evening coffees while I finish up the wedding planning?" Cady's rosebud mouth turned downward at the corners.

Gemma cleared her throat conspicuously.

"I mean, I totally love your version of the Dirty Earl," Cady quickly added, resting a hand on Gemma's forearm. "It's just that Darby has that homemade Madagascar vanilla-bergamot syrup that I love."

This subtle ribbing between the bookstore proprietress and her best friend was only one more tick mark in the column labeled Reasons to Get the Fuck Out of Townsend Harbor.

Darby couldn't bear the thought of unintentionally driving a wedge between two of the four women who had welcomed her with arms thrown unapologetically wide.

"We tried," Gemma said, squeezing Cady's shoulder.

"Well, if you're really going, then I guess you better take this with you." Stiffly bending at the knees, Cady reached behind the beautiful old credenza register and came back with a purple gift bag tufted with black and lavender tissue paper.

"What's this?" Darby asked.

"Nothing much." Gemma shrugged. "Just a little something to remember us by."

An ache woke in Darby's throat. "As if there's a single chance in hell I'd forget you two," she said, eyeing the bag. "Should I open it now?"

"Yes!" Gemma and Cady said in unison with cheerleader-like zeal.

"All right, then." Darby set the bag on the credenza and began pulling out the tissue.

One by one, she unwrapped smaller tissue-wrapped packets bearing a surprising assortment of items for the bag's small size. She had only reached the fifth of approximately thirty packets when she covertly glanced at her cell phone and felt a jolt of alarm.

She had a forty-five-minute drive to Kingston to catch the 4:15 p.m. ferry, and it was already 3:20 p.m. Darby didn't want to seem rude by tearing through the remainder of what Cady and Gemma had so thoughtfully assembled, so she relied on an old Dunwell standby.

"Actually, would you mind if I use your restroom right quick? I already have all the water drained from the camper's sanitation tank."

Gemma and Cady exchanged an oddly pleased look.

"Of course," Cady said. "I just got some got some brand-new lavender soaps from Secret Garden. You should definitely try them."

"Oh! And the vanilla-blueberry sandalwood," Gemma added. "If my mom had had that soap growing up, my language would be even worse."

"There's an alarming thought," Cady said, elbowing her friend.

"I'll just have to wash one hand with each," Darby said, wanting to throw them a bone to soften the sting of her departure, even one as ridiculous as this.

In the small, moody, maximalist, subway-tiled and sumptuously wallpapered bathroom, Darby quickly set an alarm on her phone using her very recognizable ringtone as the notification sound. She then washed her hands using the aforementioned soaps and returned to the foyer.

Gemma and Cady pasted twin overzealous smiles on their faces as she approached, causing Darby's antenna to twitch. She made a show of returning to the process of opening her gifts. Exactly three minutes later, her phone began to tinkle out "The Java Jive."

"I love coffee, I love tea."

I love...Ethan Townsend.

No the fuck you don't, Darby warned her Judas of a brain. She couldn't afford to give that line of logic even one inch of space.

She quickly opened her handbag and glanced down in it, hoping the expression of dismay was more convincing than Gemma and Cady's respective performances.

"Oh, shoot," she said. "That's Mr. Whatshissack from the Mountain Thunder Coffee Farm. I'm going to have to take this on road."

Gemma and Cady finally seemed to catch on to her haste.

Darby held out her arms, and they both squished in for a quick group hug before helping to restuff the gift bag while Darby faked the beginning of a phone call. Phone sandwiched between her chin and shoulder, she stepped out into the spring air and waved before climbing up into the camper and closing the door. She made sure she was down the block before transferring it to the apparatus mounted on the dash.

"Thank God," she said with a sigh when she finally reached the roundabout at the end of Water Street.

Taking a long, slow breath, she indulged in a long, slow look at the quaint assembly of shops in the rearview mirror.

"This is for the best," she said, her eyes misting over as she watched Nevermore's gothic shingle swing in a gust of air off the water.

Darby let her foot off the brake and turned into the roundabout.

And nearly ran over Caryn Townsend.

The former first lady had materialized out of nowhere, and was now waving to Darby and miming rolling down her window.

"Son of a bitch," Darby muttered without moving her lips and teeth.

Still.

She couldn't ruin her son's life *and* leave without so much as a goodbye.

With effort that made her sorely regret not getting the upgraded power windows, Darby pulled back out of the roundabout and cranked the old metal handle to roll down the foggy sheet of glass.

"Hello there," Caryn said brightly. "I was hoping I would see you before you departed."

Tempted to point out that Caryn could have seen her any time in the two weeks leading up to her imminent departure right this fucking second, Darby bit her tongue. "I guess you're in luck," she said. "I'm just on my way out of town right now. In fact—"

"I just wanted to thank you." Caryn's lacquered fingernails folded over the window.

"For what?"

"I'm... That is, my son and I—"

"You really don't have to tell me," Darby said. "I'm so glad you two have been able to patch things up."

"I have you to thank," Caryn said, her blue eyes fastened earnestly on Darby's.

"I'm not sure I can take credit for that."

"Whether or not you did so intentionally, the end result is the same. And I just needed you to know that I'm grateful. Between that and my conversation with Roy," she said, a sly look giving her elegant features a distinctly foxlike cast, "my life has taken a rather dramatic turn as of late."

"I'm so glad to—"

"Oh, would you look who it is!" Caryn glanced toward the rear of Darby's camper and waved.

Checking her side mirror with a sinking heart, Darby spotted Roy coming up the sidewalk.

Or, at least, a creature wearing an alarmingly accurate facsimile of Roy's face. Because that was where the resemblance to

246

the man she'd spoken with in the cluttered, dusty junk shop ended. He moved at a pace markedly different from the lumbering gait that had brought Roy and his insulated coffee thermos to her service window each morning. His trim figure was now fitted out in a beautifully cut dove-gray suit.

"I'll let you two catch up," Darby said breezily, shifting her camper back into drive. "We'll have to keep in touch."

"Wait!" she heard Roy shout.

Oh, for the sake of all fucks—3:22.

"Well, isn't this a pleasant surprise," Caryn said with a warmth and sincerity that caused Darby's heart to squeeze despite her suspicions that it was not, in fact, a surprise at all. "And where are you headed looking so dapper?" Caryn asked with a saucy wink.

Roy shifted his weight, and for the first time, Darby saw the enormous bouquet hidden behind his back.

"Oh, you shouldn't have," Darby said, reaching for the bouquet.

Roy jerked them away just as Darby's fingertips brushed the cellophane wrapper likely made of plastic bottles fished out of the Puget Sound. "I didn't."

Aaaaaand there he was, ladies and gentlepeople.

"These are for her."

Caryn's cheeks flushed with obvious pleasure. "For me?"

"Yes, indeedy." Roy transferred the impressive jewel-toned bundle of blooms. "I was going to give them to you tonight, but I just couldn't wait to see you."

"Well, I won't keep you two." As much as Darby was intrigued by this development, she was in imminent danger of missing her ferry if she ran into any traffic.

And the way her day was going, that was looking extremely bloody likely.

"But I never I gave you the information I promised," Roy said. "And a deal's a deal."

"You know? Seeing as I sold Raven Creek and am actually

right this very minute driving the business the town council wanted to shut down out of Townsend Harbor, I don't think I'm actually going to need it after all. So as much as—"

"It looks like Miss Dunwell is in a bit of a hurry. Perhaps we should let her go," Caryn said.

Gratitude the size of the Olympic Mountains swelled Darby's chest. At least one person in this town had a fucking clue.

Roy inclined his neatly barbered head deferentially. "I'm afraid this affects you too."

"Me?" Caryn batted her lashes at Roy. "What on earth could this have to with me?"

Darby could just drive away.

She could wedge her platform sandal down on the gas pedal and rocket right the hell out of here.

Could, were it not for one small complication: Caryn's hand was still fastened on the window well.

She could see the headline now.

Exotic Dancer with Mob Ties Drags Former First Lady, Receives Fuck-ton of Jail Time.

"Could you maybe text it to me?" Darby suggested.

"This is the kind of information I'd only feel comfortable disclosing in person, if you catch my drift," Roy said.

"Speaking of catching—"

"Of course," Caryn interrupted. "Please, go ahead, Roy, so we can get Miss Dunwell on her way." She squeezed his forearm encouragingly.

Crinkles appeared at the corners of Roy's gray-blue eyes. "As you know, I've been a devoted amateur historian for some time."

"Why yes," Caryn said. "The historical society has relied on your expertise on several occasions."

Roy's clean-shaven cheeks glowed with the compliment. "In my research on the Townsend family, I've discovered something rather, rather shocking."

Darby's knuckles whitened on the well-worn leather of her steering wheel.

Caryn's eyes widened. "Shocking?"

Roy nodded. "You see, before the Townsend family founded Townsend Harbor, they were p-puh—" He paused, emitting an embarrassed chuckle.

Only on two occasions had Darby heard him struggle with a slight stutter, and both times, in the wake of a verbal confrontation.

Odd.

"Prostitutes?" Darby suggested, trying desperately to hurry him along. "Priests? Plumbers?"

That the last in this series earned her a sharp look from Caryn, Darby found more than a little amusing.

A gull wheeled overhead, its harsh cry seeming to echo Darby's frustration.

"They were p-p-puh-puh *pirates.*"

Caryn gasped, her eyes widening to the size of saucers as her hand flew up to her neck to clutch at the string of very real pearls. "No."

"Yes!" Roy said in a harsh whisper. "Sailed with C-Captain C-Cook himself."

"There, there." And damned if Roy's hand didn't cover Caryn's *on the damn door.*

Darby's right foot twitched.

The headline quickly rewrote itself.

Exotic Dancer Traumatizes Elderly Veteran, Is Sentenced to Hell.

"I'm sorry to have to tell you like this," Roy said gently.

"As fascinating as this has been, I really, really—"

Another gasp from Caryn sent Darby's heart into borderline atrial fibrillation. "Does Ethan know?"

The name reverberated through Darby's head like an echo, exposing the cavernous volume of the space the sheriff had occupied. A liminal space between who she had been, and who she would be in the aftermath of her heartbreak.

A thousand times she'd been tempted to text him.

A thousand times she'd slapped the phone out of her own hand.

She was not, refused to be, *that* girl.

The one who let her heart rule her head. The one who muted her colors to match a man, to blend into a community.

To find a home.

"I thought that you should really be the one to tell him," Roy said. "I know this will come as quite a shock."

The words were a pin popping the bubble of Darby's inner monologue.

She cleared her throat and glanced up at the sky. "It looks like it's going to rain," she said lamely. "I should probably get going."

When neither acknowledged her, Darby accidentally on purpose nudged the metal window crank with her knee.

Caryn looked down at her hand still in Roy's and blushed. "Yes," she said, withdrawing quickly. "Yes, I suppose you should."

Roy lifted the hand from the passenger-side window and reached into the paper bag slung over his arm. It returned holding a beribboned hatbox she recognized from his shop. "For the cloche," he said. "I think Helen would want you to have it."

Speechless, Darby looked at the beautiful box, then at Roy, whose mouth curved in a surprisingly handsome smile.

It was the first time she'd ever seen it.

"You make sure you drive safe, young lady."

"Thanks," Darby croaked in daddy issues. "I will."

"Do keep in touch," Caryn added.

"Will do."

Pebbles shot out from Darby's rear tires as the stomped on the gas, and her speedometer needle quivered as she steered her vehicle around the bend.

She pressed the gas pedal all the way until she spotted the tree tunnel ahead.

Home stretch, she told herself. Another hundred yards and she'd be free of this place. Free of the home it had promised to be.

Free of disappointment that covered the landscape she'd once loved like moss.

Trees blurred in her peripheral vision as the tears spilled over Darby's lids.

Almost there.

Red and blue lights flashed in her rearview mirror.

"Oh, come on!" She slapped her palm against the dash hard enough to send the grass-skirted plastic hula girl mounted above her air vents into a manic twerk. Apropos, as it had been the kitschy secondhand shop purchase that had given her the idea for her move farther across the Pacific.

Squinting at her side mirror to see the cruiser behind her, she felt a rush of relief.

McGarvey.

She slowed her speed and pulled to the side of the road, hoping like hell she could keep their encounter brief and uneventful. Turning on her hazards, Darby quickly dashed the tears from her face and tugged her sweater down to reveal another inch of cleavage.

She'd sooner lick the barnacles off a trash barge than cry her way out of a ticket, but if her sweater kittens happened to put McGarvey in a more generous mood, all to the good. Her days of trading distress for consideration were long fucking gone.

And good riddance.

Deputy McGarvey's boots fell heavy on the asphalt as he approached the driver's-side window. He rested his arms on the doorframe and leaned in, his face a mask of mock sternness. "Ma'am, do you know how fast you were going?"

Darby bit her lip and met his gaze with an apologetic one of her own. "Not exactly," she said, tapping her ancient speedometer. "This thing can be a little hinky."

"Forty in a fifty-five is hinky," he said, a smirk tugging one corner of his lips. "Seventy in a fifty-five is a high-speed chase."

"I'm so sorry," she replied in a honeyed voice that sounded nothing like her own. "The thing is, I'm actually supposed to be catching the 4:15 p.m. ferry because I have to drop my camper off in storage for a seven p.m. flight out of Sea-Tac. If I miss it, I'm screwed until tomorrow morning, and I really, *really* need to get there today."

Until she'd said it out loud, Darby hadn't realized just how true this statement was.

McGarvey nodded slowly, his expression unreadable. "I'm sorry," he said. "But I'm afraid that's not going to be a possibility."

Darby felt her heart drop into her guts with a sickening splat. "Why is that?"

"Because I have to give you this." McGarvey handed a white envelope through the window.

If she never saw an official-looking document as long as she lived...

With trembling fingers, she pried open the flap and pulled out the tri-folded sheaf.

She flattened them out against her steering wheel, reading the text at the top several times before her brain unpacked their meaning.

Petition to Declare Darby Dunwell a True Townsendite

On the very first line, in a signature so obsessively neat that she could actually read all the letters, was Ethan Townsend's name.

Many more followed.

Caryn. Cady. Gemma. Myrtle. Vee.

She got as far as Roy Dobson's when her eyes began to blur and hot tracks slipped down her cheeks.

Ethan had his land. He'd build his brewery. The small space she'd occupied in Townsend Harbor would close over as quickly as grass on a grave.

As it should be.

"I'm sorry," Darby said, handing the papers and envelope back to McGarvey as the broad smile slid from his face. "But I can't."

"Are you sure?" McGarvey asked, meeting her streaming eyes.

She nodded, fiercely dashing the moisture from her cheeks. "Please. Just let me go."

Before I lose my nerve.

McGarvey shook his head sadly. "Okay. But I'd cool it on the gas if I were you. The 101 is crawling with cops from here to Poulsbo."

Darby waved as he walked back to his cruiser and waited until he was inside to ease back onto the road at a more moderate speed.

So long as he didn't follow her into the tree tunnel, she should be able to resume her steady clip within a minute or two.

3:32 p.m.

She could still make it.

Provided another Townsendite didn't show up to slow her down in some inexplicable way.

But as luck—or the lack thereof would have it—someone did.

There, at the mouth of a canopy studded with spring green buds, was Ethan Townsend.

He stood tall and broad-shouldered, staring down the length of the highway, a quiet determination in his gaze as he watched her approach. Though it had only been two weeks since she saw him, Darby drank him in like a woman starved. The familiar contours of his jaw line, his sharp cheekbones, eyes the blue of the summer sky after a storm.

Darby's foot slid off the gas pedal, and the camper's sudden deceleration made her stomach flip.

That was her story, and she was sticking to it.

At the precise moment that it occurred to her to wonder what the fuck Ethan was doing standing on the side of the road with no car in sight, his arm lifted from his side and a small cardboard sign appeared from behind his back.

Maui or bust.

TWENTY-TWO
Runoff

THE LIQUID YOU SEPARATE FROM THE SPENT GRAIN HUSKS DURING LAUTERING

OH SHIT.

She wasn't going to stop.

Ethan had been sure that this would work, and when the ancient muffler told him she'd decelerated at the sight of him, he filled with an elated hope.

Should have known it wouldn't be so easy.

Recovering immediately, Darby had reapplied the gas pedal, and Ethan knew if he didn't do something quickly, she'd get away.

Welp. Here went nothing.

Stepping onto the sun-dappled asphalt, he stood in the middle of the lane and held the sign up to his chest like a man in a mug shot. Death by Airstream wasn't exactly how he thought he'd shuffle off his mortal coil, but if Darby drove the vehicle that turned him into roadkill, then call the road crew and pour him a drink in Valhalla, because he was all the way dead.

Without her, what was the fucking point?

She left more rubber on the road than her tires as she screamed to a stop so close, Ethan could have kissed the grille.

Speaking of holy shit, he almost had to buy himself a new pair of board shorts.

Allowing a moment for his balls to crawl out of his body

cavity, he locked eyes with the woman who was going to kill him one way or the other.

Judging from the look on Darby's face, this was going to be a harder sell than he'd initially expected.

Nostrils flaring, lips compressed into a hyphen, hair up in a bandana like Rosie the Riveter, she was a pin-up nomad goddess with one hell of a temper.

At least life wouldn't be boring.

"Out of the way, Ethan. I'm going to miss my ferry," she called, gesturing angrily.

"Let me come with, and I'll show you a secret shortcut," he replied. "You can yell at me all you want on the way."

She looked at him as if he'd lost his goddamn marbles. "You can't just pick up and leave, Ethan."

He shrugged, shoving his hands into his pockets. "Turns out I can."

"You're just going to abandon the county without a sheriff? Real nice." Her expression darkened from unimpressed to pissed off.

"I resigned," he explained, pressing his palms to the warming hood of her Airstream. "Kiki will be running things until the fall election, where she'll likely run unopposed. At least, unopposed by me."

Darby poked her head out the window and tossed a dismissive gesture at him. "That's the dumbest thing I've ever heard! Did it even occur to you that I'd say no before you made these plans for you? For us?"

If by *occurred*, she meant kept him up for two nights in a row...then yes. "Well, I'd take it as a kindness if you didn't, what with the grand gesture and all. But if you did, I'd just have to spend the rest of my life trying to change your mind."

"You had two weeks to change my mind!" she yelled. "I've heard nothing from you. *Nothing*."

Now was not the time to mention that he'd tried her at her camper and never found her home. Nor had she been alone when he'd found her in town. She'd ignored his texts. Phone calls. Voicemails. And two apology bouquets.

He looked forward to squabbling about that later. But for now, he only had one thing to say.

"I love you."

He'd like to have thought the earth moved, but Darby's foot must have slipped off the brake, because the Airstream nudged into him before halting again. Deciding against tempting fate further, Ethan circled around to her driver's window, which was already rolled down.

She smelled fantastic and looked even better. Her presence, once a thorn in his side, was an instant balm. His muscles and guts unclenched. His heart gave up ten beats a second, though the rhythm became the syllables of her name.

"Hi," he said, thoroughly enjoying the expression on her face, somewhere between thunderstruck and antagonized. "I love you."

She grappled with her seatbelt and, after an adorable struggle, was finally victorious.

When he thought she'd open the door, she rolled out of the captain's chair and disappeared into the bowels of her trailer.

In the middle of the road.

Looking down the tree tunnel, Ethan noted McGarvey had already started setting up traffic cones at the back of the Airstream.

"She's mad enough to park in the middle of the road? She's mad enough to be here a while," the deputy called sagely.

Ethan thanked him with a nod before turning back to the crashing and clanging from behind the serving window.

"I should have pressed the issue sooner," he said loudly to the tempered glass. "But I was giving you some space. I was figuring out how to disentangle myself from who I thought I should be so I can become who I am. We can talk about that... not in the middle of a highway," he offered carefully. "I love you."

Finally, the service window slid open with a protest and

Darby appeared, her pretty lips pursed into a perfectly peachy-glossed slash of feminine fury.

Damned if she didn't look exactly like she did that first day at Raven Creek.

"I don't have the words, Ethan," she gritted out. "What do I even say to that?"

"I'll talk, then," he offered. "I know that I haven't—"

"*When?*" she exploded, shaking some words out of her pocket lint, apparently. "*When* did you fall in love with me? When haven't we been in the same room that we weren't fighting or fucking?"

Ethan didn't even need to think about his answer.

"It was the second you tore up that paperwork I served you into fuck-you confetti. You amused, confounded, transfixed, and infuriated me all at once. Most women can only produce two emotions at a time. *Tops.*"

"Bullshit," she growled, her eyebrows meeting in consternation. "You're in love with the sex we can't stop having."

He shook his head, placing his hands palms up on her counter, begging her silently to take them. "You and I aren't strangers to one-night stands. To the amnesia that can accompany them," he said, ignoring her sharp look. "But since that exact moment you swiveled around to speak to me in Canada, I haven't been able to stop thinking about you."

"Yeah," she said, her fury melting into a watery skein of hurt in her eyes that threatened to shatter his heart. "Yeah, you thought about me so much you made it your personal mission to kick me out of your entire town."

Ethan inhaled, reached deep for strength and courage, and hoped that he could get through this without bungling every word of the truth he'd kept hidden, even from himself.

"That's where I went wrong. It's where I should have stopped and taken a good look at what was really important, rather than what I'd allowed others to assign importance to."

He was getting through. Probably. It was all but impossible to tell.

"A part of me knew—" He had to clear a gather of nerves and emotion from his throat before he could try again. "I knew you were trouble with a capital T. That you were going to change Townsend Harbor—change *me*—irreparably."

She planted her elbows on the counter, resting her chin in one palm as she listened intently, her expression giving away nothing. No encouragement. No disincentive.

Well, good. He had more groveling to do.

"I hate change," he confessed, surprising exactly no one. "In my life, change has always meant loss. It's always torn down everything I thought I knew, and then left me with the lone responsibility to rebuild. I don't know what to expect from strangers anymore. I don't know what my country will look like tomorrow. What the geopolitical landscape will do at any given moment. There are dangers too big to comprehend and too small to see. When I look at this world, how it changes so fast, I don't have time to get used to the last seismic shift before the next one hits... and, ultimately, that's what you were, Darby."

"An earthquake?"

"A force of fucking *nature*." Forgetting himself, he reached in and covered her free hand with his, craving the feel of her. Loving that he'd identify the specific silk of her skin even blindfolded. "If the last several years have taught us anything? It's that we all know less than we think, and we control less than we want. But I do know something, Darby. I can't stop thinking about you. I will *never* stop thinking about you. Worrying about you. Caring about you. Being curious about you. Marveling at you—"

"What are you doing? What do you want from me, Ethan?" The questions escaped barely above a strangled whisper as, even though she stubbornly refused to blink, the well of her tears overflowed her spiked lashes and spilled down her cheek.

"This," he answered. Meaning it with every single part of himself.

Ethan lifted his hand and skimmed her fingers with the barest brush of his lips. "I want to be the one that holds your hand. I want to eat meals with you. I want to meet all your friends and hear all your stories. I want to go to your oncologist follow-ups, and I want to be the one who takes care of you when you need it. I want to talk with you all night. I want to sleep next to you and wake up with you—"

"I get up at, like, four thirty," she warned around an unlady-like sniff.

"I want to wake up a couple of hours after you," he quickly amended, his heart both glowing and aching at the sight of her tears. At what else began to gather in her eyes.

Hope.

"The point is, I've tried for two weeks to let this town be big enough for the both of us, and I realized that was never the problem. Darby, I can't stop picturing a life with you, and as much as I love Townsend Harbor, that life doesn't have coordinates. I want *you*, Darby. I want to be with you. If that's here? Fine. If that's in Maui, well, *aloha*, let's do this. If you say no..." He had to breathe through a surge of panic. "If you drive away, you'll take all the color in my life with it."

He thumbed away her next tear, shaping his palm to a jaw clenched tight with unspent emotion.

"But...this is your home." It was a feeble argument on her part, meant to talk him out of it, to remind him that she was a woman who didn't hold still, and he was a man who'd spent his entire life doing what was expected.

"My home will be where you are," he said, and meant it.

"What about your dreams? The property?" She gestured past the tunnel opening to the corner of the vast land Ethan still loved. That he still held sacred in his heart.

He shrugged. "I have it on good authority that Rhonda and Sylvio at Townsend Title and Escrow aren't going to be able to make things work, and the property will revert to you any day now."

Her mouth dropped open, and she made a sound of pure surprise.

"Someday..." He gave a little side-eye to the cars building up behind where McGarvey directed traffic slowed down to one lane.

Fuck it. They could wait. His heart and soul, hell, the *rest of his life*, was on the line here.

"Someday, I hope you let me build a brewery on the land. But if that isn't where you're planning on ending up, that's fine with me. I'm just asking to be along for the ride."

Sniffling, she stood up and regarded him with eyes gone liquid and softer than he'd ever seen them before.

Then she slammed the service window closed.

Ethan was contemplating throwing himself in front of one of Fertile Myrtle's sanitation trucks cruising up the way when the door to the camper opened. He barely had time to brace himself before Darby launched into his arms and wrapped her limbs around him, clinging like a barnacle.

Her lips crashed against his in a searing, desperate kiss, and Ethan felt every wall he'd built around himself come crashing down. Her tongue tangled with his as her fingers dove into his hair and scored at his scalp. She tasted like salt and tears, but their teeth wouldn't stop clashing through their wild, almost-hysterical smiles.

It was one of those moments where words weren't needed. Where language failed to express the relief, joy, elation, bliss...

After several seconds of devouring each other—and even more honks of encouragement and/or impatience from the peanut gallery—she dragged her lips from his and frowned down at him. "Well, you've made me miss my ferry." She looked back at the tree tunnel. "But I still have reservations for one of those glamping huts over a crystal-blue lagoon where women go to mend their hearts after losing a life-altering love."

"What if I booked two first-class tickets to Maui for tomorrow?" he said. "We'll dream of the future over froofy drinks, and I'll take you bikini shopping, which is a win for us both."

"Deal," she said, wriggling like a toddler to get down.

Ethan enjoyed her sliding down his body a little too much for an audience. He saluted McGarvey and turned to adjust the havoc she'd created in his pants.

All right... Time to hit the road.

He opened the driver's door in time for her to hop up into the cabin.

He didn't have to look back at the tree tunnel as they drove down the Coastal Highway toward a brand-new destination.

Toward a future neither of them dreamed about, and neither of them could wait for.

Townsend Harbor would always be there to welcome them back.

But home was wherever Darby wandered.

Because she took his heart with her.

Epilogue

FINISH: THE SENSORY EXPERIENCE OF COFFEE JUST AS IT IS SWALLOWED.

KAPALUA VILLAS, MAUI, TWO NIGHTS LATER

A GENTLE BREEZE SIFTED THROUGH THE GAUZY curtains, carrying with it the ecstatic chorus of tropical birdsong. Between the sex, the sun, and steady stream of heavenly, heady Kona coffee, Darby wasn't exactly sure what time it was.

And to be honest, she didn't care. In fact, she might never care about anything ever again except staying exactly where she was, doing exactly what she'd been doing for as long as humanly possible.

Provided fresh trays of beautiful food kept arriving on their private balcony overlooking an endless bolt of crystal blue that might very well be forever.

Or so a girl could hope.

"Ethan?" Despite his name being half absorbed by the pillow where Darby's sweat-kissed face was buried, Ethan lifted his disheveled head. The rest of him remained heavy and slack, and their limbs were intertwined in a position that mimicked two sky divers colliding in midair.

"Yeah?"

She rolled her cheek away from the buttery pillowcase to find eyes that rivaled the pristine Pacific. "I love you too."

His flushed cheek creased in a smirk. "Yeah, you fucking do."

With considerable effort, she peeled her arm from the mattress and caught the perfect globe of his bare ass with a resounding *smack*. "What d'you mean, 'Yeah, you fucking do? You don't know me."

"Don't have to," he drawled, despite having proven irrefutably that he knew her very, *very* well. "No one would do what you just did to me unless they loved that person."

A Cheshire Cat grin spread slowly across her swollen lips as she remembered—in detail—the sexual equivalent of a trust fall. He was surprisingly limber for a man who'd spent so much of his time obsessively hugging the straight and narrow. "Good point."

"But tell me tomorrow," he mumbled.

"I will," she said on a yawn.

"Good. Because I plan to tell you every day for the rest of our natural lives."

Eyelids that had been filling with sand only seconds before snapped open. "Are you saying what I think you're saying?"

Ethan's deep chest rose and fell in a regular rhythm that Darby had already come to recognize as his imminent departure from consciousness. "What do you think I'm saying?"

"A man like you talks about spending the rest of his life with someone, and usually there's a very different kind of legal proposition involved."

Rough, warm fingers found the back of her knee, anchoring it over Ethan's hip. "A man like me does what the fuck he wants."

"He finds out his ancestors were pirates, and all of a sudden he's a rogue," Darby said to the billowing canopy of the four-poster bed they'd rarely left except to find an alternate surface on which to bone.

"I still think Roy is full of shit." Ethan traced his fingers up her thigh to palm her ass. "But I sure do love plundering this booty."

Darby flung a dramatic arm across her eyes as she groaned. "You really are a walking dad joke, you know that?"

"How about you come walk my plank?"

"That's it." Darby began to squirm away from him. "I'm ordering more coffee."

With a burst of momentum that left her dizzy, Ethan rolled her beneath him and pinned her arms above her head. "Not until I've buried my treasure."

Then she felt him hard against the most deliciously sensitive part of her, and she forgot to protest.

Ethan sank himself by fluid degrees, moving into her like the tide. Drawing her deeper into herself.

Deeper into love.

About Cynthia

Cynthia St. Aubin wrote her first play at age eight and made her brothers perform it for the admission price of gum wrappers. A steal, considering she provided the wrappers in advance. Though her early work debuted to mixed reviews, she never quite gave up on the writing thing, even while earning a mostly useless master's degree in art history and taking her turn as a cube monkey in the corporate warren.

Because the voices in her head kept talking to her, and they discourage drinking at work, she kept writing instead. When she's not standing in front of the fridge eating cheese, she's hard at work figuring out which mythological, art historical, or paranormal friends to play with next. She lives in Texas with the love of her life and two fluffy cats, Muppet and Gizmo.

I love stalkers! You can find me here!
Visit me: http://www.cynthiastaubin.com/
Email me: cynthiastaubin@gmail.com
Join my Minions: https://www.facebook.com/groups/
Cynthiastaubins/

Subliminally message me: *You were thinking of cheese just now, right?*

And here:

Also by Cynthia

Tails from the Alpha Art Gallery

Love Bites

Love Sucks

Love Lies

Love Binds

The Kane Heirs

Corner Office Confessions

Secret Lives After Hours

Bad Boys with Benefits

The Jane Avery Mysteries

Private Lies

Lying Low

Case Files of Dr. Matilda Schmidt, Paranormal Psychologist

Unlovable

Unlucky

Unhoppy

Unbearable

Unassailable

Undeadly

Unexpecting

From Hell to Breakfast

About Kerrigan

Kerrigan Byrne is the USA Today Best-selling and award winning author of several novels in both the romance and mystery genre.

She lives on the Olympic Peninsula in Washington with her husband, two Rottweiler mix rescues, and one very clingy torbie. When she's not writing and researching, you'll find her on the beach, kayaking, or on land eating, drinking, shopping, and attending live comedy, ballet, or too many movies.

Kerrigan loves to hear from her readers! To contact her or learn more about her books, please visit her site or find her on most social media platforms: www.kerriganbyrne.com

Also by Kerrigan

A Goode Girls Romance

Seducing a Stranger

Courting Trouble

Dancing With Danger

Tempting Fate

Crying Wolfe

Making Merry

The Business of Blood Series

The Business of Blood

A Treacherous Trade

Victorian Rebels

The Highwayman

The Hunter

The Highlander

The Duke

The Scot Beds His Wife

The Duke With the Dragon Tattoo

The Earl on the Train

The MacLauchlan Berserkers

Highland Secret

Highland Shadow

Highland Stranger

To Seduce a Highlander

THE MACKAY BANSHEES

Highland Darkness

Highland Devil

Highland Destiny

To Desire a Highlander

THE DE MORAY DRUIDS

Highland Warlord

Highland Witch

Highland Warrior

To Wed a Highlander

CONTEMPORARY SUSPENSE

A Righteous Kill

ALSO BY KERRIGAN

How to Love a Duke in Ten Days

All Scot And Bothered